Colors Running

Robert A. Minor

Writing is exciting and challenging, leading your mind into a new, almost unconscious dimension that those never venturing into the realm of fictional writing will ever experience. Even though exciting and stimulating, the task of completing a manuscript would be doubtful at times without the love and support of family and friends.

This book is dedicated to my beautiful wife, Paula Kay, and my best friend, Mark Zurwell. Both have encouraged and supported me in writing this and other stories.

Chapter One
Chance Meeting

A lone rider stopped on top of a knoll at the edge of the forest to watch five white men, about fifty yards away, bind the hands of a black man and put a noose around his neck. The men forced him atop a bareback stallion and looped the other end of the rope to a tree branch.

The lone rider pulled his rifle from its sheath and took careful aim just as one of the men grabbed a whip and prepared to smack the rump of the horse,

The man on the knoll took careful aim. The whip snapped, the horse bolted forward, the gun fired and the rope broke as splinters flew from the tree limb. With hands tied behind his back, the black man was carried away on the frightened horse.

The rifle slid in its sheath, and the lone rider pulled his revolver, spurring his horse on. One of the five startled men went for his gun, dropping it as a bullet ripped through his shoulder, and he fell to the ground. When the sound of gunfire filled the air, a second man's horse reared as he pulled his gun, but a bullet found its mark in the man's leg. He screamed in pain. The panicked horse dashed away with the wounded man. A third man tried to draw his gun but fell to the ground when a bullet creased his head, sending his hat flying. The other two men rode off in fear.

The rider from the knoll sped past the two injured men on the ground and pursued the panic-stricken horse with the black man, bouncing from side to side, trying to stay on the terrified animal. About a mile from the attempted hanging, the frightened horse passed through trees and ran up and over a small hill. As the frightened horse bolted over a fallen tree the black man crashed to the ground. The lone rider reined in beside him as he rolled onto his back, looking up at the rider.

"Why'd you do that? I ain't got no money. Can't ya sees I's a slave? When they catches up with ya they gonna hang you too!"

The rider dismounted and began removing the noose from around the man's neck. "Would you rather I'd let you hang?"

"No, sir, I's much obliged but why do you care if they hangs a slave? Most would stop and help."

He untied the man's hands: "I don't know ... It just didn't seem right."

"Yeah, but now you's gonna die just like me."

"I will if we stay here." He looked at the bareback horse grazing a hundred yards or so away. "Money isn't the only thing you don't have; you need a saddle."

"Ain't got no horse neither; he belongs to them. Now they'll hang me for being a horse thief, too."

"Which is worse, being hanged as a horse thief or for being a runaway slave? Come on, let's get that horse before your friends show up."

The lone rider mounted his horse and helped the black man up behind him then started toward the grazing horse.

"Hangin' is hangin' so's guess it don't make no never mind; when we get the horse, you'd better high-tail it so's you don't hang with me."

"You going to let them catch you?"

"No, sir, I's gonna get!"

"I'm heading to Texas, want to come along?"

"Danged if you ain't dumber than me." The black man slid off the mount when it stopped beside the grazing horse. "Does ya wants ta hang?"

"After what I did, do you think they will just let me ride away? They're looking for a double hanging now. Where will you go?"

"Danged if I know."

"Might as well tag along with me."

The black man struggled to mount the bareback horse.

"Try grabbing his mane and swing your leg over his back." With the reins in his left hand, the man grabbed the horse's mane with both hands and swung his right leg over the horse. The horse whinnied, rising on its hind legs; the black man slid over its back onto the ground on the other side. The rider suppressed a laugh, "Not much of a horseman, are you?"

The black man got up and talked softly to the horse, rubbing its neck and nose. "I knows horses. You think they let slaves ride 'em?" He continued to talk to the horse as he got the reins. "Whoa boy easy, boy." He grabbed the mane and swung onto its back, this time staying on the nervous animal. He continued to comfort the horse.

"You know how to handle him?"

"I knows." The rider started north at a slow pace. "How you gonna get to Texas goin' north?"

"The ground is soft."

"Gonna be soft goin' West, too."

"Our horses are leaving tracks. Your friends will be able to follow us. We'll go north until the ground changes then head southwest."

"You pretty smart, Mr. ..."

"Thad Walker," he replied.

"Mr. Walker."

"That was my father, call me Thad."

"Okay, Mr. Thad. How'd you get so smart?"

"It's not Mr. Thad, just Thad. My brother Bill found an Indian boy with an injured ankle once, and we took him to his village, and they invited us to stay. We stayed a few months, and they taught us how to hunt and track."

"How come he not with ya?"

"Died of snakebite a few years back."

"Oh. I sorry to hear that."

"Thanks. What's your name?"

"Buford Owens. My mama gives me the Buford part and the plantation master gives me the Owens."

"Ever think of changing it?"

"Why'd I do that?"

"They're looking for Buford Owens not... Buford... Chance."

"Whoa...you sure is smart. Do ya thinks Buford Chance is okay?"

"How about William B. Chance?"

"Ya means William Buford Chance? Why I need three names?"

"Most free men have three names. People may not question you being a free man if you have a name like others. William B. Chance sounds kind of sophisticated."

"What that mean?"

"A successful man. One that owns a business or property; someone important."

"Ain't gonna believe that about no black man and it don't matter cause they gonna hang me when they catches me."

"That's if they catch you. You run away before?"

"Two times, but they catches me and takes me back."

"But you keep trying. Where did you go the other times, you ran away?"

"North. We all go north cause we hears those folks up there tries to help us."

"All the more reason to go to Texas with me; they may think you will go north again since that's what runaways do.

***

While Thad and Buford were getting the horse and heading north, the three men rode back to the two men on the ground near the tree in the clearing. The man with the leg wound was the last to return.

"I'm going after them," a tall thin man said, one of the two not wounded.

"Not until we get these men to a doctor," the big man on a white-spotted horse said as he got down to help the two wounded.

"They're not hurt that bad. I've never let a slave get away from me and I'm not starting now."

"You're not going anywhere, Stanley. I need help getting these men to a doctor. Now get down and help me get them on their horses."

Stanley Lynch reluctantly got down and helped the man with the head wound back up on his horse. Frank Owens, the big man with the white-spotted horse, held the horse for the man with the shoulder wound who groaned with pain as he mounted. The five men started back through the forest in the opposite direction Thad and the runaway were going.

***

It became quiet as Thad and Buford continued north for several hours before the ground became firm and rocky. When it did, Thad started west. Eventually the terrain became a gentle slope down toward a small stream heading in a southern direction, about a mile in front of them. When they got to the stream, Thad guided his horse to the middle and started south. Buford fell in behind Thad.

"I knows what ya doin'. Can't see no hoof prints in the water."

"You catch on fast. We'll follow the stream for a few miles and look for a good place to exit."

They walked their horses downstream for about an hour then left the water heading west, riding side by side, on a meadow covered with short turf.

"You's smart all right but it don't matter none, they's comin' that's for sure. I don't know why you don't go off on your own. How many of 'em did you kill?"

"None, but three will be hurting for quite a while so they may not start looking for a few days, which will make it more difficult for them to track us."

"Some maybe, but not Mr. Lynch. He gonna come sure as the sun gonna rise in the mornin'. Huntin' runaway slaves is how he gets paid. He comin' that's for shore and he's real mean."

"All the more reason to keep moving and since we're heading west instead of north, there's a good chance he will never find you."

"Since you don't kill nobody don't make no sense you takin' me along."

"I'm doing a little running of my own. I killed a gambler outside of Atlanta. It was self-defense, but I'm not sure the sheriff will see it that way, so I left. I don't know if he is after me or not. I decided to head west. Maybe go to California."

"But ya don't needs to take me along. I just slows ya down."

"How far do you think you will get on a stolen horse without a saddle and no provisions?"

"That's what I mean. You could be long gone. I just makes it easier for 'em to catch up with you."

"Let me worry about that."

"You shore has my head all messed up."

"How so?"

"Here I'm a thinkin' ain't no good white men, 'cept maybe those up north, that want ta help us, then you go and save me from hangin' and help me getaway. How am I gonna hate all white men when you go and do a thing like that?"

"I'm sorry Buford, next time I'll let them hang you."

Buford looked at him. "Don't think you would. Somehow I thinks you'd do it again."

Neither spoke as they rode across the meadow and started through a wooded area until the sun hung low in the western sky. Thad dismounted. "We'll stop here for the night."

"Ain't no good place to build a fire," Buford said, sliding off the horse, "Too many trees."

"It will be a cold camp. If they are looking for us, they may not look in here. A fire would give us away. I have some jerky and hard biscuits. Maybe tomorrow we can shoot a rabbit."

***

Frank Owens, Stanley Lynch, and the three wounded men rode until the sun began to descend before a small town appeared a few miles away. Long shadows filled the street when Owens stopped in front of the doctor's house. After Owens and Lynch helped the three wounded men inside, Stanley Lynch turned to go.

"It's getting dark, Stanley," Frank said "You better wait until morning. Let's go to the restaurant and get something to eat."

"Guess you're right, but I'm going after them at first light, and I'll bring them both back."

The two men headed toward the restaurant: "You better be careful, that man could've killed us all. He got the rope with one shot. He won't be easy to take. You better hope Buford took off on his own."

"I want them both. I can handle him."

"Like you did back at the tree?" It became quiet as they crossed the street to the restaurant.

The following morning, Thad and Buford rose with the sun as did Lynch who began backtracking, heading for the forest and tree in the clearing where they tried to hang Buford.

***

When the light was bright enough to see through the forest, Thad saddled his horse and they continued on through the trees. About an hour later the trees gave way to open country with scattered trees and brush. About noon they came to a small stream and watered the horses and themselves. Thad refilled his canteen before crossing the creek.

"I think we should avoid towns until we are farther west," Thad said as they finished the last of the jerky and biscuits, under a large oak tree.

"Ain't nobody gonna think I'm a free man no matter where we go."

"Yeah, I've been thinking about that." Thad went to his saddlebag and removed a gun belt and holster. He handed them to Buford.

"Whoa! I ain't never shot no gun. You trust me with it?"

"You wouldn't shoot me after saving you from hanging, would you?"

"No sir, but I might shoot myself since I don't know how to use it."

"You'll look more like a free man if you have a gun. I'll teach you how to use it later."

"You takes this from the gambler you shot?"

"No, it was my brothers. Put it on but leave the gun in the holster until I show you how to handle it."

Buford put it on. "You's do too much for me, Thad. How I gonna repay ya?"

"That's the other thing. We need to work on your speech."

"Huh?"

"The way you talk."

"I's just talk like all my people."

"That's the problem. It will give you away. Time to go." Thad swung into the saddle.

Buford handed Thad the reins to his horse. "You's go ahead I's sees if I can catch a rabbit."

"It's 'I'll see if I can,' not 'I's sees.'" You don't know how to shoot."

"Don't need no gun." He started through the brush mumbling to himself, "I's sees ... I'll see, didn't know being free would be so hard." As Buford walked away, Thad moved on, walking his horse, leading the bareback horse.

***

It took Lynch the better part of the day to reach the tree in the clearing then start following the trail left by the horses. Less than two miles from the tree, he came to the place where Buford fell from the horse when it jumped the fallen tree. From the fallen tree Lynch followed the trail north, at a slow pace.

***

The sun was high in the western sky when Thad saw Buford, far off to his right, carrying a rabbit. He stopped and waited for him. "Ain't goin' hungry tonight." He held up the rabbit.

"Good man. We'll camp under those trees up ahead."

When he got to the wooded area, Thad dismounted and began building a fire.

Buford came up behind him: "Uses gots a knife?"

"Do you have a knife," Thad answered.

"No. That's why I's asks you." Thad stood and looked at Buford then pulled a folded knife from his pocket and handed it to him. "Ho. "It's my talk." Thad smiled. "I's try Thad, I's... I'll try to do better." Shaking his head, Buford walked away from their camp to clean the rabbit.

The rabbit was a welcome change from jerky but their water ran out as they ate. With the remnants of the fire buried, Thad and Buford started west, following the sun, now approaching the horizon. As the sun disappeared below the horizon, Thad reined in at the edge of a lake to camp for the night.

***

Lynch continued to follow the hoofprints until they began to fade, along with the light, so he stopped and setup camp. The next morning Lynch continued north as the ground became hard and the hoof prints were no longer visible. He continued north looking for the trail but it never reappeared. Even so, he continued north, looking for a town.

***

Thad and Buford started southwest about the time Lynch started north. With Buford beside him, Thad followed the edge of the lake before going west. Later that morning Buford caught another rabbit, and they stopped for a late breakfast.

While Lynch continued north looking for a trail, Thad set up a few pinecones and a piece of a limb on a fallen tree and began teaching Buford how to shoot: "Hold it like this." Thad pulled his revolver from the holster. "Now hold it out in front of you and cock the hammer." Thad cocked his gun and Buford cocked his. "Point it at the chunk of wood on the fallen tree. Close your left eye and sight down the barrel." Buford followed instructions. "The piece of wood should be just above the end of the barrel. Now squeeze the trigger."

The gun sounded with a loud bang and dirt flew up below the fallen tree, nowhere near the piece of wood. Buford jumped as the gun went off: "Whoa! It kicks like a mule."

"You'll get used to it. Your aim is good but a little low. Try again and remember to squeeze the trigger." Buford cocked the gun and fired again, this time hitting the fallen tree. "Better, now a little higher. Buford fired again and this time hit the chunk of wood. "That's great. Now aim for a pinecone." The next shot hit the fallen tree, then above the pinecone, sending dirt flying behind the fallen tree with the next shot hitting the pinecone. "I'm impressed." Buford cocked and tried to fire again, but nothing happened. "Time to reload. It's a six-shooter, not seven. Come over here and I'll show you how to load it."

Buford watched Thad reload the first chamber then handed him the gun. "That's a little scary. I's... I'm kinda afraid of it."

"That's good. You should always treat the gun with respect. It can kill you as easy as someone else." With the gun reloaded, Buford tried to hit the other pinecones. He missed with some but seemed to be improving with each shot. "That's enough for now. Reload, and we'll move on. I don't want to use up all my supplies. We may need them if your friends catch up with us."

"You keep sayin'...saying that. They ain't...are no friends of mine."

Thad smiled. "We'll go another day then start looking for a town."

Two days later Lynch was still going north, even though the trail never reappeared, as Thad and Buford topped a hill with the outline of a town appearing off in the distance, several miles away.

"Get off your horse," Thad said. Puzzled, Buford slid off the horse. "Remove its bridle." He removed it and when he did Thad hit the horse on its rump with his hat. "Haa get!" The startled horse ran off, and Thad chased it a short distance yelling and waving his hat before returning to a dumbfounded Buford.

"Why'd you chase my horse away?"

"It's a stolen horse. You don't want to be seen riding a stolen horse. If Lynch is following us, he can describe it to people and know we came through here. We'll get you a horse in town." He removed his foot from the stirrup, extending his hand toward Buford.

"You's can't's...you can't buy me's...me a horse. How's...how am I gonna...going to repay you? I'll just go off on my own."

"If you do, you'll be caught and go back to the plantation or hanged. Once we get you looking like a free man, we'll look for work. You can pay me back if you want and then take off on your own."

"If my mama had told me someday I'd meet a white man I'd like I would never have believed her."

"You need to be careful of how you say things when we get in town, and you're doing better, I don't know how the folks here feel about people of color. If things go bad and a firefight starts, just draw slow point and shoot."

"Maybe I's... I made a mistake; being free is hard."

"Life is hard my friend, no matter what your color. I don't think it will come to that. Be polite when speaking to people but not submissive."

"What does submissive mean?"

"Talk to them as if you are their equal, not as you would talking to your master." Thad glanced over his shoulder. "I think the first thing we'll do is get you some new clothes."

"I'll never get you paid back."

"Want to be my slave?"

"Might as well be, I owe you everything including my life."

"No man should be able to own another. I never could figure out how the founders could write a paper claiming all men are created equal and then let some remain slaves. Don't forget you're William B. Chance, when we get there."

"That's going to take some gettin'...getting used to."

The town grew larger and larger as Thad continued down the gentle slope, not knowing what to expect, once there. A dirt road went straight through town and they passed a sign that read Prairieville as they entered. Even though Buford needed a horse, Thad rode on past a livery stable looking for the general store. About halfway through town, he reined in at a hitching rail in front of the store and both dismounted.

"What can I do for you, Mister?" the proprietor said, looking at Thad.

"Bill here needs some new clothes. Think you have some that will fit him?"

"Never sold to a black man before. Not sure I want to."

"What do you have against money?" Thad walked over and picked up a wide-brimmed hat.

"If he puts it on, he's bought it."

"Then I guess you will sell to him." He started looking through clothes and Buford joined him. "Do you have a place Bill can change? He will also need boots."

"Room in the back but don't leave his old clothes there. Don't want them in my store."

Buford went to the room and came back carrying his old clothes and Thad placed the hat on his head. "What do we owe you?"

"Boots five dollars; pants three; shirt two and the hat seven."

Thad paid the man: "We'll be back. We need provisions."

"Don't stay long. This town doesn't like Negroes."

A smile appeared on Thad's face as he looked straight at the man: "That's a shame. I'm beginning to like it here. Maybe we will stay."

"We should just go," Buford said, leaving the store.

"You need a horse." Thad headed for the livery stable leading his horse. As they entered the gated stable, a man came out of the office and stopped on the porch. "We need a horse," Thad said.

"I don't deal with no coloreds."

"You sell horses, don't you?"

"That I do but not to the likes of him."

"You'll sell to me, won't you?"

"I got one over here." He pointed to a scraggly horse in a corral to his left.

"I like the stallion over there." Thad pointed to a gray horse in a corral to their right.

"I've kinda taken a likin' to him."

"What about the horses in the corral across from him?"

"They're kinda special to me too."

Buford walked over to the gray stallion and rubbed its nose.

"I'll give you sixty bucks for the stallion," Thad said.

"That's a hundred and fifty-dollar horse."

"The nag you tried to sell me is a five-dollar horse and the stallion a forty-dollar horse, but I'll give you sixty, and I'll need a saddle and saddlebags, also."

"You know horses, don't you? But I didn't say I'd sell to ya."

"You may be biased but not stupid. No one will give you sixty dollars for a forty-dollar horse, and I don't think you're in business to lose money."

The man looked at him for a moment: "I'm sellin' to you?"

"Yes."

"Saddle is twenty-five and bags fifteen." He turned and went into the office. Thad and Buford followed.

"I'll give you twenty for the saddle and saddlebags," Thad said.

"How you expect me to earn a living at that price? I told you what they cost."

"Saddle is worth fifteen and the bags five. You'll be earning a living, not stealing it."

The man looked down shaking his head then looked at Thad. "You owe me eighty dollars."

"Write it up, and I'll pay you. I want a receipt."

"Not very trusting, are you?"

"We ride out of here, and you start shouting horse theft. Damn right I want a receipt."

"Mister, I swear, I'm an honest man."

"I caught that right from the start when you tried to sell me a forty-dollar horse for a hundred and fifty dollars."

The man sighed, sat at the desk and began writing.

The stable owner put a bridle on the stallion and led him out of the corral. Buford saddled it then both mounted their horses and Thad looked at the man: "Nice doing business with you."

"Don't come back anytime soon."

"I think we'd better get while we have a chance," Buford said as they rode out of the stable.

"We need provisions, and I'm hungry." Thad headed for the restaurant. "I'd like to have a decent meal before we leave."

"They's ain't gonna ... they won't serve me, and you know it. You're just causin' trouble."

"Aren't you hungry? Let's see if you're right." He reined in at the hitching rail in front of the restaurant.

When they entered, a large woman wearing an apron glared at them: "What are you doing in my restaurant?"

"We're hungry," Thad said.

"Your kind is not welcome in here."

"What about out back? Okay if we eat there?"

"The lady grinned then yelled at a lady serving tables: "Mable, move a table to the far corner with two chairs." She looked at Thad. "You can eat there but don't take too long."

"Much obliged."

"Everybody's got to eat." She walked away.

"I don't like this," Buford said, following the server to a dark corner in the back.

"We're going to eat, aren't we? Just don't turn your back to the others."

From the restaurant, Thad headed for the store: "That was a great meal."

"Taste good, but my stomach is still shaking. You ... you're beginning to scare me. You tryin'... trying to get us killed?"

"When we get our provisions, we'll go." They entered the store, and Thad walked over to the counter where the proprietor stood, glaring at them. "We need salt pork, flour, beans, coffee, and hardtack biscuits. Do you have canned peaches?"

"I got them."

"We also need powder and bullets, a lot of it."

"Going to start a war?"

"We like to target shoot. How far to the next town, west?"

"West Gap is about a day and a half ride from here."

"Is it as friendly as this town?"

"Might think you're still here."

Thad paid the man, and they walked outside: "I'd like a beer."

"Me too but you know they'd most likely shoot me if we go in the saloon, and maybe you too."

"Let's see if you're right."

"No, Thad. Let's just go."

"Maybe this is like the restaurant. He started for the saloon and walked through the swinging doors, followed by a nervous Buford.

The bartender stopped wiping the top of the bar and two men leaning against the bar turned toward them as four men at a table stood. "No Negroes allowed in here," the bartender said.

"We just want a beer," Thad answered.

"I'll wait outside." Buford left the saloon.

"Thad walked to the bar. "Give me two beers."

"You can only drink one at a time, and I ain't givin' you one for your black friend."

"Okay, make it one."

The man poured a mug of beer and sat it in front of Thad. He paid for it, picked up the mug and headed for the door.

"Where ya going?"

"I'll bring the mug back." Thad walked outside.

"You gonna let him get away with that" one of the men at the bar asked.

"He paid me. There is no law against drinking a beer on the street."

Outside, Thad found Buford standing with his back to the wall and Thad leaned against the wall beside him then handed the mug to Buford.

"You're gonna get us killed," Burford whispered, watching people stare at them as they walked by, some leaving the boardwalk to avoid going past them.

"Take a drink." Buford took a sip and Thad took the mug, taking a long swig. "Now that's a good beer." He handed it back to Buford, still looking up and down the street. Buford tried to hand it back. "The sooner we finish it, the sooner we'll go." Buford took a long drink, half emptying the glass. Thad took the mug and drank half of what was left. "Sure is a beautiful day," Thad said, as the sheriff crossed the street, heading toward them.

"Damn it, Thad, drink it so we can go!"

"Afternoon, Sheriff," Thad said.

"You boys have business here?"

"Leaving as soon as we finish our beer."

"Make it soon."

Thad finished the beer and walked inside and placed the mug on the bar. All eyes were on him: "Thanks for the beer." He turned and went outside to a nervous Buford with the sheriff standing in the middle of the street, looking straight at them.

"Mighty friendly town you have, sheriff," Thad said, as they mounted their horses.

"Don't come back."

As the sun continued its westward journey with a cloudless sky overhead, Thad and a nervous Buford rode out of town heading west.

"You's...you're either the bravest man I've ever know'd, or just plum crazy," I can't believe they didn't kill us."

"They wanted to, but knew they would have to kill both of us and would hang for killing me." He looked at Buford. "Not sure about you."

"So, you put my life in danger for what?"

"They knew I wouldn't let them shoot you and would have to kill both of us, as I said. I figured it would help give us cover. If Lynch comes looking for you, he wouldn't believe a runaway slave would do the things we just did. It also should convince the town you are a free man."

"Maybe, but I don't want to be free and dead. You're crazy, that's for sure. If you'd been wrong, we'd be dead. I don't want to go to West Gap and have you try to get us killed again."

"I won't, I promise. If they run us off, we'll go to the next town, and we'll take our time getting there, I want to make sure you know how to use your gun if it comes to that, and sooner or later I'm sure it will."

Chapter Two
Fire Fight

Several hours passed before Thad and Buford stopped for the night. The sun, now far to the west, continued its descent, taking the crepuscular light with it, as Thad set up camp near an oak hammock, not far from a small stream.

"I think we'll stay here for a while," Thad said the next morning as he placed a pot of salt pork and beans over the fire. "Time for some target practice. Let's see if you can still hit where you aim." Thad placed the empty peach can in the crotch of an oak tree limb and stepped off thirty paces. "See if you can hit the can." Buford stood beside him and aimed at the can. His first shot hit the tree a couple of inches away from the can. "Close; try again." He aimed again and this time sent the can flying. "I'm impressed." Thad threw a hardtack biscuit on the ground about fifty feet away. "Hit the biscuit." The biscuit broke in pieces as Buford took aim and fired. A big smile appeared on his face. "Think you're pretty good, huh?" Thad threw another biscuit in front of them. "Holster the gun, draw point and shoot. Don't fast draw and don't aim just point and shoot. Don't raise the gun above your waist."

Buford holstered the gun drew and shot with the bullet kicking up dirt a few feet beyond the biscuit. "Dang. How can I miss so far?"

"It's not easy shooting offhand, but someday it may save your life. You see how far you missed. Try to compensate."

He holstered the gun, drew, and shot again, this time sending dirt flying in front of the biscuit.

"You overcorrected." The next shot was to the left and a little long.

"I ain't never gonna hit it."

"And you're never going to sound like a free man talking like that."

"Well, it makes me mad."

"Getting mad and losing control may get you killed someday. Don't take your eye off the biscuit and this time, see the bullet hitting it before you shoot."

"That don't...doesn't make any sense."

"Mind over matter my friend, mind over matter."

This time the biscuit skidded across the ground when Buford drew and fired: "I hit it I hit it."

"Keep shooting."

Buford shot again sending dirt up next to the biscuit then broke it in pieces with his last shot.

"Whoa! That made me tingle."

"Reload. You're just getting started."

Thad made Buford continue offhand shooting until he could hit the biscuits with almost every shot.

"You need to be ambidextrous when it comes to shooting. This time use your left hand."

"Ambi...huh?"

"You need to be able to shoot with either hand. If your right hand is injured, you don't want to be killed because you can't shoot with the left."

"Oh, okay." He put the gun in his left hand and shot, missing the biscuit.

"You need to train your left hand to follow your eye just like your right."

When Buford was hitting most of the time with his left hand, Thad made him switch to his right. The practice continued, switching from hand to hand until Buford had destroyed many biscuits and gone through a lot of powder and lead. By noon, Buford was exhausted, so they stopped for lunch.

"You work me as hard as Master Owens."

"But I'm doing it for you, not for him or me. These are skills you'll need as a free man, especially since you're a free black man. You'll get a lot of respect because of your size, and if you can shoot fast and straight, no one will mess with you."

"I hear you, but can we take a break?"

"We'll take a walk after lunch and have a look around. Maybe you can find a rabbit for dinner. If we do, I want you to make it run before you shoot it. You've never shot a moving target."

"Don't sound like no break to me," Buford said, taking a sip of coffee. "Won't find a rabbit this time of day."

"I think you're right. The sun is too hot to explore in the middle of the day. We'll go later. More coffee?"

"Now you're talking like a friend, not a master." Buford extended his cup and Thad filled it then Buford sat, leaning against an oak tree. Thad sat beside him.

"Were you born on the Owens plantation?"

"No. Born and raised on the Gaylord plantation but they sold me when I turned fifteen. Don't like to keep families together. Mama and Daddy are still there, but I was getting too hard to handle, so they sold me."

"Is that why you ran away, because they sold you?"

"No. I'd a run sooner or later. I didn't like being whipped for no reason sept ... except to keep me afraid and not cause trouble."

"How old were you when you first ran?"

"Eighteen. I made it to Kentucky before they caught me. Didn't try again until I was twenty."

"How old are you now?"

"Twenty-three. Thought I'd make it this time but they caught up with me real fast. I fought 'em real hard too. I made up my mind I wasn't goin'...going back, that's why they decided to hang me."

"You would rather die than go back?"

"That I would. Being a slave is more like being in hell than being alive. Might as well be dead."

"Glad I came along."

"I prayed real hard, and God sent you. You're still helping me. Not sure you're a man...maybe an angel from God."

Thad smiled. "God knows I'm no angel., Butte. I'm just a man like any other."

"After what you did in that town back there, I kinda believe you. No angel would do the things you did and no man either. I don't think you are afraid of anything."

"Fear is our worse enemy, Butte.

If we let it control us, we're lost, and others will control our lives. You're a brave man. You proved that when you fought the men that tried to take you back. Freedom was more important to you than your life, so you fought."

"You're wrong, Thad. I was scared out of my mind, but I fought anyway."

"Of course. That's what conquering fear is all about. You control it, not let it control you."

"Are you saying you were afraid back there, in that town?"

"Not fear, concern. I wanted them to believe we are free men, just trying to be accepted. If we had acted as if we had something to hide, they may have arrested us and checked to see if you were a runaway. When we pushed our way into the restaurant and bar, we showed them we had nothing to hide, so they tolerated us and tried to get us to leave."

"You did all that, not me. I was so scared I almost pissed myself."

"Well you hid it well, and I think it worked. No one is following us, and if your friend Lynch comes looking for you, I don't think they will believe it is you he is looking for."

"Dang it, Thad. He ain't my friend. He wants me dead. Don't you know that?"

Thad smiled. "Where's your control?"

"You did that on purpose, didn't you?"

"Anger and fear go hand in hand, Butte. You must control them both. Lynch wants you dead, but anger and fear will kill you before he does if you don't learn to control them."

"You got it all figured out, don't you? How old are you, a hundred? Don't look much older than me."

"I'm twenty-six."

"So, how did you get this control you're talking about, or is it just that, talk?"

"It's a long story."

"I'm listening."

"My father owned a farm in North Carolina and made a good living on it until a mule kicked him in the head and killed him. Ma tried to run it for a year after he died, but it was too much for me and Bill, we were too young to keep it going without help, so Ma hired a man to run it. After a year she married him. He treated us well until he married Ma. After a few months, he began treating us mean, especially Bill. We took it for a couple of years then one day when Hiram started on Bill, Bill beat him with an ax handle. He was afraid he killed him and took off. I was afraid to stay there alone, so I ran with him. We made our way to Florida and went to work on a cattle ranch. Mr. Fields is a good man and treated us well. Taught us to ride and herd cattle. The first thing we bought with our pay were guns. After that, we spent most of our money on powder and lead to practice shooting. There are lots of pine trees in Florida, and we loved shooting pine cones off the trees. We practiced drawing on each other but with empty guns. The more we practiced, the better we got, but Bill was always better than me.

"Bill was worried he killed Hiram until we heard he lived, not hurt as bad as Bill thought. Not long after we left, Ma divorced him, sold the farm and moved in with Aunt Betty, her sister. We had nothing to go back to, so we stayed in Florida.

"But Bill never got over what he did to our stepfather. He was afraid if he lost his temper again, he might kill someone. At first I didn't understand, I thought he was afraid and that is why he didn't stand up to others. I was wrong; he was exercising control. Some of the other hands would pick on him, and he just took it. I felt sorry for him and wanted to fight for him, but I was too young to fight a grown man. One day one of the hands, Harold, somewhat of a bully, started on Bill. He took it for a while, but when Harold got in Bill's face again, Bill put him down with a right to the jaw. Harold got up and come at Bill, but he put him down again. 'I don't want to fight you, Harold,' Bill said, looking down at him, 'but if you don't back off, I'm going to hurt you.' No one picked on him after that."

"You really loved him, didn't you?"

"Very much, he was my hero."

"Is that why you named me Bill?"

"Never thought about it. Could be. We worked for Mr. Fields for over a year then decided to see more of the country. We worked for other ranchers but not as long as for Mr. Fields. We were camped along the Saint Johns River when the snake bit him. The nights were cool, and I guess the snake crawled under his blanket to keep warm. When Bill got up, it bit him in the chest. I got him to town, but there was nothing the doctor could do. I... I watched him die."

"I know that almost killed you too."

"I wanted to die; I can tell you that. I sold everything except his gun. I drifted from ranch to ranch after that and never forgot what Bill taught me about anger and fear. At one of the ranches, a hand taught me to play poker, and I discovered I was good at it. I gambled in between jobs and found I could make more money gambling than working. What Bill taught me about anger and fear came in handy gambling. If you were losing and the others saw fear or anger in your eyes, they took advantage of it. But if you didn't let it show, when your luck changed and you won a big pot, they thought you were losing on purpose because you were a card shark. I never cheated, I'm just good at the game, but I got into a lot of fights because I won so often.

"I tried to talk to the man in Atlanta before I shot him. He accused me of cheating, so I offered to give him his money back, but he burst into rage and went for his gun. He didn't even get it out of his holster and one of the other players said I just shot him, and he never went for his gun, that's why I ran."

"That's some story, Thad. You've been through a lot. I'll give you back the gun when I get a job and buy my own."

"Keep it. I think Bill would want you to have it."

"You too good to me. I don't know how I will ever thank you."

"You just did."

It became quite, and before long their eyelids became heavy, and they drifted off to sleep. When they woke, the sun had moved far to the west, and shadows began to stretch across the landscape. Buford stretched and groaned as Thad opened his eyes.

"I think I can find a rabbit now," Buford said.

"I'll go with you." Thad put more wood on the fire, and they started off through the brush and trees.

About fifteen minutes later Buford stopped: "Look under that bush up there."

"I see him. I'll spook him and make him run."

"But I got a good shot."

"I want you to shoot a moving target." Thad picked up a rock and threw it at the bush making the rabbit run, and Buford began firing.

"I'm kicking dirt up his butt; why can't I hit him?"

"Because you're aiming at him."

"Of course, I am."

"When you squeeze the trigger, the rabbit has moved away from where you are shooting. You need to lead him before you shoot."

"Huh?"

"When we find another one, follow him with the gun then move it ahead of him as you shoot. By the time the bullet gets to where you shot, so will the rabbit."

"Makes sense... I think."

Time passed as they continued through the brush and trees and the light began to fade before Thad saw a rabbit grazing not far away. "See him?" Buford nodded, Thad clapped his hands, and the bunny ran. Buford followed him with the gun then swung the barrel ahead as he squeezed the trigger and the rabbit did a summersault then lay still.

"Good shot," Thad said.

"You were right. I pulled through and shot."

"Let's see how good you did." They walked up to the rabbit, and Buford picked it up. "Right through the head. I'm impressed."

"Thanks. Sure going to taste good with those beans."

"We can have biscuits with it."

"You sure there's some left? We shot a bunch."

"I have flour and oil. I'll make some."

As Buford cleaned the rabbit and put it on a stick over the fire, Thad made biscuits. When the rabbit was almost done, Thad placed the pan of biscuits over the fire. The sun disappeared below the horizon when they began to eat.

"Rabbit is good," Buford said, and the beans too."

"And my biscuits?"

"I thought the store-bought ones were bad, but I think you beat 'em."

"Thanks. Next time you can make them."

"Most likely be worse. I don't know much about fixin' food. We leaving in the morning?"

"No. More practice."

"Why? You said I'm doing good."

"There's a few things you haven't tried."

The following morning Thad put some dirt in another empty peach can. "When I throw this in the air I want you to see if you can hit it. You ready?"

"I'm ready."

Thad tossed the can into the air, and Buford shot and missed. "Try again." Thad retrieved the can and threw it high above them. Buford shot, causing the can to spin, scattering dirt through the air. "Not bad." Thad filled the can with dirt again and threw it high and in front of them. The can exploded when the sound of the gun filled the air. A big grin appeared on Buford's face. "Think you're pretty good, huh?" Thad threw a biscuit and Buford shot, missing the small target.

"It's too small," Buford said.

After retrieving the biscuit, Thad threw it high over their heads. Buford shot and missed again.

"Remember what I told you before? Keep your eye on the target and see the bullet hit it before you shoot."

"I'll try." This time when Thad tossed the biscuit, it exploded when Buford shot. "Whoa! I can't believe I hit it!"

"You better believe. You must always believe you are going to hit your target. See it in your head before you shoot. Get the thought of missing out of your mind. You must train your gun to follow your eye. When you do, you will never miss again. Reload, and I'll get another biscuit."

Buford reloaded the gun. "Is those the store-bought or yours?"

"Store-bought."

"My stomach's gonna hate me for this."

"You're a cruel man, Butte." Buford laughed as he finished reloading. The first shot missed but the biscuit exploded with his second. "Okay, holster the gun," Thad said after Buford hit the next two biscuits. "When I throw the next one draw and shoot." Buford's first shot missed but hit the biscuit with his next shot. "Reload, and we'll try again."

"Ain't gonna be none left for supper," Buford said as he reloaded

"There won't be any left for dinner," Thad said.

"That's what I said." Thad just looked at him. "Oh, okay, I'll try to talk better."

When Buford was able to hit two in a row, drawing and firing, Thad tossed two biscuits in the air, starling Buford and he missed both.

"That ain't ... isn't fair. No one can hit two."

Thad handed him three biscuits.

"You want me to throw them all at once?"

"That's the plan."

"You're crazy. You can't hit all three."

"Throw them."

Buford tossed them, and all three exploded into pieces as Thad drew and fired in rapid succession.

"How did you do that?"

"Practice. Holster your gun. I'm going to throw a rock at a tree behind you. I want you to turn and fire at the sound when it hits the tree, but don't turn toward me, turn the other way."

"Why do I need to do that?"

"If you ever hear a gun being cocked behind you, it may save your life."

"You think of everything."

"Not me, Bill. He was always trying to protect me and taught me how to protect myself." He paused. "He thought of everything...except a snake crawling into his bed."

"I'm sure sorry about that, Thad."

"It's just life, Butte. Are you ready?"

"Sure."

Thad hit a tree with a rock, behind Buford, he turned and fired, missing the tree. Thad threw another rock and Buford missed again. On the third try, he nicked the tree. "Better, but you need to hit closer to the sound."

"You don't ever back off, do you?"

"I lost a brother. I don't want to lose a friend. You ready?"

He nodded, and Thad threw another rock. He continued throwing rocks at different trees, making Buford shoot toward the sound in a different location behind him until he could hit close to the sound, consistently.

The sun was high overhead by the time Buford's shooting pleased Thad, so they stopped for lunch, finishing off the rabbit and beans from last night, along with Thad's scratch-made biscuits.

"What now? You want me to do more shooting?"

"We'll quit for now, but later I want you to practice shooting more than one biscuit out of the air. Right now, I'm thinking about going for a swim."

"I'm not good at swimming."

"What I've got in mind is a bath. I'm hot and sweaty, and my clothes are filthy."

"I could use a bath and clean clothes, too."

"Yeah... I was going to talk to you about that." Buford glared at him, and Thad grinned, rose, and started for the river.

Buford rose and followed. "Well you don't smell like no field of clover ya know."

"I know. My horse keeps shying away from me when I approach him. I think he's trying to tell me something."

Thad removed a bar of soap from his saddlebags and both stripped to their long johns and entered the water. About an hour later they were sitting on a saddle blanket under an oak tree, waiting for their clothes and themselves to dry.

"I want you to try to shoot something different for dinner tonight," Thad said, "I'm tired of rabbit."

"We scared up some strange looking birds when we were looking for rabbits. Look like some kinda chicken. They could be good to eat."

"They're grouse. We'll need at least two. They're not very big."

"You shoot one, and I'll shoot one."

"You shoot all of them, and I want four."

"Four! You're the good shooter you shoot 'em."

"You need the practice. And try not to waste bullets."

"You keep making me shoot we won't have none left."

It became quiet except for the occasional sound of a bird singing off in the distance. Both drifted off to sleep as they had yesterday. When they woke, their clothes were dry. After dressing they wandered through the country looking for grouse. After walking for quite some time, a bird flew up from some brush a few yards in front of them, and Buford shot. The bird fell to the ground, and a big grin appeared on Buford's face.

Thad picked up the grouse: "Nice shot. You need three more."

Time passed without seeing another bird as they wandered through the sparse brush. The sun continued its journey west and Buford began to think they wouldn't see more game when a rabbit appeared ahead of them. He started for his gun, but Thad stopped him, grabbing his hand before he could draw and shoot.

"No rabbits."

"We only got...have one bird. Don't look like we's...we're going to see more."

"Then I guess you will go hungry."

"But I shot it."

"Your job not mine, keep going."

Long shadows of evening began to appear as they continued walking. Without warning, a few feet in front of them, three grouse took flight, startling Buford. He managed to get off two shots before the birds were out of range, missing with both shots: "Dang. They scared the fire outta me."

"You wasted two bullets."

"You shoulda shot. You'd got all three. I told you I didn't know they were there."

"You must be ready at all times. You never know when danger is near."

"Birds ain't...aren't dangerous."

"What if they were men?" Buford sighed and they continued through the open country.

More time passed before two birds flew up in front of them. Buford shot, dropping one of them but held off shooting as the other flew out of range.

"You should have shot both."

"I didn't want to waste a bullet."

"You wouldn't have if you'd hit him."

"What if I'd missed?"

"What if it was a man shooting at you?" Buford sighed again as Thad picked up the bird before continuing.

The light started to fade before three birds burst from the brush not far in front of them. Buford downed one, then a second as the third made its escape to the safety of the trees, far ahead of them.

"You should have got all three."

"Dang, you're a hard man, Thad. I got two and didn't waste no bullets."

"If the third was a man he wouldn't have wasted a bullet either. He would have killed you."

"You keep saying that, but they're only birds. Can we go back now? It's getting dark."

After cleaning the birds in the field, they returned to camp. The beans were gone and much to Buford's objection, Thad made more biscuits. Surprisingly this time the biscuits were better. After eating, they sat drinking coffee as the sun disappeared below the horizon.

"Either you're doing better, or I'm getting used to them, the biscuits were pretty good."

"Thanks, Butte, but I'm not letting up on you."

"Ain't no surprise to me. Are we leaving tomorrow?"

"More practice. We'll leave about noon. I think West Gap is about a day's ride. I don't want to get there at night, so we'll camp out one more night." Neither spoke and the only sounds in the dark night were the crackle of the fire and an owl hooting off in the distance.

Both awoke to a campfire of smoldering embers as the sun appeared in the east, chasing away the starlit dark sky. Thad rekindled the fire. Breakfast was cold biscuits washed down with coffee. Thad made Buford practice each shooting technique before dousing the fire and starting west. That night they finished the last of the biscuits then rose early the following morning and continued toward West Gap.

"I'm proud of you, Butte. You shoot better than most men I've met, for no longer than you've been shooting. You should be able to defend yourself if necessary."

"Are you feeling okay, Thad? You said something nice about me."

"Don't let it go to your head. I want you to have confidence in yourself if you ever need to use your gun in a fight. Knowing you can handle a gun is half the battle. Having bullets buzzing around your head is the real test."

"Then you don't mean it."

"Of course, I do. I wouldn't say it if I didn't. I think you're a natural when it comes to shooting, but shooting targets is a whole lot different than facing a man with a gun."

"I ain't...not sure I could shoot a man."

"Killing is easy, Butte; it's living with it that is hard."

"Hope I never find out and I'm not as good shooting as you."

"Give it time, Butte, or should I say, Bill. When we get to town don't forget you're William Buford Chance."

"I know. Not sure I'll ever get used to it."

"If I call you Bill be sure you respond, or people may become suspicious. I don't know if West Gap is like the last town or not. The man in the store said it was, but he didn't like us. Remember you're a free man, so act like one."

"It was me not you, they didn't like. I still don't know why whites don't like us."

"People can be afraid of things that are different, and your size will cause some to be afraid since you're different. Just treat them with respect but show them you're their equal."

Neither spoke for a while and as the sun made its way high over their heads the town came into view. A dusty dirt road divided the town and they walked their horses' past people walking along the boardwalks on both sides of the street. A few horses were standing at hitching rails while three riders rode by on horseback. Thad went straight to the store. Tethering the horses at the hitching rail, they went inside.

A lady said, "May I help you?"

"We need some supplies," Thad said.

"Not from around here, are you?"

"Just passing through. I didn't expect to see a woman running a store."

"My husband is working in the back. I'll get him if you want."

"Not necessary."

"What can I get for you?"

"Powder, bullets, salt pork..." Thad ran down a list of food supplies, and the woman started through the store gathering them. While she worked, six men rode in and stopped in front of the bank across the streeet. Four men got off their horses and went inside.

"How's the food in the restaurant?" Thad asked as he paid the lady.

"Best in town." She smiled. "Only one in town. I've never heard anyone complain."

"Will they serve me?" Buford asked.

"You going to pay?"

"I'll pay."

"Then I don't see a problem."

"Some don't like people of my color."

"Don't think we've ever had a black man here before. I don't see Bertha having a problem, as long as you pay. You're kinda sensitive about your color, aren't you?"

"No ma'am. Most white folks don't like us. I just don't want to cause trouble."

"Well..." before she could finish, shots were heard outside, and Thad bolted for the door, followed by Buford. Four men ran from the bank, shooting, one shot a deputy standing in the middle of the street and another shot the sheriff in the shoulder. The four, still shooting, ran toward two other men on horseback, holding the reins of four horses.

"Take the left!" Thad said, as he drew and shot two men on his right, trying to mount their horses. Without thinking Buford shot the other two men as they mounted their horses, both fell to the ground, limp and still, along with a bag of money. A man down the street shot one of the men on horseback, trying to ride out of town, and he fell to the dusty street. The sixth man spurred his horse on, heading out of town, but a large man in a wide-brimmed hat drew his gun, took aim, and fired. The man fell to the ground, dead.

"You men probably saved my life and a few others," the sheriff said, walking up to Thad and Buford. Buford was shaking and still holding his gun.

"Put it away," Thad said, and Buford holstered his gun, trembling.

"I need to talk to you boys in my office," the sheriff said, holding his shoulder.

"Don't you think you need to have that wound dressed?" Thad asked.

"Doc will be here shortly. Follow me."

The sheriff went to his office and sat behind a desk. Thad and Buford followed. The doctor came in and started helping the sheriff remove his shirt. He winced as the doctor probed the wound. He looked at the doctor. "How's Ben?"

The doctor continued to work on the shoulder: "You'll need a new deputy."

The sheriff looked at Thad and Buford. "New to West Gap, aren't you? You two shot and killed those four robbers so quick I barely saw it."

"I didn't want to kill no one, sheriff," Buford said with a quiver in his voice.

"What's your name, mister?"

"Bu... William Buford Chance, sir."

"You killed two vermin, not men," he said, wrenching as the doctor continued to work on his shoulder.

"The bullet went straight through," the doctor said. "You're lucky, an inch to the right and you would lose the use of your left arm. He cleaned and bandaged the wound. "Shot of whiskey will help the pain." He folded his bag and left.

The sheriff began writing on a piece of paper: "Where you from?"

"I's—"

"We're from Florida," Thad said, interrupting Buford.

"What's your name?"

"Thaddeus Walker."

"What business you boys have in West Gap?"

"Just passing through. We need supplies."

"You did the town a service. You can go."

"Aren't you going to talk to the men that shot the other two bank robbers?" Thad asked.

"No need. The big man is Mr. Chase. He owns the largest cattle ranch in the state, and also, the bank. The other man is his top hand. Enjoy your stay in West Gap."

On their way out, Buford looked at Thad: "I don't like killing. When you said 'take the left' and started shooting, I was shooting before I knew it. It kinda makes me sick."

"Killing another man is a hard thing, but sometimes necessary," Thad said, heading for the store. "Unfortunately, as I said before, killing is easy. Living with it is hard. We'll get our supplies and go." They entered the store.

"Tom Goash," a man said, extending his hand to Thad. "The whole town is talking about you two."

"Nice to meet you. We came for our supplies."

"You can leave them here," the lady that waited on them said, "if you're going to the Restaurant. Bertha is expecting you."

"My wife is right. Your supplies will be waiting for you when you return."

Thad looked at Buford, and he smiled. "Thank you. We won't be long."

"Take your time," Tom said as they left. Two men stood and left when Thad and Buford entered the restaurant.

"I bet you boys are hungry after all that shooting." The middle-aged woman wearing an apron said. "Sit where you please."

"I's... I'm causing you to lose money," Buford said. "I'll wait outside."

"What's your name?"

"William Buford Chance."

"This is my restaurant, Mr. Chance. If some don't want to eat here, they can go hungry." They sat at a nearby table. "What are you boys drinking?"

"Beer," Thad answered.

"You'll have to go to the saloon for beer. I've got whiskey."

Thad smiled. "Even better."

"Know what you want to eat? I'd guess steak, potatoes, and greens."

Buford smiled. "Sounds good."

"Great," Thad said.

"Be right back with the whiskey."

"Food sounds good," Buford said, "but my stomach is still shaking some. I know those were bad men, but I still don't like knowing I killed them."

"Life is hard, Butte. And to survive, sometimes you have to do things you don't like, but you do them. You'll be fine. A sip of whiskey will calm you down."

The whiskey helped Buford relax, and the food was good, but when Thad tried to pay, Bertha refused. "This town owes you for what you did. This meal is on me."

"That's very kind of you," Thad said, "but not necessary."

"Most people around here know better than to argue with me, Mister. I'll overlook it this time. Come back again, and it won't be free."

"The food is great, and I've learned my lesson, Bertha. I'm looking forward to coming back."

They left the restaurant and headed for the store.

"Hold up a minute."

Thad looked behind him and saw a big man approaching, the same man that shot the last robber. He extended his hand to Thad. "I'm Tim Chase, and I'm mighty beholding to you for saving my bank."

"Just trying to be good citizens."

"You not only saved my bank but more than likely some lives, also. Ever work cattle? I'm getting ready for a drive, and I could use another hand."

"What about Bill?"

"Can't use him."

Buford looked at him. "What you're a sayin', Mr. Chase is, a black man is good enough to save your bank but not good enough to work for you."

Chase looked straight at Buford then at Thad. "I like his tenacity, I'll hire both of you, but I want you up with the herd." He looked at a man a few feet behind him. "Darrel."

"Yes, Sir, Mr. Chase."

"Take these men up to the herd."

"Have Brian do it, sir."

"You're my top hand, Darrel, but if you can't follow orders, I can't use you."

"Yes, sir."

Chase looked at Thad. "We're leaving in five days. You can camp out with the other hands till we start."

"We have some supplies waiting for us at the store."

"Get 'em. Darrel will be waiting for you when you come out."

"Thank you, Mr. Chase. We won't be long."

With their supplies loaded on the horses, they followed Darrel out of town: "What's this ten... ten, thing he called me?"

"Tenacity. He means he likes your boldness, not afraid to stand up to him."

"I think it was the whiskey talking. Surprised myself when I said it."

"Whatever it is, keep it up, you need to be like that with everyone. That's the way a proud free man that's not afraid of anything, would talk."

"Ain't gonna work when we get up there. I don't know why you got us into this? You know I don't know how to work cattle. I'm still learning to handle a horse."

"Me? You're the one with tenacity. We have five days. I'll teach you everything you need to know. You're smart. You'll catch on fast. It's really not that hard."

"I hope you're right. Ain't nobody ever called me smart before."

Chapter Three
Move 'em out

When they got to the herd, Darrel stopped near the chuck wagon and looked at Buford. "Camp over by those trees." He pointed toward a grove of oaks about fifty yards from the main camp. Buford and Thad headed for the oaks, unsaddled their horses, and removed the saddlebags and supplies.

"Since we will be eating from the chuck wagon," Thad said, "I'm going to give our food supplies to the cook." Buford agreed, and Thad headed for the chuck wagon with the supplies.

"I think you could make better use of these than we can," Thad said, placing the supplies on the tailgate of the wagon.

"Thank ya kindly," the cook said extending his hand, "Just call me Cookie."

"Thad Walker." He shook Cookie's hand.

"Heard what you and your friend did in town. Four rapid shots four men killed and not a bullet wasted."

"You can camp over here with the others," Darrel said, walking up behind Thad.

Thad turned. "I'll stay with Butte."

"Butte? I thought his name was Bill?"

"His friends call him Butte. If I were you, I'd call him Bill." He turned and walked away.

Darrel looked at Cookie: "I think Mr. Chase made a mistake hiring them."

Cookie returned to his work: "Not my business."

The light had started to fade when Cookie rang the dinner triangle. Thad rose and looked at Buford. "Let's get something to eat."

"You go."

"I guess I should have bought a bottle of whiskey at the store. Remember what I said about standing up for yourself? This is going to be a long drive. Don't let Darrel intimidate you."

"What are you going to do when he sees I can't work cattle?"

"I told you I'd teach you. Come on, I'm hungry."

Thad and Buford walked to the chuck wagon but waited for the others to be served before approaching Cookie. "It's gonna be a long drive," he said as he filled Buford's plate. You should be over here with the other wranglers."

"Mr. Barter don't like me. I'll be okay where I am." He headed back towards the oaks as Cookie filled Thad's plate.

"You can eat with us," Darrel said, walking up beside Thad.

"I guess you weren't listening earlier. I stay with Butte."

"I give the orders around here."

"And I'll follow them...as long as they don't conflict with Mr. Chase's orders. If they do, I'll follow his." Thad walked away to join Buford.

"You got your hands full with them two," one of the wranglers said.

Darrel sat down with the others: "I'm gonna hate this drive."

Everyone rose with the sun except Cookie. He had been up before first light preparing breakfast.

"After we eat, we'll ride out to the herd," Thad said, "and I'll show you a few things about handling cattle." They went to the chuck wagon then returned to their camp. After eating Thad returned their plates and cups to Cookie then walked over to Darrel. "We're going to ride out and look at the herd. We'll work the night watch if you want."

"Got all the help I need for now. Be plenty to do when the drive starts. Just don't get in the way."

"Sounds fair. We'll be around if you change your mind."

Thad and Buford saddled their horses and started for the herd about a mile away. The herd seemed to stretch to the far horizon as the cattle came into view.

"Ain't that many cows in the world," Buford said.

"One of the wranglers said it's about five thousand head."

"And owned by one man?"

"Mr. Chase is a very rich and powerful man."

"If I'd know'd that I wouldn't have talked to him the way I did."

"He respects you for talking to him as his equal. Let's see if we can find the front." Thad and Buford rode at a slow trot along the side of the loosely spaced herd with steers grazing in all directions. After riding for more than half an hour, open grassland began to appear in front of the herd. "I'll show you how to separate cows from the herd," Thad said when they got to the front, "and then bring them back to the others. Once your horse learns what you want him to do, he'll do most of the work."

"How am I going to teach him when I don't know?"

"You will learn together. I can see a lot of improvement since we bought him. He is catching on to what you want him to do, and he likes you, so he wants to please you. I want to get you and the horse used to having cattle around you, so I'm going to start walking Buck through the herd. You follow a few steers away."

"It's kinda scary having cows all around me," Buford said, "and my horse is a little nervous."

"You will get used to it. Just keep walking and talk to him in a soft voice, so he knows you're not afraid."

"But I am."

"Don't let it show or he may get spooked and start running. Control, Butte, control."

Buford began stroking and petting the horse on his neck and talking softly to him. In time, both Buford and his horse seemed to adjust, continuing through the herd in a calm manner.

"Okay," Thad said, "let's go back to the front, and I'll show you how to cut some out."

Thad showed Buford how to move a few head from the herd then return them. He showed Buford how to cut out a single animal then put it back

After a few lessons, Thad situated Buck a short distance away from the herd and made Buford practice working the herd.

"Bring me six," he said, and Buford tried to cut them out. "Not so fast you're spooking them. Take your time." Buford took more time, talking to them and using his rope the way Thad showed him. "Better. Now bring them to me."

Buford started them toward Thad.

"Now put them back."

"Bring me one."

"Now put it back."

This routine of cutting cattle in and out of the herd continued for several hours with Buford improving as morning turned into noon then late afternoon.

"Aren't we ever gonna quit?" Buford asked. "Water's not enough, I need some food."

"Okay, we'll head back, but we've missed lunch. I want you to walk through the herd for a while."

"We'll miss sup...dinner too if you keep messing around. You're really enjoying this, aren't you?"

Thad smiled at him. "In spite of all my doubts, there just might be wrangler in you after all."

"Is that a compliment or more of your smart talk?"

"You're doing good, Butte. By the time we start the drive, you should be ready."

"You mean we're going to do this every day till the drive starts?"

"You're just getting started. You've got a lot to learn."

"And you're gonna enjoy every minute of it, aren't you?"

"You don't want Mr. Chase to fire you when he gets here, do you?"

"No."

"Then grin and bear it."

"I'll bear it all right, but I won't be grinnin.'"

"I'm hungry," Thad said as the light began to fade. "Come on, let's get out of the herd and get back to camp."

Everyone had finished eating when they got to camp, and Cookie was cleaning dishes.

"I saved you some," he said when he saw them ride in. Buford dismounted, and Cookie handed him a plate. "Been gone all day."

"That we have." He took the plate and headed for their camp as Cookie handed Thad a plate.

"You've been gone all day," Darrel said, walking toward Thad.

"That's the largest herd I've ever seen," Thad replied.

"Five thousand," Darrel answered. "Murphy said it doesn't look like your 'brother' knows much about cattle."

"My brother, huh? That's a good way to put it. I guess we are like brothers. In God's eyes, we are all brothers, so that makes him your brother also." Darrel glared at him. "Bill is a little rusty, but he'll be ready when the drive starts."

"If he's not he's gone."

"If I remember right," Thad said, still holding the plate and the reins to Buck, "Mr. Chase hired us, not you." He turned and walked away.

"Why don't you let it be, Darrel, they ain't done nothin' to ya."

"Just tend to your job, Cookie. It's none of your business."

For the next three days, Thad worked Buford hard and he began to enjoy working cattle, improving every day. His horse could almost anticipate his every move and command. When they rose the morning of the drive, everyone was up before first light, and the camp was abuzz with activity. Mr. Chase arrived with five more wranglers, a second chuck wagon, and a supply wagon.

"Ain't too sure those new men will work out," Darrel said to Tim Chase. "The Negro don't seem to know much about cattle."

"We will know in a couple of days. What are they doing over there?"

"Some of the boys don't like being around Bill."

"They're part of the crew. I want them over here with the rest."

"Yes, Sir, Mr. Chase."

"Where did you put them?"

"At the back of the herd."

"I want the herd moving by the time the sun hits the horizon."

"Yes, sir. We'll be ready."

***

Wranglers were up eating, talking, smoking, and saddling their mounts, long before the light began to appear beyond the eastern horizon. Buford and Thad saddled their horses then ate, waiting for the drive to start. Cookie was busy cleaning up and loading the chuck wagon. The cook from the other chuckwagon helped Cookie douse the fire and finish loading the wagon. As the sky brightened and the sun just touched the eastern horizon the command came.

"MOVE 'EM OUT!"

"Move 'em out," came the cry from each wrangler as he mounted his horse and headed for the herd. The chuckwagons and the supply wagon moved at a fast pace trying to get ahead of the herd. The wagons would find a place, miles ahead, to stop and prepare lunch as the herd moved by very slow, and wranglers stopped to eat, a few at a time, as the drive continued.

Darrel rode over to Thad and Buford. "The boss wants you in with the others so tonight camp with them. You know your job, get moving."

As wranglers approached, the cattle became nervous seeing the wranglers moving toward them, shouting and whistling and some animals were breaking away from the herd. Buford went after two steers heading away. One returned with little effort but the second was stubborn, avoiding Buford's maneuvering, trying to drive it back to the herd. In time Buford and his horse won the battle, and the reluctant steer rejoined the sea of animals.

"Didn't think I was gonna get that one," Buford said, riding up to Thad.

"Some are more stubborn than others. You did good. Go left, and I'll go right."

Before long the wranglers had the herd moving in a northern direction. As the sun rose higher in the bright morning sky, the herd and the wranglers were moving in unison at a slow pace. If all went well, they would arrive at their destination as planned, but drives seldom were completed without problems.

By the time the sun was high overhead, the wranglers saw smoke rising far ahead, off to their left. When the herd was close, a few wranglers at the front of the herd spurred their mounts and headed for the chuck wagons, still ahead of the cattle. As the herd passed, wranglers came and went, changing positions around the herd so others could eat.

"Go eat," Thad yelled to Buford, as the rear of the herd approached the chuck wagons.

"I don't want to be with others by myself."

"It's going to happen sooner or later. Might as well get used to it. Go. You'll be fine."

"Okay." Buford left the herd and rode to the chuck wagons. When he dismounted and picked up a plate, some of the wranglers moved away from him.

"Goin' OK out there?" Cookie asked as he filled Buford's plate.

"Seems like." Buford filled a cup with coffee and walked away from the other wranglers and sat down.

"You're the one that shot those banks robbers, ain't ya?" A young wrangler said as he sat down beside Buford.

"I didn't do it alone."

"I know, your friend got two. Benny Ellis," He said, extending his hand.

Buford sat his cup down and accepted the handshake. "William Buford Chance."

"Nice ta meet ya, Mr. Chance."

"My pleasure Mr. Ellis. Most call me Bill."

"Thank ya. Please call me Benny."

"You look kinda young to be a wrangler, Benny."

"I'm fifteen. This is my second year working for Mr. Chase. When Pa left, Ma had to move to town. Mr. Chase hired me. Wouldn't let me work cattle at first. Had me doin' chores then started teachin' me to handle cows. This is my first drive. I'm still tinglin' inside."

"I'm surprised he'd let you come along since drives can be dangerous."

"He's got some of the others watchin' me, and he checks on me a lot. Why you sittin' over here by yourself?"

"Some of the others don't like me. Just trying to give them space."

"What did ya do to 'em?"

"Nothing. Some don't like people of my color."

"That don't make no sense."

"People can like and dislike who they want, Benny. I got to get back so others can eat. Thanks for the company."

"You're welcome, sir... I mean Bill."

Buford returned to the herd and Thad rode off when he saw him coming. When the last wranglers were fed, the chuck wagons put out the fires, loaded the wagons and rode past the herd again, looking for a site far ahead to camp for the night. Tim Chase wanted to make it to the first water on the drive, by nightfall, a small stream about twenty feet wide, so that is where the chuck wagons would stop. The small stream would allow the cattle to drink before starting out the next day. It would be several days before they would cross water again.

The sun continued its descent behind the western horizon, far to their left, as the cattle approached the stream. All the wranglers except those on the night watch rode into camp, about half a mile to the left of the herd.

"My butt's sore from sitting in the saddle all day," Buford said as they dismounted.

"You'll have saddle sores before this drive is over," Thad replied.

Most of the wranglers avoided Buford as they sat to eat, but a few sat close, and Benny came over and sat next to Buford. He looked at Thad. "You're the one that shot the bank robbers with M... Bill, aren't ya?"

"Thad, this is Benny Ellis, this is Thaddeus Walker, Benny," Buford said looking at Benny. He looked back at Thad. "Me and Benny ate lunch together."

"Nice to meet you, Benny." Thad looked at Buford a little puzzled.

"I'll tell you about it later."

"You two are heroes. Must be excitin' fightin' bank robbers."

"Nothing heroic about killing another man, Benny," Thad said, "but sometimes it's necessary."

"He knows what he's a saying, Benny. I don't like killing. Hope I never have to do it again."

"Real heroes are men like George Washington, Thomas Jefferson, and Benjamin Franklin," Thad said.

"I never met 'em," Benny answered.

"You don't know about the founding of this country?"

"I ain't never had no school housin' and Ma and Pa never told me about it."

"You should be in school and not on this drive," Thad replied.

"Mr. Chase has talked about sending me to school, but I'm kinda scared since I'm so dumb."

"You're not dumb, Benny, just uneducated. You should go."

"Never been to school myself," Buford said.

"Maybe we should do something about that," Thad answered, looking at Buford.

Buford rose. "I'm gonna get some rest."

"I'm going too, Benny," Thad said. "Nice meeting you."

"I'm proud to know ya," Benny replied.

As Buford and Thad were unrolling their bedrolls Darrel walked over to them: "I want you two up early and relieve the night watch."

"We'll be there," Thad said.

***

Stanley Lynch was returning home from his trip north, looking for Buford, as Thad and Buford turned in for the night. He rode up to the front porch of the Owens' plantation house and dismounted. After ascending the stairs, Stanley knocked on the door. The butler let him in and took him to Mr. Owens. Frank was sitting behind his large desk smoking a cigar. "Been gone quite a while." He offered Lynch a cigar. He accepted it, lit it, and sat in a chair in front of the desk.

"I followed their trail north until the ground became too hard to leave tracks. I never saw their tracks again. I stopped at every town I came to, but no one had seen a runaway or a black man with a white man. Runaways always go north. He must be up there somewhere. He may be in the Underground Railroad. I'll go back in a week and keep looking. He'll come out sooner or later. I don't think he will go to Canada, but I guess it's possible."

"He wouldn't be the first runaway to go to Canada," Frank said. "I heard a story about two men that showed up in a west Texas town and shot four bank robbers."

"What does that have to do with Buford?"

"Most likely nothing, but one of them was black."

Stanley sat up in his chair: "You think he went west? They always go north. You think he is still with the man that freed him?"

"Doesn't seem reasonable," Frank replied. "Buford has never held a gun let alone fired one. The only reason the story made it back east is because one of them was a negro. I heard both killed two men in seconds and never wasted a shot. There's no way it could be Buford."

Stanley's eyes narrowed as his brow furrowed. "It's beginning to make sense to me now. I never could figure out why I never found their trail again. That friend of his tricked me."

"Think about it, Stan. There's no way Buford could learn to shoot that quick and that good and why would that man give him a gun? It must be someone else. A free black man that's been shooting all of his life could do it but not Buford."

"That part is hard to believe, I agree, but how often have you heard of a white man and black man running together?"

"Never but that doesn't mean it's them."

"I'll rest a couple of days then head west."

"I'll pay you for your time and trouble going north looking for him. I won't pay you to go west on a wild goose chase. He's no good to me if you do bring him back. I'll have to hang him. Forget about him, Stanley."

"I'm going. I've never let one get away from me, and I'm not starting now. If I don't bring him back, how are you going to keep the rest from running? He needs to come back so they know it does no good to run."

"Let me worry about that. Go home and rest. Put this behind you, Stanley. It's over."

Stanley stood. "I'll go home and rest and then head west. Buford ran from me three times and he ain't going to get away with it, and his friend has his coming too."

"If it is Buford, Stanley, and he shot two men on horseback in a split second, what chance do you think you have?"

"I'm going Frank, and nothing you say will stop me."

***

Even though it was later in the east than in West Texas, Stanley was home sleeping the following morning when Buford and Thad awoke as they heard the cooks getting ready for breakfast. Both rose, put on their boots, and went to the chuckwagon. "Coffee ready?" Thad asked.

"Yep and got some victuals too." Cookie fixed them a plate as four more wranglers approached. Thad and Buford sat close to the fire. Cookie served the others, and three of them walked away, but the fourth sat next to the fire with Buford and Thad.

"You're the new men Mr. Chase hired, aren't you?"

"Good guess," Thad replied.

"Everybody knows what you did in town. Gotta be some crack shots to take them down like that."

"Thanks," Thad said, "Mr. Chase and Darrel did some good shooting also."

"Name is Stanford Brown, but everybody calls me Stan."

"Nice to meet you, Stan," Buford said.

"Likewise," Thad added.

"Heard you were relieving the night watch with us. Gonna be a long day."

"You're right about that," Thad said. "Been working for Mr. Chase, very long?"

"Five years. He's a fair man. Don't think there's many like him." It became quiet, and they ate in haste then Stan rose. "See you at the herd."

Buford and Thad put their plates and cups on the back of the chuck wagon. "Thanks, Cookie," they both said and went to their horses.

"You're welcome. See ya at lunch."

The six riders started for the herd, searching for the night guards, spread far apart. Each located a guard who walked his horse through the herd to the campsite, only visible by the light of the fires near the chuck wagons. The dark morning made it impossible for the relief guards to see each other, scattered around the herd. Even the cattle were indistinct shadows around them. Once the eastern skyline began to push away the black of night, cattle began to appear across the vast open range. As the sky brightened, steers made their way to the stream for the last drink they may have for several days. The cattle were reluctant to leave the cool water in the stream, and it took some effort to get them moving again. By noon the relentless heat of the sun drained the strength of both wranglers and cattle, but the drive continued. That night Buford and Thad were exhausted, falling asleep right after they ate. The third day felt better since a cloud layer reduced the heat of the sun. Even so, it seemed the day would never end since the light refused to fade. At last the sky darkened and the light from the campfires began to glow left of the herd, and the wranglers stopped the herd for the night.

Clouds still covered the sky when the drive started the following day. Buford and Thad were in their normal place at the back of the herd, far apart, when Mr. Chase approached Buford.

"I've been watching you ever since the drive started," he said, "and I like what I see. I'm glad you talked me into hiring you."

"Thank you, sir. I didn't mean to offend you when I spoke out the way I did."

"I liked your boldness. It showed me you're a man of strong character. That's why I hired you, and I see you're a hard worker also."

"You're most generous, sir, and I want to thank you for what you're doing for Benny Ellis."

"Met Benjamin, did you?"

"Yes sir. I can tell he is a fine young man."

"You're a good judge of character. I had to foreclose on their farm when his father took off on his own. He was too lazy to work hard enough to make the place pay and fell way behind on the mortgage, so he just ran off, leaving his wife and son to fend for their selves. They had little in the place, but I gave Margret a small house I had in town and gave her the money from the sale of the livestock. It wasn't much so I hired Benny to do chores at my place so they would have enough to live on."

"Somehow, I feels you pays him more than you should."

Tim smiled at him. "I discovered he's like his mother not his father, she's a fine hard-working lady, so I started teaching him to work cattle. He's coming along very well. Drives can be hard and dangerous, so I keep an eye on him and so do most of the wranglers. Life is hard Bill, and I think the younger you learn that the stronger you become. I think he will mature by the time the drive ends. He's going to be a fine man."

"I know you're right about that. He sat with me at lunch and treated me with respect, no never mind I'm different. Liked him from the start."

"You mean I was reluctant to hire you because of your color?"

"You gotta think about your business and your men. Might cause you problems hirin' a black man."

"I never met anyone of your race before you showed up in town, Bill. Not sure why I was reluctant to hire you. Thank you for helping me make the right decision."

"I'm much beholding to you sir for giving me a chance, but I think I'd better get back to work before my boss fires me."

"Yeah, I hear he can be a real ass at times."

"Not the boss I'm talking about," Buford replied then returned to the herd.

The sky continued to darken as the day wore on and they could hear the roar of thunder far in front of them. The cattle became a little nervous, so the wranglers pushed them into a tighter herd before the rain began. Not hard at first, just a few large drops, even though they could see a sheet of water about a mile ahead of them. The wranglers donned their slickers before the sky opened with a roar of falling rain. The cattle were a little spooked at first but settled down when the thunder disappeared, seeming to enjoy the cooling effect of the rain. The rain was relentless and continued throughout the day. The drive slowed even more as the hard prairie soil turned to mud. As the herd advanced, the cattle's movement in the middle and rear of the herd almost stopped, becoming mired in the deep thick muck. The heavy rains forced the drive to end early.

Without a fire, dinner became hard biscuits and beef jerky without coffee to wash it down. Wranglers found it impossible to rest because no one could lie in the quagmire that used to be a prairie. Some tried to sleep against trees and others on their mounts in the rain that refused to end. In the wee hours of the morning, the rain slowed then stopped. By daylight, some of the surface water began to disappear. Even so, the cooks couldn't build a fire with water-saturated wood, so again everyone ate biscuits and jerky.

The blessings of the rain came when the sun glistened off a small lake not far in front of the herd. A slight depression in the prairie had filled with rainwater creating the artificial lake. Steers began wandering forward into the water to drink their fill. The wranglers moved the rest of the herd into the water as the chuck wagons tried to drive through the deep mud beside the lake, hoping to find a dry location for lunch. Wranglers led their horses into the water to drink as well. About two hours later they began to move the herd forward, wading through the water toward the deep mud in front of the lake. Several miles ahead, the ground became dry once again.

Everyone looked forward to a hot meal for lunch even though the drive would continue as any other day. That night men slept for the first time in two days.

"Sometimes I think being a slave was easier," Buford said, as they prepared their bedrolls for the night, "but here I know I can quit if I want."

"Is that what you want to do, quit?"

"No, sir, I'll keep going. Mr. Chase is counting on us."

"You're staying because of Chase?"

"Some, but for me too. When you're a slave, you work cause they makes you. When you hire on to someone, you are promising to do what they hired you to do. You gives your word. A man keeps his word. It don't matter how many times they called me boy on the plantation, I knows I'm a man. I'll stay all right. I like Mr. Chase, but I got to do this for me too. A man keeps his word, and a man don't quit."

"Are you going to preach all night, or sleep?" Thad asked, lying on his blanket with his hat over his eyes.

"I ain't preaching. Never been to no church but Mama read the book to me some."

"If I'd known you were going to talk so much, I'd a let you hang."

Buford rolled toward Thad then lay back down: "Okay, I'll shut up."

"Thank you."

"You don't mean that, did ya?"

"Buford!"

"Okay-okay."

The next morning the drive started with the first rays of light, and once again as the day progressed, the sun beat down with intense heat. Noon came and went, and by nightfall the herd came to its first major water crossing, the Red River.

"The last few days have been rough on the men," Tim Chase said to Darrel. "We'll let them rest tomorrow. Have them spell each other guarding the herd. Have some men cut a steer out of the herd, clean and dress it. I want it on a spit roasting in time for an early dinner. Tell the men before they go to sleep."

"Okay, Mr. Chase. I'll get right on it."

A cheer went up when Darrel told the men. To have a day of rest was unheard of on a cattle drive.

"Ain't that something," Buford said, "Don't think nobody would give their men a day off in the middle of a cattle drive."

"After what we've been through, they would, if they want to get their herd to market," Thad said.

"Then you don't think he is a good man?"

"Better than most, I'd say, and smart as well. If he doesn't let them and the cattle rest, he may lose cattle and men before we end the drive. I'm sure he has compassion for his men, but he is a businessman. If he drives the cattle too hard, they will lose weight, and he won't get a good price for them."

"What should we do tomorrow?" Buford asked.

"I'm going to the river and cool off," Thad said, "bathe and wash my clothes. Look at the mud on my pants and boots."

"Guess I'll join you. Mine don't look no better than yours."

By morning, a steer roasted over hot coals near the chuckwagons, and back east Stanley was on his way west to resume his search for Buford. As Stanley rode toward Texas, one of the wranglers kept the steer turning while the cooks added wood to the fire and prepared breakfast. Men rose and ate at their leisure. After eating, some relieved the guards but most went to the river to swim and wash. All were laughing and talking, some splashing each other like kids. Every two hours they changed the guard and relieved the man turning the steer. When the steer finished cooking, all ate their fill. The first wranglers to finish relieved the cattle guards without being told.

Before the sun cleared the horizon the following morning the drive began, prodding the cattle across the river about the time Stanley rose and resumed his journey to Texas. He knew his chances of finding Buford were slim, even if he was the black man that shot the bank robbers in West Gap, but his hatred for Buford and the man that helped him escape would not let him quit. He'd pursue them to hell if necessary.

Darrel rode over to Thad at the back of the herd: "You two are on night watch."

Buford rode over as Darrel left, heading for the front of the herd. "What did he want?"

"We got the night watch."

Chapter Four
Raid

The drive continued unabated now that the rain and mud were behind them. Everyone felt well rested after a day of leisure. Spirits were high. Clouds scattered across the sky gave them some relief from the heat. As the sun descended to the western horizon, the sky cleared, revealing a full moon, bathing the prairie and cattle in an eerie glow. The six cattle guards were scattered around the perimeter of the herd to discourage cattle from wandering off during the night. Buford caught himself dozing off at times, and some wranglers sang, helping to keep the cattle calm and themselves awake.

Hours passed in the peaceful night with the full moon still high overhead and the guards looked forward to a rising sun, still hours away. The peace of the tranquil night vanished as shots rang out to the right and toward the front of the herd. The lowing of steers also filled the air as the frightened herd began to scatter. Shocked awake by the bark of guns, the guards rode toward the gunfire, with frightened cattle crisscrossing in front of them. Buford and Thad raced through the spreading cattle toward the shots. The guards were firing at six rustlers trying to cut out a large section of the herd. The rustler's fired back as Darrel, riding bareback, came through the herd firing at them, not far from Buford. One of the bandits pointed his gun at Darrel as Darrel shot a rustler to his left. Buford fired, and the man aiming at Darrel fell into the panicking cattle.

Darrel saw the gun pointing at him then drop from the man's hand as the outlaw fell from his horse. Startled, Darrel looked at Buford as more wranglers arrived, and Thad shot another bandit, sending him to his death. Another wrangler wounded another rustler, and he and the remaining two bandits sped away across the prairie with wranglers firing at them.

"Let them go!" Tim Chase shouted as he rode through the scattering steers. "Get the cattle."

The rustlers disappeared, through the eerie glow of the moon, into the trees about a mile away. Wranglers began rounding up the scattering herd. Thad and Buford joined the others, returning the frightened cattle to the main body then going out into the night looking for more. The eastern sky began to change from the eerie glow of the moon to a reddish band along the horizon by the time the herd was reformed and calm. With the herd calm, Darrel rode over to Buford at the rear of the herd.

"You saved my life."

"That I did. Same as you woulda done for me."

"Sure," Darrel replied then rode away.

"You're welcome... I think," Buford said to himself.

"What should we do with their bodies?" Darrel asked, with the dead rustlers slung over the backs of their horses.

"Keep their guns and bury them," Mr. Chase said. "No towns close by and no law out here."

"What about the horses?"

"Any markings?"

"They're not branded. Stolen, more than likely."

"Put them in with ours, we'll put the bar C on them when we get back. No telling where they're from."

The drive ended that evening without water for the cattle, but about noon the next day they crossed the Washita River. The following night they camped on the banks of the Canadian River, a very wide body of water that would be difficult to ford. To prevent losing cattle, they took them across in small groups, taking until almost noon to complete the crossing. The drive ended that evening next to the North Canadian River, a much smaller river and easier to cross.

***

While the drive progressed, Stanley Lynch started through Texas, stopping at every town asking about a black man and white man but no one had seen them. He continued heading west until he came to the small town of Prairieville and stopped in front of the general store, going inside.

"I'm looking for two men, one black and one white," he said to the proprietor.

"Yep. Come through a while back and bought some supplies and clothes for the black one."

"Clothes, huh? Do you know where they went from here?"

"Only had one horse. Went to the livery and bought another."

"Thanks," Lynch said and turned to go.

"They friends of yours? If you find them tell them not to come back. They're not welcome here."

"Lynch opened the door and looked at the man: "If I find them, they won't be coming back. You can count on it." He closed the door as he left. His new friend is pretty damn smart, Stanley thought, new clothes and a different horse, but it won't do them any good. I'm sure it's them. He mounted his horse and rode to the livery stable. As he rode through the gate, he saw a man sitting on the porch of the stable's office and reined his horse in at the hitching rail.

"The man in the store told me you sold a horse to a black man a while back."

He sat up in the chair: "I did no such thing! I sold to a white fella that was with the colored. Ain't got no use for no coloreds. Most arrogant men I ever knowed. White one went in the saloon bought a beer and come out on the porch and shared it with the colored! Right there in front of the whole dang town, till the sheriff run 'em off."

"Where did they go when they left?"

"Ta West Gap and killed four bank robbers. Damnedest thing I ever heard of. You know 'em?"

"I know the negro and can't wait to meet the other one."

"Can't understand how you can like coloreds."

"Didn't say I liked him. How far to West Gap?"

"About a day's ride due west."

"Much obliged." Lynch turned his horse and rode away, heading west.

***

Stanley stopped for the night as the drive reached the edge of the North Canadian River and Darrel rode over to Mr. Chase: "I saw an Indian off in the trees a few times and some on the bluff to our right."

"I know. Saw then myself. This is turning into one hell of a drive. Maybe I'm not supposed to get this herd to market. Make sure the men are well armed."

"If they're going to attack it will be when we cross the river in the morning."

"I've been thinking about that. I think we should cross tonight. I've never heard of Indians attacking at night. Use the normal number of guards until midnight then have the rest of the men join them. Tell them not to make a sound, and I want them armed. Start them across as quiet as possible, and I want extra men at the back of the herd in case I'm wrong about the Indians. Once across, keep the herd moving at a walk until daybreak, then pick up the pace."

"Okay, Boss. I'll tell 'em."

The sky, filled with stars and no moon, made it difficult as the men walked their mounts in stealth silence toward the almost indistinguishable herd. The touch of a rope started them moving, along with soft whistles from the wranglers. Slowly the herd began to move through the river and up the other bank. It took a couple of hours to ford the river. By the time the hint of day began to appear in the east, the herd was only a few miles beyond the river. As the sky lightened, the wranglers increased the pace of the cattle. When the sun was about to break over the far horizon, they began to hear war cries from a band of about fifty Indians far to the right of the herd, heading toward them. The men started the cattle running as the warriors sped closer still screaming, with rifles held high. As the distance between them disappeared, both wranglers and Indians began firing, causing the herd to panic, running faster. The Indians began penetrating the scattering herd, still shouting and firing. Darrel, now caught on the edge of the panic-stricken steers, stood in his stirrups twisting backward and firing at the advancing warriors, lost his footing when a steer crashed into his horse, throwing him to the ground. He jumped to his feet dodging the oncoming cattle. Buford, not far away, spurred his horse forward, coming up beside Darrel with his foot out of the stirrup and an outstretched hand. Darrel grabbed his hand and swung up behind Buford, continuing on, chasing Darrel's horse, as the battle raged on. When Buford pulled in close to the riderless horse, Darrel changed horses with an almost impossible leap from Buford's horse to his.

The battle continued, and three Indians fell to the ground as others cut cattle from the herd and headed toward the bluff a mile away: "Let them go," Chase yelled. "Reorganize the herd but keep them moving!"

The wranglers managed to regroup the herd and slow the pace, watching the bluff and surrounding prairie for signs of Indians.

"We have two wounded," Darrel said, coming up to Mr. Chase. "One with a leg wound and the other shot in the arm. I don't think they are serious; no bones broken."

"Have them attended to, we may have to send them ahead."

The drive continued, with wranglers looking for Indians but none showed. The drive ended early that evening to let the men rest.

"The men have missed another night's rest," Mr. Chase said. "We'll start late tomorrow. I think the Indians got what they came for, so I don't think they will come back. But I wouldn't bet my life on it. Have someone go back a few miles and have a look."

"Okay, Mr. Chase."

Most of the men lay down in the grass to rest while the cooks prepared dinner. Thad and Buford were two of the first to go through the line and sat close to the fire. As they ate, wranglers began sitting down beside them.

"Saw what you did out there, Bill," one of them said. "You're a very brave man."

"Thanks. Don't see me being any braver than y'all."

"Eric's right," another drover said, "I've been watching you ever since the drive started and you don't turn away from nothin' no matter how hard or dangerous it is. I'm proud to be on the drive with ya."

"That's nice of ya to say, but I haven't seen no slacker working this drive."

While they were talking Darrel sat across from Buford with his plate and looked at him: "You saved my life, twice, and I haven't even thanked you for it."

"Ain't no need, Mr. Barter."

"The name is Darrel and there is a need. You know how I've treated you ever since Mr. Chase hired you, and you still saved my life. I didn't want you here cause of your color. I never thought about why nobody liked you folks, where I was raised. No blacks lived in my town, and I never knew a black man or woman. Saw some, slaves mostly, so I don't know why I was not supposed to like ya, it's just the way it was.

"Then you save my life, killing a man that was goin' to kill me. The truth is, if it was the other way around, I don't know if I'd a saved you. Then when I'm knocked off my horse while the Indians were attacking, you risked your life to save me again. When I was fighting to keep the cattle from stomping me into the ground, I started praying, 'Lord if you let me live, I promise to be a better man'...and He sent you to save me! He not only used you to save me but to show me how He wanted me to be a better man. To not judge people by their color. God is the judge, no one else. He made us all. Can you ever forgive me?"

Tears were running down Buford's face: "Nothing to forgive... Darrel. I was sure you were a good man watching how hard you work and how loyal you are to Mr. Chase. But I didn't know how big of a man you are until now. It takes a mighty big man to say the things you did. I'd be mighty proud to call you my friend."

Darrel stood: "I consider it an honor to call you my friend and be your friend, Mr. Chance."

"Buford stood and accepted the handshake: "My close friends call me Butte."

"Thank you, Butte. I'm gonna sleep good tonight."

Later, as Thad and Buford spread their blankets and stretched out on them, Buford asked, "am I dreaming, Thad? The men are treating me kindly, and Darrel is proud to be my friend."

"You're just reaping the benefits of being yourself. You know some people don't like you because of your color, but in spite of that, you treat them well. In time they see what kind of a man you are and forget about their prejudice and accept you for the good man you are, color and all."

"Are you going to preach all night?" Buford asked, pulling his hat over his face.

***

As the drive resumed late the following morning with no sign of Indians, Stanley was entering West Gap and stopped at the general store.

May I help you?" Tom, the proprietor asked, as Stanley entered.

"I heard two men shot some bank robbers here a while back."

"That they did. Killed four of them quick as lightning."

"One of them black?"

"Yes, he was. Both big men. Saved the bank's money and most likely some lives."

"Know where they went?"

"I heard Mr. Chase hired them for his cattle drive. He owns the bank and a large cattle ranch. Most likely in Springfield by now."

"Springfield?"

"Springfield Missouri, that's where they sell the cattle, could be back in maybe a week."

"How do I get to Springfield?"

"Go north then east and you'll find the cattle trail. Can't miss it. Are they friends of yours?"

"Much obliged," Lynch said as he turned to go.

"Wonder why he's in such a hurry?" Tom said to himself as the door closed.

***

The two drover's wounds had been cleaned and dressed. The one with the arm wound insisted on taking his place with the others, working the herd. The man with the leg wound rode the chuck wagon with Cookie. Later that day they crossed the Cimarron River before stopping for the night. At the close of the next day's drive, they were approaching the Missouri line with their destination, Springfield, about a day away. Chase sent the two wounded men on ahead with the supply wagon to have their injuries properly treated.

The following day the cattle drive stopped early, a few miles from Springfield. This allowed the cattle to rest and reach the stockyards by mid-morning with enough daylight left to count and sell the large herd. With the light beginning to fade, except those guarding the herd, Chase assembled all the wranglers near Cookie's chuck wagon.

When the last wrangler arrived, he climbed onto the wagon: "Tomorrow your work will be done. This has been one of the hardest drives we've ever made. You've all worked hard, and I'm proud of every one of you, and I know you deserve time to relax, unwind, and have fun. Most of you have been here before, so you know it's a wild town with other drovers here from other ranches. You know to stay together and help each other if there is trouble. You also know if any of you cause trouble you will no longer work for the Bar C."

The men began to disperse as he got down from the wagon and approached Thad and Buford. "You both have done a great job. I think I might have lost more cattle and perhaps some men without you. I can never thank you enough. However, after we deliver the cattle tomorrow, I'll have more men than I need, so I'll have to let you go. If you're around West Gap next year, come and see me, I can use you again. See me at the stockyard office tomorrow for your pay."

"We'll be there," Thad said.

"It's been an honor to work for you, sir," Buford said.

Chase looked at him: "The honor is all mine, Bill."

"I wouldn't be here if it weren't for you, Butte," Darrel said. "I'll always be in your debt not just for saving my life but making me a better man. If you come back next year, I'd be proud if you would use the bunk beside me in the bunkhouse."

"Thank you, Darrel. You becoming my friend has made all the trouble on this drive worthwhile. I'm proud to know you." They shook hands.

The final leg of the drive began early the next morning. By mid-afternoon, the cattle had been counted, and the drovers paid.

"Sure was nice of Mr. Chase to gives us all a bonus," Buford said as they rode down the dusty, noisy main street of Springfield. "Feels good to earn my first pay and the first thing I'm gonna do is buy us a beer."

"Are you sure you want to go into a saloon? This is a wild town."

"I'm a free man. It's time I act like one."

Tethering their horses at the hitching rail in front of a noisy saloon, Buford and Thad walked through the swinging doors and up to the bar: "Two beers," Buford said.

A big gruff looking man walked up to Buford. "Your kind ain't welcome in here!"

"I'm just gonna have a beer friend—"

"I ain't your friend."

The man swung a fist at Buford who ducked and caught the man on the chin with his left fist, sending the man to the floor. He jumped to his feet, and Buford sent him down with a right to the jaw, and this time the man was dazed, struggling to get up. Buford grabbed him by his shirt collar and belt at the seat of his pants, ran him to the door and threw him out into the street.

"That felt good," Buford said with a big grin on his face walking back toward Thad.

"Be ready to shoot."

"Huh?"

The doors burst open as the man came through, gun in hand. Thad shot, and the gun went spinning to the floor as the man screamed with pain.

"You almost blew my hand off!"

"Be glad it was me. Bill would've killed you. Better have it looked at, you could lose a couple of fingers."

The man went back outside holding his hand and moaning. Another man picked up the gun and followed him out of the saloon.

Buford, still stunned, looked at Thad with eyes wide open. Thad grinned: "You're welcome."

Buford turned and looked at the man behind the bar, staring at him: "I don't see no beer!" The man hurriedly drew two beers and placed them on the bar. Buford paid for them and leaned against the bar, feeling weak: "I think I want to go."

"Not yet. You need to drink your beer and do it slow. You don't want anyone to think you're scared."

"But I am," he whispered."

Thad picked up his beer and took a sip: "Try not to shake when you pick up your mug." Buford took his time in picking up his mug, took a sip and put it down quick before his hand began to shake.

"How'd you know he'd come back?"

Thad sighed, "you have so much to learn, Butte."

The saloon was noisy, filled with talking, laughing, and the sound of a piano playing off in the corner, but neither spoke as they finished their beer.

"Let's get a real bath," Thad said as they left the saloon. "We'll go to the store and get new clothes before we go."

"Okay and I's... I'm going to get me a cigar."

"You ever smoke?"

"No, but I saw them plantation men smokin' 'em. Made them look real important and successful, so I told myself someday I'm gonna have me one, too."

"Smoking a cigar won't make you successful."

They went to the store then to the bathhouse. As they sat back in the hot steaming, soapy water Buford struck a match against the side of the tub, lit a big cigar, and took a puff then bit down with his teeth, smiling: "This is the life all right."

"Did you inhale?"

"Huh?"

"Take the smoke into your lungs."

"No. I'm just puffin'."

"A real smoker would breathe it in."

Buford drew on the cigar, filling his lungs with smoke and started coughing. He continued coughing and choking for a while. Thad had a big grin on his face. "You tryin' to kill me? I feel sick." He doused the cigar in the tub and threw it on the floor. "Guess I ain't cut out to be successful."

A young, pretty girl, stuck her head through the curtains and smiled. "Anybody in here want their back scrubbed?

Buford jump and grabbed a towel, putting it across the tub: "I ain't got no clothes on!"

"I know," she said smiling. "Want me to scrub your back?"

"NO! Just get! It ain't proper!"

"Are you sure? I'm real good at scrubbing backs."

"I'm sure, now get! Go!" She disappeared through the curtain. "What she doin' here, Thad?"

"Running a bathhouse isn't the only way these ladies earn their living."

"You mean ..." Thad smiled. "I'm as clean as I'm gonna get, let's go."

"Are you sure?"

Buford got out of the tub and started drying off. "I'm sure all right. hope my Mama never finds out about this. Let's get some dinner, I'm hungry."

"Okay, but first we'll drop our dirty clothes at the laundry.

The restaurants were so crowded it took them an hour to get a table: "What you boys drinking? The woman asked when she came to their table.

"Whiskey," they both said.

She stood looking at Buford for a moment. "You're the first black cowboy I've ever seen."

"Does ya want me to leave?"

"No ... you're kinda cute." Buford's eyes opened wide. "Be back with your whiskey."

"Why'd she say that, Thad?"

"I guess she likes you."

"Sometimes being free scares the fire outta me. I didn't know there could be such a place as this. Cowboys runnin' around the streets drunk. Pretty little girls tryin' ta scrub your back. Must be the craziest place in the world. I'll be glad when we leave."

The light was beginning to fade when Buford and Thad left the restaurant and walked to the hotel. The street was still filled with revelers, cowboys walking down the street with a bottle in their hand. Some talking to ladies of the evening or heading for the next saloon escorting a lady in a frilly dress. They entered the hotel and went to the desk.

"We need two rooms for the night," Thad said.

The man looked at Buford then back at Thad: "Got one with two beds."

"We'll take it."

"That'll be ten dollars."

"The sign says 'Clean Rooms a dollar fifty,'" Thad said.

"Price just went up."

Buford threw a ten-dollar coin on the desk. "Show me the room."

"Up the stairs to the right at the end of the hall."

"It's too much, Butte. We'll sleep in the stable."

"I want you to show me the room," Buford said ignoring Thad, looking the man straight in the eye.

The man picked up a lamp and the key and started up the stairs with Buford and Thad behind him. He unlocked and opened the door. Thad went in and lit the lamp on the nightstand, and Buford grabbed the lamp from the clerk and walked around the room.

"Sign says clean rooms, floors dirty."

"Looks clean to me," the clerk said.

"Look in the corner. Kinda dusty."

"My housekeeper won't be back until tomorrow."

"You have a broom?"

"I'll get you one."

"Not for me, for you. You clean it!" Buford said, looking down at the man. The man hesitated then left and returned with a broom and began sweeping. He swept what little dust he could find out the door.

"Does that satisfy you?"

"It'll do." Buford handed the clerk the lamp and shut the door in his face.

Thad sat on one of the beds. "I like the way you handled that."

Buford removed his boots and flopped down on the other bed: "He kinda ticked me off. I just wanted to rub his nose in it, some."

Both rose with the sun and went to the restaurant for breakfast then to the laundry before retrieving their horses from the livery stable.

"We going back to West Gap?" Buford asked as they left the stable.

"We'll go through there, but I want to go farther west, I think we should continue on to California."

"If you say so, but West Gap is friendly. We might not find another town like it."

"Where's your spirit of adventure? We'll stop at Fort Arbuckle tonight. We can stay in the settlement outside the gate. I don't feel comfortable sleeping in open country in Indian Territory."

Chapter Five
Starting over

The light disappeared as they rode into the settlement outside Fort Arbuckle. Thad and Buford dismounted and went into the store. "Is there a place we can spend the night?" Thad asked.

"Rooming house three doors down, stable at the end of the street," The proprietor said.

"Thanks. Any place to eat?"

"You missed supper at the rooming house. Ruth's across the street is open. You'd better hurry, she's getting ready to close."

"Much obliged," Thad said. From the store, they walked their horses across the street to the small restaurant.

"I'm beginning to feel like a free man with nothing to worry about," Buford said as they began to eat. "I got paid for my first job and looking forward to whatever is ahead of us. I can go wherever I want and do what I want. Yes sir, Thad, life is good."

"You were almost shot by rustlers and Indians, and drenched for a day in a monsoon rainstorm; what if there is more of that ahead of us?"

"Don't matter. You said life is hard. What is good is I'm free. Whatever is ahead I'll deal with it."

Before the sun rose the following morning, Thad and Buford went to the restaurant for breakfast. Afterwards, as they walked down the middle of the street heading for the livery, Buford heard a familiar voice: "Take off the gun, Buford. I'm taking you back."

They both stopped. "That's Mr. Lynch," Buford said without turning.

"Let me handle it."

"Not this time. I gotta do this myself." He turned and faced the horsemen. "What you doing out here, Mr. Lynch?"

"You know why I'm here; you're a runaway, I'm taking you back. Remove the gun belt."

"Ain't no civil law out here, Mr. Lynch, so why don't you just go back home and forget about me?"

"I do my job," he said getting off his horse. "Law or no law I'm taking you back. Now take off the gun."

"No, sir. I ain't goin' nowhere."

"You're going back, Buford, dead or alive. Take off the gun!"

"I don't want ta hurt ya, Mr. Lynch. Please...just go, I ain't doing you no harm."

"I didn't come all the way out here to go back without you. Take off the gun, or I'll kill you right here and now."

"Please don't go for your gun, Mr.—" Lynch reached for his gun, Buford drew and fired as Lynch's gun cleared the holster. Lynch pulled the trigger as he fell forward and the bullet ricocheted off the dusty street into the cool morning air a foot away from Buford's head. Within minutes the fort gates swung open and four soldiers came running out, guns drawn, with an officer not far behind them.

"Drop the gun, Mister!" The officer yelled. Buford dropped his gun.

"It was a fair fight, Captain," A man on the boardwalk said. "I seen the whole thing. This here black fella told him not to draw but he did, and now he's dead. He had no choice but ta kill him."

The captain looked at Thad: "Is that what you saw?"

"The man is right, he warned him, but he wouldn't listen. If he had shot Bill, I'd a killed him. He was dead either way."

"Pick up your gun, Mister..."

"William B. Chance," Thad said.

"Is that your name?" the captain asked as Buford picked up and holstered his gun.

"Yes, sir. That's me all right."

"I'm Captain Watson, commander of the fort. Why was he trying to kill you?"

"Bill and Lynch had a disagreement a while back," Thad said, "I guess Lynch never put it behind him."

Captain Watson looked at Thad then Buford: "You knew him?"

"Some."

"Do you know if he had family?"

"He don't have no wife, I know that, but don't know about other kin."

"He's a drifter," Thad said.

"I'll bury him in the fort cemetery. What's his full name?"

"Stanley Lynch, sir," Buford said.

"You're free to go, Mr. Chance. Try to stay out of trouble."

"Yes, sir. I'll do my best." Captain Watson walked away, and two of the soldiers carried the body into the fort with another leading Lynch's horse. Buford looked at Thad. "What disagreement?"

"He thought you should hang and you didn't. Let's get our horses and get out of here before the captain changes his mind and starts asking more questions."

Thad and Buford went to the stable and got their horses but when they were in the saddle, Buford looked at Thad: "It ain't right, Thad. We lied to the captain. I know where he's from."

"You didn't lie I did, and it wasn't a lie just not all the truth."

"I need to tell him, Thad. I can't just go. What if Mr. Lynch has family back home?"

"What good will it do? He's dead and telling won't change anything. You know the law says runaways must be returned to their owners. If you tell the captain he is duty-bound to send you back. If Lynch has family, they will figure it out when he doesn't return. You tell and that freedom you were so happy about yesterday may be lost."

"I gotta tell him, Thad. It ain't right. His family should know and be able to bury him."

"You said you would never go back. Don't do it, Butte. Think of yourself. You don't owe Lynch anything, or his family."

"You go. I'm going to talk to Captain Watson." Buford turned his horse and rode to the fort gate. Thad went with him as he approached the guard. "I need ta talk to Captain Watson."

"Open the gate," the guard said, and the gate opened. They followed a soldier to a log structure, dismounted and followed the private up the stairs. He knocked on the door.

"Enter."

The private opened the door and saluted: "Begging your pardon, sir, a Mr. Chance to see you, sir."

"Send him in."

They walked to the desk and Watson, pen in hand, looked up at Buford.

"We didn't tell you the truth out there, sir."

"You had an eye witness. He said it was self-defense. Are you saying it wasn't self-defense?"

"That part is true, sure enough, but... I know Mr. Lynch. I know where he comes from." Watson put down his pen. "I... I'm a runaway slave, and Mr. Lynch was trying to take me back."

"You're a very honest man. Why are you telling me? You could be free with no questions asked."

"If he has kin they should know, and you should know. It don't feel right lying to you, sir."

"You know the law says all runaways must be returned to their rightful owners. And as an army officer, I'm duty bound to uphold the law."

"Yes, sir, I know."

"You feel compassion for the family of a man that was trying to return you to slavery?"

"Lynch tried to hang him," Thad said.

Watson looked at Thad then back to Buford: "And still you feel compelled to tell me?"

"Well... I... I...yes sir, I guess I do."

"God must love you very much, or this is your lucky day, Mr. Chance. At Fort Arbuckle, I'm charged with protecting people migrating west and civilized Indians from hostiles. Since we are in a territory and not a state, national and state law does not apply. Therefore, I'm not compelled to enforce them here. Tell me where he is from and I will have his body and his belongings shipped there." He paused, looking at Buford for a moment. "You're also fortunate that I don't believe in slavery. A different officer may have taken a different approach."

"Thank you, sir. You are most kind."

Buford gave Captain Watson the information, and then he and Thad left, riding toward Texas.

"Watson is right," Thad said. Buford looked at him as they rode. "You're either lucky or blessed. Don't ever do anything that stupid again."

"Stupid! My Mama told me always to tell the truth, and I feel bad for killing Mr. Lynch."

"Do you think she would tell you it's better to tell the truth than to be free?"

"No. I don't know... I didn't want to kill him."

"I know that, but he gave you no choice. He tried to hang you, and he would've shot you and felt no remorse. He wouldn't have told your parents and most likely hung your rotting carcass in the public square."

"I know... I know, but it don't make it no...any easier. I feel real bad about killing him."

"Well ask God to forgive you then let's ride. We have a lot of ground to cover."

Both picked up the pace and rode in silence until they stopped for lunch. Thad began collecting wood to build a fire: "Do you want me to shoot something?" Buford asked.

"Maybe for dinner. We'll have jerky, biscuits, and coffee for lunch. I want to spend as little time in Indian Country as possible."

Two days later they rode into West Gap and people greeted them with respect. Everyone remembered how they killed the bank robbers with lightning speed and possibly saving a few lives along with the bank's money. It felt comfortable there, but Thad wanted to continue west.

"This is a nice place," Buford said. "We should stay here and make it our home."

"You have a point except for one thing." Buford looked at him. "Texas is a slave state. If someone else comes looking for you, the town won't be able to stop them from taking you back."

"I'll take my chances."

"Then I guess I'll take my chances too."

"You're not a runaway."

"True, but I helped you get away and shot three men doing it. You think they will forget what I did? The least they will do is put me in prison if not hang me along with you. Helping a runaway is against the law. I think we should go to California."

"Okay. I guess I was just thinking about me. I'll go."

Early the next morning after breakfast, Thad and Buford started west. The first day was uneventful, then the following day, as the sun moved from overhead toward the west, a small town came into view. The town grew larger as they rode.

They entered on a dirt street with a few people on the boardwalks on either side of the street. Farther down the street, two horses were standing in front of the general store, one with a rider and another man mounting the other horse with a bag in his hand:

"You can't walk out of my store without paying!" A man said coming out of the store.

"What you gonna do about it? Ain't got a sheriff no more."

The man from the store started toward the thief, and the man drew his gun. Thad drew and fired knocking the gun out of the man's hand. The other man started for his gun, but Buford drew first: "Go for it, and you're dead." The man moved his hand away from his gun.

"Where's the law?" Thad asked.

"Don't have a sheriff anymore," the store owner said. "Some men disarmed him, took his badge, put him on his horse, and ran him out of town about a week ago."

"This man is guilty of stealing and attempted murder, and his friend is an accomplice. Who's the law without a sheriff?"

"Guess I am," a man said, walking up the boardwalk toward them. "I'm Mayor Bryant Trent, but I'm no lawman."

"Where's the jail?" Thad asked.

"Four doors down, but I'm not sure it's a good idea to put them in jail."

"Robbery and attempted murder is about as good as it gets, to go to jail."

"I wasn't gonna shoot him, "the man still holding his hand said. "I was just trying to scare him."

"You're lucky the bullet hit your gun," Thad said, "the judge will decide your intent, but there's no doubt you're a thief. Off your horses and head for the jail—both of you."

The two men along with Thad and Buford dismounted and followed the mayor to the jail. Thad and Buford took the guns from the accused and put them behind bars, locking the cell door.

"Mr. Philmoor is gonna be real mad when he hears about this," one of them said. "He'll come and get us out, and you'll be sorry you got involved in something that is none of your business."

"He's right," the mayor said, "that's why I didn't want to put them in jail. Brian Philmoor's men have been trying to run the town ever since he established his cattle ranch a few miles from town. Every time I find a sheriff, they run him off."

"Why don't you get help from the Rangers?" Thad asked.

"You're not in Texas anymore, Mister; this is the New Mexico Territory. The only law here is what we can provide for ourselves."

"You can't let them take over your town. You need to find a sheriff that can enforce the law."

"They've run off the last three sheriffs I've hired, and the town's people are afraid to stand up to them. You want the job? That way when they come and run you off or kill you, they won't blame the town, but if I were you, I'd get on my horse and keep going. I'll let them go when you leave. I'm sure one of his boys is halfway to the ranch by now. Won't be long and he'll come riding in with some of his men."

Thad looked at Buford.

"You're gonna do it, ain't you?" Buford said.

"No, we are." Thad looked at the mayor. "We work together. Do you have badges?"

The mayor opened a drawer in the desk and removed two badges: "I think you're making a big mistake," he said as shooting and yelling filled the air outside the jail. Thad looked toward the door. "That's Joey Smyth. He gets drunk and starts shooting in the air before going back to the ranch." Thad took the badges and pinned on the sheriff's badge, handing the other badge to Buford. "Do you swear—"

"We swear," Thad said and walked out the door. He took a rope from his saddle and walked out into the street. When Joey rode by Thad lassoed him, pulling him from his horse and he hit the ground hard. The youth looked up at him as Thad pulled him to his feet. "You're under arrest for disturbing the peace." He walked the drunk, and now dazed young man, into the jail, removed his gun and put him in a cell.

"Joey is one of Philmoor's favorites," the mayor said, "he's going to be real pissed when he gets here."

"Do you want the town to belong to him or the people? If you don't stop him, he will own you. The town needs to stand up to him."

"I don't want dead people in the streets. Up to now he hasn't killed anyone, but no one has done what you are doing to his men. He may come in shooting."

"Can you get a few men to back us up?"

"Not a one. Like I said the town is afraid of him."

"Not even you?"

"I don't want the town looking for a new mayor after he kills me. I told you I'm no lawman."

"If he kills us, you'll become his puppet, or he will kill you too. Is that the kind of mayor you want to be?" Thad looked at Buford. "Get that shotgun from the rack and load it."

"Sometimes I almost wish you'd let them hang me." Buford got the gun and began loading.

"What happened to all that talk about freedom and not a care in the world?" Thad asked as he loaded his revolver.

"Should've knowd better, being with you."

Silence prevailed as they waited for what seemed hours as less than an hour passed before they heard the noise of horses hooves growing louder and louder. Thad stepped out onto the boardwalk.

"He's either the bravest man I've ever seen or the stupidest," the mayor said.

"Both." Buford followed Thad outside, carrying the shotgun.

Six men came to a stop in front of the jail. A big man in the center glared at them: "I've come for my men."

"Come back after the trial. Two are charged with attempted murder and stealing."

"I don't know you, mister. You must be new, so I'm going to overlook what you've done to my men, if you let them go. I'm Brian Philmoor, and I run things around here."

"You may run things at your ranch, Mr. Philmoor, but not this town."

"You must not be too smart. I have five men with me, and there are only two of you. If you know what is good for you, you'll let my men go."

"Are you threatening me?"

"Call it what you want."

Thad snapped his gun from his holster, pointing it at Philmoor's head and Buford snapped the shotgun to his shoulder, pointing it at the other men. "Anyone draws, your boss is dead," Thad said. "You're under arrest for threatening an officer of the law. There's nothing I like better than killing. Take off your gun and drop it and dismount, nice and slow. If anyone goes for his gun the first to die is your boss." Philmoor looked at him with a stunned expression. "Do it!" He removed his gun and dropped it then got off his horse. "Up here." Philmoor stepped onto the boardwalk. Thad placed his gun next to Philmoor's head and looked at the five men. "You have two choices. You can go back to the ranch and wait for your boss to be released or come back with more men but if you do, the first to die will be your boss; I'll shoot him in his cell when you ride up. The choice is yours."

"You're the law; it's illegal to kill a man in a jail cell," one of them said.

"And it's illegal to break a man out of jail." He looked at Philmoor. "You want to tell them?"

"Go to the ranch and stay there," he said. The men turned and rode away. Thad escorted Philmoor into the jail and locked him in a cell. "You're the ones that killed the bank robbers in West Gap, aren't you?" Philmoor said.

"That's us." Thad took the shotgun from Buford and handed it to the mayor. "Watch the jail; we're going to introduce ourselves to the town."

"I'm not the law, you are. What do I do if his men come back?"

"You can start by getting a backbone. They won't come back. They know their boss will be the first to die. We won't be long."

The new sheriff and deputy went outside and started down the boardwalk: "I almost pissed myself when you drew," Buford said. "What would you do if they started shooting?"

"Kill them all. You would've killed at least three and I'd got the rest. They were too slow."

"But you didn't know that until you drew. We could be dead."

"We're already dead. You died when they hanged you, and I died with my brother." They walked into the saloon, and Buford looked at the man playing the piano. He looked at the badge on Buford's chest and stopped playing. Everyone looked at them. "I'm Thad Walker, and this is Bill Chance. If you don't cause trouble, there won't be any trouble. If you do, you're going to jail. Nice meeting you." They left the saloon and started for the store.

"Are you sure his men won't come back?" Buford asked.

"I'm sure. If they do, they know their boss is a dead man. With Philmoor dead who's going to pay them?"

"You wouldn't really shoot him, would you?" Thad looked at him. "Yes you would—damn!" They went into the store.

"I'm Bruce Olson," the proprietor said. "Thanks for what you did."

"You're welcome. Do you think he would've shot you?"

"No. I think he was trying to scare me like he said. So far, they haven't shot anyone, just intimidate everyone. They're mean and have roughed up a few men at times, but that's all."

"That could change if they decide they want to own the town. Are you saying you won't press charges?"

"No. I just want to be paid for the merchandise he took. I don't want to cause trouble."

"He broke the law."

"Brian Philmoor is kind of a bully and lets his men be the same, but we need the business from the ranch."

"You're forgetting the ranch needs the town as well. Why doesn't the town stand up to them?"

"They're a rough bunch of men and roughed up the mayor once along with running off three sheriffs. We know it could be worse, so we just take it."

"Maybe it will change now that we're here."

"I saw you take Mr. Philmoor to jail. When he gets out, he might be mad enough to come back and destroy the town."

"You said he's a bully, not an outlaw. He may try something, but if he hasn't killed anyone so far, chances are he won't start now."

"I hope you're right. You going to let the man go that robbed me?"

"How much does he owe you?"

"He took chewing tobacco, cigars, bullets, powder, and some hard candy. About five dollars."

"I'll see you get your money."

"Much obliged. What about Mr. Philmoor?"

"He'll have to serve his time."

"I wish you'd think about it. He brings a lot of business to my store at times, and he always pays his bill. It's just some of his men that steal from me at times."

"He broke the law when he threatened me. I'll think about it."

Thad and Buford left the store and took all the horses, their horses and those belonging to the people in jail, to the livery stable.

"Howdy," A man said coming out of the blacksmith shop.

"I'm Thad Walker, and this is Bill Chance. As you can see we're the new law in town. How much to board the horses?"

"Fred Barns," the man answered. I saw what you did to Philmoor's men and saw you lock him up. Don't expect to live a long life, do you? Two bits a day or dollar a week."

"These two by the week." Thad handed him the reins to his and Buford's horses. "And the rest by the day." He put his hand in his pocket.

"I'm paying," Buford said and handed Fred ten dollars.

"Five weeks. I hope you live that long. What about the other four?"

"See the mayor," Thad said. "Nice meeting you."

When they returned to the jail Thad looked at the man that robbed the store: "Mr. Olson isn't going to file charges if you pay for what you took from his store."

"I'll pay. How much?"

"Ten dollars."

"I didn't take that much!"

"Paying up front is the store price. Stealing is twice the price."

"That's not fair."

"But stealing is? Suit yourself. You can stay in jail until the judge arrives."

"No, I'll pay." He took some money out of his pocket and handed it to Thad.

"What about me?" The other man asked.

"You're free to go, but I'd be a little more careful about who you hang around with if I were you. Your horses are at the livery. It'll cost you two bits a piece to get them out."

"Why? They haven't been there for a day?"

"The cost of stealing is higher than being honest." Thad handed them their guns.

"Are you going to let me out with my men?" Philmoor asked.

"You'll have to wait for the judge."

"That could be weeks."

"Should have thought about that before you threatened me. I'll give you a choice. Pay a hundred-dollar fine or a week in jail."

"A hundred dollars? That's robbery!"

"Threatening a law officer is a serious offense. You can stay for the week if you want."

"If you think I'm going to sit around in this jail for a week you're crazy."

"Then pay the fine."

"You think I carry that much money on me?"

Thad unlocked the door. "You can pay it the next time you come to town."

"You trust me?"

"I take you for an honest man."

"You don't know me. I could go back to the ranch and come back with all my men and kill everybody I see. You first."

Thad handed him his gun belt. "You could do it right now."

Philmoor's face turned red as he took the gun belt. "What about Joey?"

"I'll let him sleep it off and send him home in the morning."

Philmoor turned to go.

"Your horse—"

"I know...at the livery."

"Mr. Philmoor," Buford turned and looked at Thad. "tell your men if they come to town and behave themselves, they are welcome in Mexville. If not, they're going to jail. Nice meeting you."

Philmoor turned and stomped out the door.

"I know he is coming back and wipe out the whole town," the mayor said.

"I'm a gambler, Mr. Trent, and I know a bluff when I see one. I'm betting he won't come back except to pay his fine."

"What if you're wrong?"

"Then you can bury me. We haven't talked money. What does it pay?"

"Forty dollars a month for sheriff and twenty-five for a deputy, I guess. We never had a deputy before."

Buford looked at Thad. "Sounds fair to me."

"What about sleeping quarters?" Thad asked.

"There is a room in the back. I'll have another bunk put in it."

"That will work except he snores," Thad replied. "We're going to the store and pay Olson and then to the restaurant."

"I'll have the bunk here when you come back."

"Me snore?" Buford said as they started down the boardwalk to the store, "I wish you could hear yourself. Do you think we should stay? I thought you wanted to go to California?"

"We can use the money, and the town needs someone to keep the peace. We'll stay a while and see how it goes. We're not in Texas, so I don't think we have to worry about slavery." As they entered the store, Olson, busy arranging things on shelves, stopped working and looked at them. Thad handed him ten dollars.

"This is too much. I said five."

"Things cost more when you steal them. He'll think twice before he does it again."

"Mr. Philmoor looked awful mad walking to the livery. You think he will come back with his men?"

"He likes pushing people around. He's not used to being pushed back. He is fuming mad, but I don't think he is a violent man or a criminal. If I'm wrong, I don't think the town has anything to worry about, he'll come for Bill and me."

"Well... I kinda agree with you, but he's not the type that likes eating crow."

"No one does, but the thing about eating crow is...if you eat enough of it, it becomes a delicacy."

Olson chuckled. "Thanks for the money."

Thad and Buford left the store and headed for the restaurant. "I don't know why you saved me from hanging if you're gonna keep trying to get me killed."

"What slaves don't understand is freedom isn't free, you have to fight for it. If you let people walk all over you, you're still a slave."

"I heard that, but do you have to go looking for trouble? Sometimes I think you enjoy it."

Buford opened the door to the restaurant and a robust woman with a deep, strong voice, greeted them. "Well it's about time you boys come to see me. What took you so long?"

"Sorry," Thad said, "we had other priorities."

"Frances Stone," she said, extending her hand to Thad. "Just call me Fran. You must be Walker and you Chance." She shook Buford's hand. "I bet you boys are famished."

"I got a big appetite," Buford said.

"Have a seat. Steak, potatoes, greens, and whiskey to wash it down?"

"You're a woman after my own heart," Thad said.

She smiled. "Careful what you say, I just might believe you. I've been waiting a long time for someone to put Philmoor in his place."

"His men give you trouble?"

"They know better. I'd kick all their butts if they mess with me."

"I believe you, and I want you to know I'm as docile as a kitten."

"You're about as docile as an enraged mountain lion, Walker. I saw how you handled yourself out there. This meal is on me but don't think it will become a habit."

"I'll pay," Buford said.

"Not this time, tall dark and handsome. I want to do this, but someday I might make you pay me back." She winked at him then left.

"She kinda scares me," Buford said.

"Why? I think she likes you. You seem to have a way with women."

"Don't want nothin' ta do with a woman," Buford said as Fran returned with a bottle of whiskey and two glasses.

"Enjoy, it'll be a few minutes before your food is ready." She walked away.

Thad poured them each a drink, and Buford took a sip: "Oh that do taste good."

"Don't overdo it. Remember you're on duty."

"I know. Does...do you really think Mr. Philmoor will just pay the fine and forget it?"

"He'll pay it but not forget what has happened. I think he will try to get even somehow. We will have to be on guard. After we make the rounds tonight, I think we should take turns sleeping."

"Rounds?"

"Walk the town and make sure all the doors are locked and nothing suspicious is going on."

Fran returned and placed two plates with large steaks and plates of potatoes and greens on the table. "This should hold you till breakfast."

"Whoa! That it will," Buford said, "thank you most kindly."

"My pleasure." She walked away.

By the time they left the restaurant, the sun was far to the west, and long shadows from the buildings filled the street. Thad decided to walk through the town before going back to the jail. They stopped at the store and bought coffee and oil for the lamps, on their way to the jail. Later, after the streets were empty and businesses had closed for the night, they walked the town again.

"You want first watch?" Thad asked when they returned to the jail.

"Don't matter. What am I going to do sitting here by myself? Gonna be a long night."

"Wake me in a few hours, and I'll take over till sunup." Thad looked through the desk drawers and found a deck of cards. "You can play cards to pass the time and when you get tired of that, clean the guns, but make sure you always have one loaded."

"How do you play cards by yourself? I watched the men on the drive play cards with each other but not alone."

"It's called solitaire." Thad shuffled the deck and began arranging the cards on the desk, explaining the rules of the game to Buford.

"Don't look like much fun to me, but I guess it's better than sittin' doin' nothing."

"Give it a try, you might like it." Thad headed for the back room.

Buford tried playing solitaire for a while but became bored and began walking around the office. He looked through the door and searched the empty street, finding the buildings almost invisible in the dark moonless night. He closed the door. The only sound in the jail came from Joey's snoring, and Buford shook his head and sighed, mumbling to himself, "I don't think I like this deputy job." He removed the shotgun, and a rifle from the gun rack, sat down behind the desk and started cleaning them. When he finished cleaning all the guns in the gun rack, with the shotgun loaded and lying on the desk, he removed the cylinder in his revolver and cleaned the barrel of his gun.

After an hour of trying to play solitaire, Buford started a fire in the stove, filled the coffee pot with water and placed it on the stove. About the time the coffee was ready Thad walked into the office.

"This job you got us ain't no fun. I like herding cows better than this."

"We won't need a night watch once Joey is gone. I'm going to walk the town then you can go to bed."

"Okay, I can barely keep my eyes open."

Thad left and when he returned Buford went to the back room.

As the light from the sun, still below the horizon, began to push away the night, Joey stirred and sat up on the bunk holding his head: "I think my head is gonna split open."

"Getting drunk is worth it, isn't it?" Thad said.

Joey stood and grabbed the bars: "I gotta go, Mr. Sheriff, real bad."

Thad unlocked the cell door. "You know where it is?"

"Yes, sir. You trust me ta go by myself?"

"Why not? I got your horse and gun."

Joey hurried out the back door and was gone for a few minutes. The back door opened and Joey started for the cell.

"Have a seat. Cup of coffee?"

"Yes, sir, I sure could use a cup." He sat in the chair near the desk. Thad poured a cup and handed it to him, and he took a big sip. "Ain't gonna lock me up no more?"

"When you finish your coffee, I'm going to send you back to the ranch. How old are you, son?"

"Pert near seventeen."

"Too young to be drinking, Joey. When you come to town, you're no longer allowed in the saloon."

"That ain't fair. All cowboys drink, and I'm a cowboy, same as the others."

"Adult cowboys don't get drunk, shoot up the town, and wake up with a hangover. One day you may be so drunk you shoot and kill someone."

"I don't mean no harm."

"I know that. You're trying to grow up, but you're going about it all wrong. When you're with the herd, you're there to protect them from wolves, mountain lions, and from getting lost. You're there to help them. You need to be that way with people as well, not cause them trouble."

"But I see the others drinkin' and laughin' and havin' a good time. I just want ta be like them."

"Would your mother be proud if she saw you drunk?"

"No, sir, she'd beat me good."

"Stop trying to be someone else and be Joey Smyth. The Joey Smyth your mother would be proud of. Be someone you are proud of. You don't want to admit it Joey, but you're still a boy. Some boys grow up and become responsible people, doing the right things. Others just grow older, acting like children all their lives. You're better than that, Joey, I know you are." He took Joey's gun belt off a wooden peg and handed it to him. "Do you have any money?"

"Yes sir."

"Go across the street and get some breakfast then go back to the ranch. Your horse is in the livery."

"You just gonna let me go? You ain't gonna fine me or nothin'?"

"I want you to remember when you come back to town you're not allowed in the saloon and no drinking. If I catch you drinking, I'll throw you in jail, and next time I won't be so easy on you."

"Yes, sir. Thank you, sir." He started to go then turned back toward Thad. "You sure I don't owe you nothin'?"

"Yes, you do. You need to take charge of your life. Don't let others think for you, think for yourself. Grow up to be a responsible man. One that I can be proud of as well as your mother, but most of all someone you can be proud of. Can I count on you, Joey?"

"Ye...ye...yes sir. I'll try... I promise."

Thad waited for Buford to rise then they went to breakfast. "What are we going to do now," Buford asked as they crossed the street.

"Wait for Philmoor to make his next move."

Chapter Six
Friends and Foes

Things were peaceful in town during the morning and early afternoon. Most were glad to have a sheriff but not sure how long it would last since Philmoor had run off three others in the recent past. Some were a little concerned about having a black man as a deputy; some were afraid of Buford, and others didn't want any blacks in their town. The prejudice in the east was also present in the west although not as severe. People moved west to enjoy the freedom the territory offered without the politics and ever-increasing laws of sovereign states. They admired others that possessed the same independent spirit, and Buford had demonstrated that when he stood up to Philmoor and his men along with Thad. Still, a few resented having a black man in town, especially one with the authority of the law. None opposed him, however. His size and strength of character kept them silent.

Philmoor came riding into town late that afternoon, reined in at the bank hitching rail, dismounted and went inside. A few minutes later he came out and walked his horse across the street to the sheriff's office. When Philmoor entered he found Thad sitting at the desk and Buford in a chair across the room.

"Afternoon, Mr. Philmoor," Thad said.

"I come to pay my fine, but I still think a hundred dollars is too much."

"Threatening an officer of the law is a serious offense. You're lucky I'm letting you off with a fine. A judge would more than likely make you serve time. But I can see you're an honest man and perhaps didn't mean to follow through, so I'll make it fifty dollars."

Philmoor glared at him and threw fifty dollars onto the desk: "If you're trying to get on my good side, forget it. I won't be happy until you get on your horse and ride out of here, taking your deputy with you."

Thad smiled. "Then I guess you're never going to be happy again, because I'm beginning to feel right at home here. Yes sir ... I just might make this my permanent home."

Philmoor glared at Thad and headed for the door, opened it, stopped, and looked back. "You're feeling pretty damn cocky right now, but that could change. You wouldn't be the first sheriff to decide to leave town."

"I guess time will tell. Be sure to tell your boys to behave if they come to town. My jail is feeling kinda empty. Have a nice day."

Philmoor slammed the door behind him, got on his horse and rode out of town.

"That man ain't nothin' but trouble," Buford said, "and you ain't helpin' things any by ticking him off."

"I don't think he is dangerous, but I'm sure he'll try something. If he can't run us off or cause us to leave, he will lose control of the town. I don't think he wants to own the town. He's just used to having his way. Maybe we should change how we do our rounds at night."

"What do you mean?"

"I'll tell you about it later. Right now, I'm going to take this money to the mayor."

After giving Philmoor's fine to the mayor, they walked the town again, but on opposite sides of the street, not together. As the sun approached the western horizon, Thad and Buford entered the restaurant.

"What'll it be boys, same as yesterday?" Frances asked.

"Does you have beans and cornbread?" Buford asked.

"That I do." She turned to Thad. "You want the same?"

"What else do you have?"

"Hunter's Stew with fresh baked biscuits."

"I'll have the stew."

"Comin' right up. Whiskey?"

"Yes ma'am," Buford said.

She returned a few minutes later with two glasses and a bottle of whiskey, followed by a woman with two plates of food.

***

The sun was disappearing below the horizon when they left the restaurant. As they walked across the street, Thad told Buford his plan for making the rounds later. Once in the sheriff's office, Thad started a fresh pot of coffee then tried to teach Buford how to play poker, with little success. Buford wasn't interested in cards and went back to cleaning and polishing the guns in the gun rack.

As the night wore on, Buford fell asleep in a chair while Thad sat behind the desk drinking coffee. In time, the sounds in the town began to diminish as merchants closed their doors for the night and people went home. The only sound they heard was faint music coming from the piano in the saloon. Shortly after midnight, the last reveler left the saloon and the bartender closed and locked the doors.

"Wakeup," Thad said as he rose and headed for the door. "I'm going to make the rounds."

"Huh, oh...okay. Be careful."

"Don't forget to lock the door."

"I'll do it."

Thad left, closing the door behind him.

As Thad walked up the street on the jail side, he checked each door finding them secure. At the end of the street, he crossed over and started down the other side. All went well until he crossed the alley between the bank and barbershop. As he did, two men jumped out of the shadows and grabbed him, one on either side.

"Got ya," one said, as he removed Thad's gun. "Now let's go to the jail and get that black deputy of your—" Before he finished, he heard a double click of a shotgun being cocked behind him.

"Ain't no need," Buford said, "I's right here, but you gone ta jail, sure enough." The stunned men didn't move as Thad retrieved his gun and disarmed them. "Get going. Jails a-waitin'."

Thad searched the men before locking them up. He put their guns in a drawer in the desk. "I'm going to finish the rounds," Thad said.

"Do you think there's more?"

"I doubt it. If there were, they would've made their move when we arrested these two."

"You take the far side and I'll take this side."

After walking the town, they went back to the jail and Thad looked at the men. "You work for Philmoor?"

"They do," Buford said before they could answer. "I seen 'em with him."

"This wasn't his idea," one of them said, "we acted on our own."

"Threatening and attacking an officer of the law will probably get you ten to fifteen years," Thad said.

"I don't want to go to prison," the other man said, with a shaky voice.

"You should have thought of that before you did this. If Philmoor is behind it, and you tell us, the court may go easy on you."

"Well—"

"SHUT UP!" The other one said.

The man looked at him then put his head down.

"Suit yourself," Thad said, "it's no skin off my nose, I'm not going to spend fifteen years in prison." The nervous one sat on a bunk with his hands on his head.

"Get some rest, Butte. I'll take the first watch."

In the early hours of the morning, Buford relieved Thad and made a fresh pot of coffee. Not long after sunrise, Thad came into the office and sent Buford to breakfast. When Buford returned, Thad went across the street to the restaurant. About an hour after Thad returned, Philmoor and five of his men rode into town and reined in at the sheriff's office. Philmoor entered the office, glanced at his men in jail then looked at Thad.

"I come for my men."

"How did you know they were here?"

"Didn't come back to the ranch last night so I figured you had 'em."

"Why would you figure that? Did you send them on a mission?"

"No. I know you don't like me or my men, so I put two and two together. Why are they in jail?"

"They attacked an officer of the law. You have any idea why they would do that?"

"How would I know...guess they don't like you. I'll see that it doesn't happen again. Let them out."

"Attacking an officer of the law is very serious. We'll see what the judge says."

"He won't be here for a long time. I need them to work the ranch."

"Mayor says it will be about six weeks before the judge comes through. They could get about fifteen years for assaulting an officer of the law."

"That's insane. I need those men."

"They could get less if they cooperate with the court."

"Cooperate with the court?"

"If they were sent, and they tell the judge who it was, he could go easy on them and they wouldn't be the only ones going to prison."

Philmoor's face reddened: "I had nothing to do with it!"

"Then you have nothing to worry about."

"Isn't there some way we can put this behind us? Can't you fine them?"

"It will cost the town quite a bit to feed them waiting for the judge," Thad said.

"I'm just trying to save the town some money. Fine them and turn them over to me, and I give you my word nothing like this will ever happen again."

"Your word, huh? You did make good in paying your fine so... I'll fine them and let them go."

"How much?"

"Hundred dollars apiece."

"Two hundred dollars! That's robbery!"

"Okay, we'll wait for the judge."

"Damn you, Walker! I'll get the money!" He stormed out heading for the bank. A few minutes later he stormed back in and threw the money on the desk. Thad unlocked the cell and let the men out, returning their guns.

"One more thing, Mr. Philmoor," Thad said as Philmoor started to leave. "You gave your word. If any of your men try anything again, I'm coming for you. If shooting starts, you're going to be the first to die."

Philmoor looked him straight in the eye. "I don't take kindly to being threatened. You have my word on it, and I keep my word."

"What I said is not a threat, Mr. Philmoor, it's a promise."

Philmoor stormed out and mounted his horse, followed by his men. Still mad, Philmoor started riding out of town at a fast pace, followed by his men. A few miles out of town they slowed their pace.

"I guess we better leave him alone," one of his hands said.

"We'll leave him alone...for now, but nobody is going to treat me like that and get away with it. Nobody!"

"He's not like the others, Boss," another wrangler said, "I don't think he is afraid of anything. I swear I see death when I look in his eyes."

"He's just a man, Jerry."

"That's true but not like any I ever met. What are you going to do?"

"I've got a plan. I'll tell you when it's time."

"Whoa," Buford said, "that Philmoor had fire coming out of his eyes. You think he got the message?"

"Maybe not. He's not the same man I saw when we first met. I think he's become more than a bully."

"Then you think he'll try something else?"

"Maybe; maybe not. I could be wrong, but we'll keep on our toes. We'll keep doing the rounds like we did last night and we'll take turns being in the open."

The town was quiet that night and nothing happened while they walked the street, one in the open and one out of sight. They started taking their meals alone and walking the town on opposite sides of the street during the day. As the days turned into weeks and Philmoor's men behaved themselves when they came to town, the citizens became more acquainted with Thad and Buford. And, Buford began to feel people accepted him as an officer of the law. His color didn't seem to matter to most in town, and they treated him with respect. If a dispute erupted in the saloon, the fighting stopped as soon as Buford burst through the door. His size was sufficient to discourage the roughest trouble maker in town. Fortunately, none of those causing trouble were Philmoor's men who had become the most docile members of the community.

***

After three months of tranquility, Thad and Buford began to relax their over-cautious routine and started eating meals together again.

Since Philmoor's men continued treating people with respect, as did Philmoor when he came to town, conducting his business and leaving, they felt their earlier concerns were unfounded. It became obvious, however, that Philmoor avoided Thad when he came to town. As peace prevailed, they began walking the town together again at night, but one would walk in the middle of the street while the other checked doors.

One day as they left the restaurant Thad looked at Buford: "I think we need to find someone to take our jobs and head for California."

"No," Buford said, stopping in the middle of the street. "I feel at home here." Before Thad could answer, four men, who were on the boardwalk outside the restaurant rushed them from behind, knocking them to the street and began beating them before either could react, as four other men sprang toward them from the other side of the street and started hitting and kicking them.

One of them grabbed Thad's hair pulling his head up from the street as two others grabbed both arms and lifted him from the ground while others began beating him again. Two men raised Buford from the dusty street, and one buried his knee in his gut, causing his legs to buckle while another beat his face with closed fists. One attacker struck him on his head with a gun, sending him to the ground. The eight men continued kicking and beating them until they both lost consciousness, lying motionless in the dust of the street.

"Don't any of you try anything," Jerry said, glaring at people looking on in disbelief, "Or you'll get the same!" People began coming out of stores when they heard the commotion, but none dared help except Fran, who started back into the restaurant to get her gun. "Don't do it, Miss Stone. I'd hate to shoot a woman." She stopped, looking at the man with disgust.

One of the men got Buford and Thad's horses, leading them next to the two unconscious bodies. The others picked them up and threw them, face down, across their saddles as Jerry, and another man mounted their horses. Jerry took the reins of the horses and started out of town as the other man followed behind. The rest of Philmoor's men mounted their horses and started back to the ranch.

"I'm going to follow them," Fran said to Mary, her server, as she entered the restaurant and got her gun. "And don't you dare tell anyone." She went out the back door, saddled her horse and started out of town.

***

When the men returned to the ranch and told Philmoor, he went to the smokehouse and unlocked it. "Okay Joey, you can go, but you made a big mistake quitting. You're a good wrangler, you had a good future here."

"I don't want to hurt nobody," Joey said.

"You need to find a new home, Joey. I don't want ever to see you here again."

"Yes, sir."

"Your horse is in the stable, now get!"

Joey got his horse and headed for town. He went into the store.

"What happened to the sheriff?"

"It was horrible, Joey. They beat 'em and beat 'em, might as well of killed them, may die anyway."

"Where are they?"

"Took them out of town on their horses, unconscious. Don't know what happened after that."

"Which way?"

"South, but I wouldn't go after them if I were you. I've never seen Philmoor's men so mean."

"Thanks," Joey said and left the store.

"That boy is going to get himself killed," Olson said.

Joey headed south, following the road out of town. It had been over an hour since the beatings, so Joey rode at a moderate pace, searching the countryside.

***

Fran followed far behind the two riders, staying off in the trees and brush, catching a glimpse now and then of Jerry and the other rider with Thad and Buford still slung over their saddles.

About the time Joey started south, Jerry and his cohort were about five miles from town when Thad began to come around. Pain surged through his body with every step his horse took as he squinted through his left eye with his right eye swollen shut. Even though he knew the horse was moving forward, all he could see was the ground spinning below him. He could hear Buford, to the left of him, moaning with each step his horse took. Thad could feel their forward motion stop, although the ground continued to spin below him, as Jerry reined in ahead of him.

"You two are not welcome in Mexville. If you live, don't come back. He dropped the reins and rode away with the other wrangler beside him.

Fran waited until the two men were out of sight before riding up to Buford and Thad, still lying across their saddles.

"Are you awake, can you hear me?" She asked.

A weak voice came from Buford: "Just let me die, Lord."

"You sure we're not already dead?" Thad moaned.

"I'll help you down," Fran said, starting to slide Buford off his horse.

"OH GOD! OH NO! LET ME BE!" Buford screamed as his feet touched the ground and Fran lowered him down on his back.

"I'm sorry, honey, but I had to get you off your horse."

"If you're going to torture me like that just leave me here," Thad said.

"Just hold your breath, honey. I'll be as gentle as I can." He screamed as she lowered him to the ground. "Sorry. You'll be okay now."

"Can you make the world stop spinning?" Thad asked.

"I..." she didn't finish and went for her rifle as a rider came into view, heading toward them.

"Don't shoot ma'am," Joey said as he came closer.

"What are you doing here? Fran asked, still pointing the gun at him. "Didn't your friends do enough? You come to take your turn?"

"I didn't have nothin' to do with it. I swear. I quit when I heard what they were going to do. Mr. Philmoor locked me in the smokehouse. Nothin' I could do. I come ta help."

"Thanks, Joey. You stay with them, and I'll go get a wagon and take them to my house." She handed him the rifle. "If they come back, shoot the sons a bitches."

"Don't tell anyone," Thad groaned as she mounted her horse.

"Not a soul." She turned her horse and rode away.

"What can I do for you?" Joey asked as Fran left.

"Kill me," Buford said, "never beat this bad as a slave. I just want ta die."

"You always want to take the easy way out, don't you?" Thad said, with a weak and mournful voice.

"I wasn't takin' the easy way when they were trying to hang me. If it wasn't for you, I'd already be dead and not suffering like this."

"You're welcome," Thad replied.

"Try ta relax," Joey said. "Miss Stone will be back soon, with a wagon."

"I can't wait to be bouncing around in the back of a wagon," Buford said.

"Yeah...gotta be better than lying on the ground watching the world spin," Thad answered.

In less than an hour, Joey saw Fran approaching with the wagon. She pulled up beside them and got down: "Help me get him up," she said to Joey as she bent down toward Thad. He took in a deep breath and gritted his teeth as they raised him up and helped him into the back of the wagon, filled with hay. Now it was Buford's turn to endure the pain of being put into the wagon. She looked at them before getting into the wagon. "I'll go real slow and try to miss the ruts. It's gonna hurt some."

"Right now, I think I'd rather hang," Buford moaned. She got on the wagon and started out with Joey following behind, leading their horses.

It took almost an hour to reach Fran's house and when they were near, Joey saw a horse and buggy at the hitching post: "Someone is here."

"I asked the doc to come," Fran said, "I trust him, and you need medical attention." As they approached, the doctor came out onto the porch. "They're in bad shape, Doc."

"Let's get them in the house," he answered.

With much effort, they took them inside, and into a room with two bed, and the doctor began removing their shirts: "I have water heating on the stove," he said. Fran got the water then returned, watching as the doctor examined them. Thad's right eye was swollen shut and he grit his teeth as the doctor opened the eye with his fingers. "Can you see anything?"

"I see you, but you're kind of fuzzy."

"Good. It will be a while before the swelling goes away but it should be fine." He continued examining Thad. "A couple of teeth are loose but you didn't lose any, and the loose ones should heal. You need to watch what you eat." The doctor continued his examination, finding many bruises all over Thad's body. When he examined his chest, Thad winced when the doctor pressed on his ribs. "You have cracked ribs. I can bandage your chest, but it's going to hurt every time you try to move." He finished with Thad and started on Buford, finding many of the same wounds except no loose teeth, closed eye, or cracked ribs. "You have a bad gash," he said when examining his head.

"Somebody hit me over the head, and it went dark till I saw the road below me slung over my horse. I could feel every step he took."

"Probably the barrel of a gun," the doctor said. The doctor began cleaning and dressing their wounds and wrapped Thad's ribs. When he finished, he closed his bag: "I'll be back in a few days to check on you."

"Money in my pants pocket," Thad said.

"I don't want your money I just want you to get well. If Frances and Joey hadn't found you, you probably wouldn't have lasted the night. The coyotes and mountain lions would've made sure of that. Try not to get up the rest of the day, and when you do, it's going to hurt like hell."

"I may never get up again," Buford said.

"Thanks, Doc," Fran said, walking him to the door. "I'll watch them as much as I can, but I need to be at the restaurant most of the day."

"I'll stay with 'em," Joey said. "I'll take care of them. Just tell me what to do."

"Change the bandages every day and if the wounds look red wash them with whiskey. It'll burn like fire, but it will keep them from getting infected."

"Yes, sir, and don't worry, Miss Stone, I can cook. I'll feed 'em and clean up the dishes too. Don't you worry about a thing."

"Thanks, Joey," Fran said as the doctor boarded his buggy and started back to town. "I need to get back to the restaurant."

"Yes ma'am, don't you worry about nothin.'"

"You're a God sent, Joey. See you tonight."

After Fran left, Joey looked in on Thad and Buford and both were asleep, so he closed the door and went out to care for their horses. When the sun was nearing the western horizon, Joey checked on them again, finding them sleeping. Fran returned after sundown and found Joey on the front porch.

"They doing okay, Joey?"

"Yes um, they're still sleeping. Didn't wake them for supper; figure they need the rest more."

"I think you're right. There's a bunk in the barn. Sorry there isn't room in the house."

"Suites me just fine. I like being close to the horses."

"I have Mary opening in the morning, so I'll fix breakfast before I go. I have a slab of bacon in the root cellar. I'll get some eggs from the hen house and make some biscuits."

"No need. I can do all that. You can go to town as usual or let me fix breakfast for ya."

"You may be right, Joey. People are used to seeing me there first thing. Might look odd if I'm not."

"Makes sense."

"Okay. I'll check on them before I go to bed. See you in the morning, Joey."

"Night, ma'am."

***

"You're up early," Fran said as she entered the kitchen the following morning.

"Mornin,' ma'am. Comes with being a wrangler. Can I fix you some breakfast?"

"No. I'll eat at the restaurant, but the coffee smells good. That's what woke me. Are they awake?"

107

"No, ma'am." He poured her a cup of coffee. "I'll wait till sunup to start breakfast then I'll wake 'em."

She sat at the table as they both drank a cup of coffee. "I'll pay you, Joey, for what you are doing."

"Don't want no money just want ta help."

"But you're out of a job. What are you going to do?"

"I'll worry about that when Mr. Walker and Mr. Chance are better. Don't you worry about me, I'll be fine."

"Okay, Joey. I'm going to go. I'll pick up more food at the store."

"Yes, ma'am and you watch out for Mr. Philmoor's men. I think they will get mean again."

"They know better than to mess with me. I'll see you tonight."

"Yes, ma'am. Enjoy your day."

***

As the sun began to peek over the horizon, Joey gathered eggs from the hen house and got the slab of bacon from the root cellar then started breakfast. While the bacon sizzled in the pan, Joey peeked in on Thad and Buford: "You want some coffee? I got breakfast started."

"Ain't no place on me that don't ache," Buford said. "Don't think I can stand."

"Can you sit up? I'll fix ya a plate."

Thad squinted at him with his left eye: "Bring the coffee first." He tried to sit up, gritting his teeth and holding his breath. Joey hurried to the bed and placed the pillow against the headboard.

"Can't move," Buford said. Joey went to his bed and tried to raise him. "Oh Lord let me die" he screamed. Joey raised his pillow, and Buford leaned back in agony.

"I'll get the coffee." Joey left the room, returning with two cups of coffee.

Whiskey would be better," Thad said through swollen lips.

"Doc said to save it for the wounds," Joey replied.

"Waste," Thad said, then tried to take a sip of coffee and winced as the hot liquid touched his cut swollen lips.

"Can't drink it," Buford said, "hurts too much."

"Would you like some water?" Joey asked.

"I would."

Joey took the coffee from Buford and got a cup of water. Thad continued to sip on the coffee.

"I'll get the food," Joey said as he left the room. He returned with two plates of eggs, bacon, and biscuits. Eating was difficult because of their bruised faces, swollen and busted lips, but both were hungry and managed to consume most of the food. Thad passed on the bacon because of his loose teeth, eating all the eggs and soft portion of the biscuits. When they finished eating both fell asleep.

Around noon, Joey heard Buford calling him and went to their room: "I needs ta go," Buford said, "where is—"

"Right this way."

"I need help getting up."

Joey helped him up and out to the outhouse. Buford moaned and gasped all the way there and back.

Thad and Buford slept most of the day, eating little for lunch and dinner. The next day wasn't much different except they were awake for longer periods. On the third day, the doctor returned and examined them and redressed their wounds. He also changed the bandaging on Thad's ribs.

"You're beginning to heal, but it will take a long time to fully recover. I want you both up and moving around. If you stay in bed too long, you won't be able to walk."

"It hurts like hell when I try to get up, Doc," Buford said.

"Learn to live with it. Try sitting on the front porch for a while then walk to the barn and back; then you can take a nap. Make it short though I want you up most of the day. Tomorrow, take the bandages off and leave them off except for your ribs, Walker, take it off to bathe then bandage them. It's going to be a long time before your ribs heal. You need to keep the wounds clean so use whiskey on them if necessary. In a week you can use soap and water."

"It seems like a waste of good whiskey to me," Thad said.

"Drink some if you want but keep those wounds clean. I'll be back in a couple of weeks. You probably won't need me after that, but it's going to be months before your ribs are healed. Remember, get up and keep moving," he said as he closed his bag. "See you in two weeks."

It took a lot of effort for them to get out of bed. Joey had to help them for the next two days before they could rise on their own. As the soreness began to ease and their stiff joints became easier to move, the walks became longer and both spent time in the barn caring for their horses. At the end of two weeks, the doctor returned to examine them and was pleased with their progress. Small wounds had healed, bruises beginning to disappear, and larger injuries such as Buford's head wound was improving.

"You're on your own now," the doctor said as he prepared to leave, "I won't be back."

***

At the end of four weeks, they began riding again, which was painful for Thad because of his cracked ribs. He endured it, however, knowing they soon could leave when he was able to ride for several hours at a time. As the sixth week came to an end, they were sitting at the kitchen table drinking coffee with Fran and Joey when Buford looked at Thad: "I think it's time we started for California."

"I thought you said you liked it here?"

"I do, but if we stay Mr. Philmoor no doubt will kill us."

Thad didn't answer as he continued to look at him. "You ain't goin', are you? You're going after him."

"He didn't kill us so I thought I'd give him another chance."

"You're insane. Ever since you saved me from hanging all you've done is try to get me killed."

"You don't have to go with me."

"I didn't tell you," Fran said, "Philmoor came into town the day after his men beat you and told everyone the town was his now and anyone that didn't like it would get worse than what you got."

"Dang!" Joey said, "I didn't know he was that mean."

"He's changed," Fran said, "Before he just wanted to bully people but now he wants total control."

"How we going to get him?" Buford said, "we don't have no guns."

"Change your mind, huh?"

"I could get guns from the store," Fran said.

"Bad idea," Thad answered, "It would look odd for you to buy guns."

"I'll go with you," Joey said.

"We're going alone," Thad replied, "If he kills us, I don't want you involved. He'd kill you too."

"You can take my gun."

"Keep it, you may need it before this is over."

"Just how do you think we're going to get them without guns?" Buford asked.

"I know where we can get guns."

"I don't like the sound of that. You're gonna do something stupid, aren't you?"

"Doing something stupid would be to ride off and leave our friends in jeopardy."

"Huh?"

"To leave and let Philmoor run over the town and abuse them is his version of slavery."

"Now you got my attention, but don't tell me what you have in mind. I don't want to know until we do it."

"I'm going with ya," Joe said.

"Sorry, Joey. You don't have the experience for this. One slip up and we're dead."

"You can have my rifle," Fran said.

"Thanks, but it won't help. If we fail, you may need it. If we don't succeed, he may turn on the town. Don't tell anyone that we're here and going after him."

"The mayor should know if the town may be attacked," Fran said. "He's a bit of a wimp, but I know he won't say anything. At least there will be two guns ready if they come."

"You're right." Tell him but make sure he keeps it to himself and don't tell him until tomorrow evening. We'll leave in the morning."

Chapter Seven
Ambush

Thad and Buford left early the next morning, riding far around the town, heading for Philmoor's ranch. Once there, they stayed in the trees on a rocky hill, lying flat on their bellies with their hats off, far above the pasture where Philmoor kept his herd.

"What we do now?" Buford asked.

"We wait."

"Wait?" Thad nodded. "It ain't much past noon. How long we wait?"

"Till dark."

"Then what we do?"

"Then what will we do," Thad said. "You still need to improve your speech."

"Won't do me no good if I'm dead."

"How many guards do you see?" Thad asked.

"Three."

"That's all I see. I think they'll go to two after dark."

"Do you think we can get them without being seen?"

"If not we're dead."

"So that's your plan. We get the guards and steal their guns?"

"Why not? They won't need them once they're tied up."

"But it won't be dark for hours. What will we do until then?"

"I'm going to take a nap while you watch."

"How about you watch while I take a nap?"

"Okay. I'll take the first watch."

"No, you sleep," Buford said. "I'm glad we're in the shade. Hope there ain't no...aren't any rattlesnakes around."

Thad moved back into the trees and placed his hat over his face while Buford continued to watch the herd and wranglers. A couple of hours later Thad returned, and Buford napped. When Buford returned, the sun was beginning to descend toward the western horizon. They ate some beef jerky and shared water from a canteen, waiting for the sun to disappear beyond the far horizon. As the light began to dim, two riders rode in and relieved the three cattle guards. In time, the sun, then its light, disappeared, replaced by an almost full moon, fixed above a few drifting clouds, scattered across the night sky.

"When are we going to make our move?" Buford asked, in a soft voice.

"Let's give it a couple of hours. Maybe they will be sleeping when we take them."

"What if they see us and start shooting?"

"Then I guess the town will bury us."

"This ain't no funny thing, Thad."

"Not trying to be funny just truthful."

"If...when we get them then what will we do."

"Go get the rest of them."

Buford sighed. "You're enjoying this, aren't you?"

"Not yet."

It became quiet as they waited. About two hours later Thad said, "it's time. You take the one on the left and don't make a sound on your way to the herd."

"I ain't even going to breathe until this is over."

With their horses in the trees, they started down the hill on foot, bareheaded, crouching down behind brush and trees as they went. As quiet as a stalking lion, Buford made his way up to the herd, staying as low as possible, trying not to spook the cattle. While the wrangler snoozed with his chin on his chest, Buford made his way toward him through the herd. Once beside him, Buford snatched the guard out of the saddle, removed his gun, then struck him over the head. The wrangler lay motionless on the ground. He removed the man's gun belt, put it on, and dropped the revolver in the holster, before peeking over the saddle. With a foot in the stirrup, Buford rose slowly over the saddle seeing the other wrangler still on his horse then watched as he disappeared. After binding the man's hands and gagging him, Buford threw him across the saddle, before making his way toward the other horse. As he made his way through the herd, he saw Thad slide the other man over the saddle, bound and gagged.

The two went up the hill, retrieved their horses and hats then headed for the line shack.

With his back to the wall of the shake, Thad removed his hat and peeked through the window. Three men were smoking and playing cards, sitting around a table with a bottle of whiskey on it. He pointed toward the door, signaling he was going in and Buford took his place at the window. A loud BANG filled the shack as Thad kicked the door open and the startled men rose and went for their guns: "Do it, and you're dead," Buford said from outside the window.

"Put your guns on the table, nice and easy," Thad said, "and move away." The three followed his command. "Now drop your gun belts." The belts fell to the floor. "Against the wall; hands over your head." They moved to the wall as Buford came in and bound and gagged the men.

"Mr. Philmoor is gonna kill ya when he hears about this," one of them said before he was gagged.

"He's about to get his chance," Thad said. "Outside and on your horses." The other two men began to awaken as Buford and Thad came up to them, leading three horses with three men on them, bound and gagged. With the five men in front, Thad and Buford started for the house. Leaving the five men in front of the house, they went up the steps, and Thad kicked the door in, Buford right beside him. As the door swung open, three startled men rose from a table and Philmoor, standing at a buffet with his back to them pouring a drink, spun around and went for his gun. Thad dropped him with one shot through the heart. Philmoor collapsed to the floor. The other men put their hands in the air.

"You killed Mr. Philmoor."

Thad and Buford turned toward the voice: "What are you doing here, Joey?" Thad asked.

I've been following ya'all day. Two of 'em out there tried to get their horses to ride off, but I tied 'em all to the rail. They ain't going nowhere." He looked at Philmoor on the floor.

"He gave me no choice, Joey. It's one less we'll have to hang."

"You gonna hang 'em all?"

"If I can find enough rope."

"We need...need to take them to town and let the law handle it," Buford said.

"We are the law, remember? And judge and jury."

"It ain't...isn't right, Thad. Let's take them in and let a real judge and jury decide."

"You getting soft?"

"Please, Mr. Walker. I think Mr. Chance is right about this."

Thad sighed. "Okay. Disarm these three and tie their hands."

"Thanks, Joey." One of them said as he tied his hands.

"I ain't doin' it for you. Most likely you'll hang anyway."

***

Midnight had passed when they got to town and Buford and Joey locked the wranglers in jail while Thad took Philmoor's body to the undertaker. No lights were on when Thad stopped in front of the building. He dismounted and knocked on the door. After a minute he knocked again much harder. Light began to show from a lamp through the upstairs window then at the top of the stairs before moving down the stairs.

"That you, Sheriff?" Doug Morris asked as he opened the door.

"It's me. Got some work for you."

116

"Thought you were dead. Who is it?"

"Philmoor."

Morris walked over to the horse with a body across the saddle and shined the lamp on the figure's face. "Danged if it ain't. Help me get him inside." Thad slid the body off the horse, and they carried it into the building and placed it on a table. "This town is going to be buzzing like a beehive in the morning when they hear about this. What happened?"

"He tried to kill me. I've got his men in jail."

"I better wake the mayor."

"Let him sleep. Go back to bed. Nothing he can do tonight. I'll tell him in the morning."

When Thad walked into the jail, Buford had lit the stove and was making a pot of coffee. He looked at Thad as he entered: "You want first watch?"

"Okay. Joey, you can go home. Thanks for the help."

"Ain't got no home now that Mr. Philmoor fired me, and since you're well, ain't staying at Fran's no more."

"There's two bunks in the back," Thad said, "you can stay here tonight, but let me warn you, Butte snores."

"Come on, Joey," Buford said, and help me take the horses to the stable then we'll get some rest. You'll see who snores when Thad takes his turn in the bunk."

***

The town was beginning to stir when Thad rose the following morning. As he poured a cup of coffee, the door opened.

"Doug told me you killed Philmoor and have his men in jail. When Fran told me you were going after him, I didn't think it would come to this."

"Morning, Mayor," Thad said, still pouring his coffee. "He tried to kill me, so I had no choice. You need to send word to the judge.

It's going to cost a lot to feed his men before the trial, and there's too many in my jail. It's not made to hold eight prisoners."

"I sent Shaffer to fetch him. Did you have to kill him?"

"No, I could've let him kill me. I'm sure that would've made him happy but not me. I want to deputize Joey until the trial. Eight prisoners and a town is more than we can handle."

"Joey?"

"He followed us yesterday and helped bring them in."

"You're costing the town a lot of money, Walker."

"Okay, you help us take care of Philmoor's men."

"I'll do what I can to help but no more deputies." While he was talking Joey came in from the back room.

"Morning, Mr. Mayor," he said as he poured a cup of coffee.

"You and Joey go to breakfast," Buford said, coming in behind Joey. "I'll go when you get back."

"Stay with Butte, Mayor, until we get back."

"I'll be here."

The restaurant was half full when Thad and Joey entered. The server came, took their orders, and left.

"I tried to get the mayor to hire you as a deputy until the trial, Joey, but he said the town couldn't afford it. Sorry."

"Ain't no never mind, I'll help anyway and got money for food too. I'll pay for breakfast."

"This breakfast is on me and thanks for the help. I'm not sure how much help the mayor will be. I'll make it up to you somehow."

"You don't owe me a thing. I'm proud ta help."

Chapter Eight
Putting down Roots

Later that day, as Thad walked through the town making his rounds, Samuel Young, the owner of the bank, came up beside him.

"Afternoon, Sheriff."

"Sam."

"You sure have this town in an uproar."

"Just doing my job."

"You're causing a problem for me as well, Walker." Thad looked at him. "When Philmoor started his ranch, he borrowed money from me to buy cattle and build some of his buildings. He still owes me, and he told me at the time he had no living relatives. If that is true, I guess I own the ranch. I know he came from Fredericksburg, Virginia and I'll check to see if I can find a relative. If I don't, I'll try to sell it. In the meantime, there's no one taking care of the place. The cattle will stray, horses need to be cared for, I don't know what to do. You and Bill know cattle, can you help me?"

"Maybe, some; after the trial. Joey Smyth used to work for Philmoor. He knows cattle. Why don't you hire him, he may be able to find some wranglers to help?"

"He's very young."

"He's young but smart and a hard worker as well. I'm sure he can find some help, and after the trial, Butte and I will take turns working the ranch. I'm a gambler, and I'd bet my life Joey will do a good job."

"Well... I don't know."

"What choice do you have? Do nothing, and you will lose the cattle and the horses. That's a lot of money. The cattle pretty much take care of themselves except for straying, and Joey knows horses."

"I guess you're right. What choice do I have?"

"I'll send Joey to see you when I get back to the office."

"Thanks, Thad. I don't know of anyone out here that would want the ranch or could afford it, so I'm hoping I find a relative."

Thad finished his rounds and when he returned to the office, Joey had just returned from taking a prisoner to the outhouse.

"Sam Young wants to see you at the bank, Joey."

"What for? I don't owe him no money?"

"Maybe he owes you."

"Can't be, I ain't never been in the bank before."

"Go talk to him, Joey. Sam's a nice man."

"Yes, sir, if you say so." Joey left the office walking very slow across the street to the bank. He stopped and put his hat in his hands and went in. In less than half an hour he walked out and almost ran across the street to the sheriff's office. "You ain't never gonna believe this, Mr. Walker! He wants me to run Mr. Philmoor's ranch. Gonna pay me and everything."

"That's fantastic, Joey."

"You had something to do with this, didn't you, sir?"

"He needed someone to run the ranch, and I couldn't think of a better man than you."

"Whoa! I'm excited but scared too. Don't know if I know enough to be a ranch foreman."

"Butte and I will help when we can. After the trial, one of us will be with you most of the time. You'll need at least two wranglers to help. Do you know of any?"

"Yes, sir, I sure do. They're not much more than boys but work hard. Don't know much about livestock, but I can teach 'em."

"I knew I was right about you, Joey. You're already making plans and thinking ahead. You're going to work out just fine."

"Thank you, sir. I'm gonna go find Bobby and Jimmy and talk them into coming to work for me, then I'm goin' ta the ranch and see what needs to be done." He bolted through the door, heading for the livery to get his horse.

"Are you sure you know what you're doing?" Buford said, "letting a boy like that run a ranch?"

"He will never learn any younger. He'll make mistakes, but everyone has a right to fail."

"Right to fail?"

"It's practice. When you were learning to walk between your mother and father, I'm sure you fell many times so you could look at that as a failure, but your parents encouraged you, and soon you were walking. That's what Joey will be doing, and we will be there to pick him up, brush him off and send him on his way. He'll do just fine."

***

Two days later the judge arrived and set up court in the saloon. Buford and Thad brought in the accused, and the judge gaveled the court into session. The saloon was full, and many crowded around the door outside. The eight men stood in front of the judge: "How do you plea?"

"Not guilty," one of them said.

"Not guilty? I have a whole town of witnesses and you plead not guilty? Assaulting officers of the law and leaving them to die is a very serious offense. If you opt for a jury trial and are found guilty, the jury may recommend hanging. If you plead guilty, you'll get fifteen to twenty and may be paroled early for good behavior. Do you still plead not guilty?" They all lowered their heads and shook them. "I can't hear you! One at a time, how do you plea?"

"Guilty, Your Honor," one said. "Guilty," another said as did all the others.

"This court finds you all guilty of brutally assaulting two officers of the law and sentences you to serve not less than fifteen years in the territorial prison." He slammed the gavel down. "Courts adjourned; bar is open. Sheriff, will you deliver the prisoners to the New Mexico territorial prison within the next week?"

"They will be there, Your Honor."

***

After delivering the prisoners Thad and Buford took turns helping Joey at the ranch. Weeks passed, and Sam Young still had heard nothing from Fredericksburg. More time passed, and Thad started thinking about a cattle drive to retrieve some of the bank's money. Joey found another youngster, and they began training him to herd cattle, which gave them five wranglers for the drive. This would make it difficult since none of them except Thad and Buford had ever been on a drive, and only one of them could go. The other would be sheriff, maintaining order in town. However, with Philmoor gone, maintaining order in town became easy.

To start a drive with four greenhorns would be risky at best. Joey knew cattle and horses but taking cattle to market was quite different from herding and branding. Anything could happen on a drive. Even so, the drive wouldn't start until they found a cook to drive the chuck wagon and feed the men. The cook is one of the hardest working people on a drive and finding one mature enough and strong enough wouldn't be easy. One day as Thad ate lunch, Fran came over to his table.

"You still looking for a cook for the drive?"

"That I am. Got one in mind?"

"Me."

"You have a restaurant to run."

"I can put Mary in charge and get Mable from the store to help."

"Thanks, Fran, but I don't think you know how dangerous a drive can be."

"That's my point. You may need another gun and you know I can shoot straight and not afraid to do it if necessary."

"You'll get no arguments from me. I know how strong and determined you are, but as a cook, you would work your butt off on a drive."

"I need to lose some weight anyway, and there's no one else around here that can do it."

"I still have a problem. I need someone to watch the ranch while we're gone."

"Why not Bill?"

"He will be sheriff while I'm gone."

"Hell...get the mayor to watch the town. With Philmoor and his men gone this place is as docile as a puppy. If there is trouble, he can send for Bill."

"Bill will have his hands full taking care of the breeding stock and horses. He should have someone helping him. Keeping the breeding stock from straying will keep him busy most of the time."

"You also could use more men for the drive, and you're the only one with experience. This whole operation is undermanned. Bill is a strong man. He'll probably have it easier than we will on the drive."

"Okay, I'll ask the mayor when I finish eating."

"When will we leave?"

"Three ... four days. I need you to come out to the ranch and look over the chuck wagon and determine what supplies we will need. The drive should take at least ten days but let's plan on twelve and probably four coming back. I also need more time to show the men the difference between herding and driving cattle."

"I'll be out in the morning."

"Thanks, Fran, for doing this. You'll be well paid and earn every penny."

"I don't want to be paid."

"I still owe you for saving our lives. You'll agree to be paid, or you're not going."

"Okay, Walker. Sometimes I think you're almost as stubborn as me."

He smiled. "I'm working on it."

Thad left the restaurant and headed for the mayor's office. Halfway across the street Sam Young came out of the bank and waved to him. Thad waited as he approached: "I heard from Fredericksburg. There are no Philmoor's there, and they couldn't find other kin. Guess I own the ranch."

"There's a safe in the house. You should go out there and see if you can open it. He may have the combination written down somewhere. There may be money in it."

"Okay. I'll be out, but I still don't know what to do with the ranch. I can't run it and don't want to. There's no one around here to buy it. If I advertise it in the east it could take years to find a buyer." He paused. "You put two thousand dollars in my bank when you came here. Why don't you buy it?"

"It's worth a lot more than that, and I'm not sure I'm ready to settle down in one place."

"Think about it. You and Bill could buy it together. I'll come up with a price and a payment plan."

"We have jobs. I'm not sure I can be a sheriff and a rancher at the same time."

"That's why you should buy it with Bill. Between the two of you, you should be able to work it out. You have Joey and three other wranglers. If he can find a couple more, you could almost run it from town."

"I'll think about it and talk to Butte, but don't expect an answer until after the drive."

"Sounds fair. I'll be out tomorrow and check on the safe."

Sam Young went back to the bank and Thad went into the mayor's office: "Afternoon Trent."

"What do you need, sheriff?"

"I need a couple of weeks off for Butte and me."

"I didn't think Bill was going on the drive."

"He's not. He will be taking care of the ranch until the drive is over."

"Then who's going to be sheriff while you're gone?" Thad just looked at him. "You want me to do it?"

"You're the mayor, who else is there? Since Philmoor and his men are gone, this is a peaceful town. There shouldn't be any trouble and if there is you can get Butte. While we're gone, you will be saving the town money since you won't be paying us."

Trent sighed. "Okay, I'll do it, but I'd rather Bill were here."

"Okay then, you work the ranch."

"I don't know anything about cattle or horses."

"Then I guess you're the sheriff."

***

The following morning Frances arrived at the ranch just after dawn and she and Thad checked over the chuck wagon and started making a list of supplies for the drive.

"As cook, you have the hardest job on the drive," Thad said, "When the drive starts, I need you to go ahead of the herd and find a place you think we will pass, around noon. The drive doesn't stop but a couple of wranglers at a time will leave the herd to eat then return so two more can eat as the herd continues the drive. We will be traveling at a walk, so it's not a problem for everyone to eat as we pass you. It will be a problem for you because as soon as everyone is fed, you need to break camp and find a place to stop for the night and set up camp again. You're the first one up in the morning and the last to bed at night."

"Damn! I guess I'm really going to lose weight on this drive."

"I tried to warn you."

"I know ... and I won't let you down."

"You're not the one that worries me. It's those four youngsters. If the herd stampedes or we are attacked, and they panic, some could be injured or even killed, and we could lose the herd. I won't sleep until this drive is over."

***

While they were checking the wagon, Sam Young arrived and went into the house. He found the safe and looked it over then started searching for the combination. It would take more than luck to find it and he looked through every drawer and cabinet in the house. He looked under the table, the bottom of the chairs, in Philmoor's clothes, and found nothing. Discouraged, he thought about going to town to get the blacksmith and see if he could open it when he decided to empty the drawers in the chest of drawers in the bedroom. With the top drawer open and everything removed, he turned it upside down. There on the bottom of the drawer were four numbers separated by dashes. He went to the safe and opened it.

Thad and Fran were still in the barn with the chuck wagon when Sam walked in: "I found it," he said walking up to Thad. "Two hundred dollars and the ranch papers were inside. You should've looked yourself you'd be two hundred dollars richer."

"Not mine. It belongs to the bank."

"Do you want to take it on the drive?"

"I have some money but I shouldn't need it, and I'll have the money from the sale when we start back. I'll bring you a receipt, but I'm going to pay the crew out of it. The rest is yours."

"Give yourself a bonus."

"I'm not being paid on the drive, and that's the way I want it."

"No, Thad. You're the only skilled member of the crew. I want you to pay yourself along with the others, and you should receive more."

"I do things my way, Sam."

"You're wasting your breath," Fran said, "If I didn't know better, I would think he was my brother."

Sam looked at Fran then back at Thad. "Have you talked to Bill, yet?"

"I will when I go back to town."

"I'm going to go," Fran said. "I'll come out tomorrow, get the chuck wagon and take it to town to get the supplies."

Sam handed her the two hundred dollars: "Use this to pay for them."

"Won't be near this much."

"You can bring the difference to the bank or keep it. You're going on the drive and don't forget this is my ranch and my drive and you're definitely going to be paid."

"Well, I'll be damn! Another stubborn cuss. Must be catching."

***

When Thad walked into the sheriff's office, Buford was sitting behind the desk with a cup of coffee. Thad poured a cup.

"I have Joey and his boys working on the fence around the south pasture," Thad said. "It should be ready by the time we start the drive. You can drive the breeding stock and those we leave, into it at night so you can get a good night's sleep. It's a little small, but they should be okay through the night."

"Might work, as long as a mountain lion or wolves don't think they've found a feast."

"You can sleep out there if you want. I think we stand to lose more on the drive as strays than to lions and wolves. Do whatever you want, but while we're gone, I got something for you to think about."

Buford gave him a hard look: "You kinda scare me when you talk like that. What trouble you getting us in now?"

Thad smiled. "No trouble. Sam thinks we should buy the ranch."

"We don't have that kind of money, and you said you want to go to California."

"I'm still thinking about going. I gave Sam some money when we got here. Not enough to buy it, but he said he would work up a price and a payment plan."

"Where did you get the money?"

"Gambling."

"You had it all the time?"

"Yes."

"Do you want us to buy it?"

"I think we should think about it and talk about it when I get back. I thought you liked it here?"

"I do, and I could stay, but you want to go to California."

"Someday. We could try ranching for a while, and if we don't like it, we could sell."

"You're full of surprises."

"It's Sam's idea. I just think it's worth considering. Think about it while I'm gone."

"If we buy the ranch what about sheriffing,' how are we going to do both?"

"That's something we will have to discuss. Think about it and write down your ideas."

"You know I don't have no schoolin', how am I going to write it down?"

"You have a sharp mind; you can remember it. You have a couple of weeks."

***

The following day Fran got the chuck wagon and filled it with everything she thought they would need on the drive. The following morning before daybreak, everyone was with the herd waiting for first light to start the drive.

"I want everyone here before we start," Thad said to Joey, standing by the fire near the chuck wagon, "even those with the herd."

"Yes, Sir, Mr. Walker. I'll get 'em."

All five wranglers walked up to the fire, leading their horses and faced Thad.

"Drives are hard, long and dangerous," Thad said. "Anything can happen and most likely will happen before it ends. When I tell you to do something you need to do it without question. Yours and the lives of others may depend on you following orders." He paused and looked each man in the eye then spoke to all. "When I look at you, I see boys. At the end of this drive when I look at you, I'll see men. Move 'em out."

All took to their mounts and headed for the herd. Fran doused the fire, finished loading the wagon, and started north, ahead of the herd. The drive began slow, with the young wranglers becoming more comfortable driving the herd with each passing day. By the end of the third day, Fran knew how far to go ahead of the cattle before stopping for lunch and at the end of the day.

The first three days went well. The weather, although hot, was clear. When they rose on the morning of the fourth day dark clouds gathered overhead. Thad told the wranglers to keep the herd tight and to increase the pace if a storm developed. The first few hours went well, but the weather continued to deteriorate with a faint rumbling coming from the clouds in front of them.

The rumbling increased as they continued and the cowboys increased the pace of the herd. A few large drops of rain began to fall with more rumbling overhead followed by a loud, bright crack of lightning, exploding a tree about half a mile to their right. The cattle panicked and began running and scattering in all directions. With too few wranglers and no experience, steers began leaving the herd, moaning and running in all directions. The scared young cowboys did their best to keep the herd together. None panicked and rode off. They used what little skill they had to keep the herd together. As they moved forward and the storm continued going in the opposite direction, the rain stopped and the rumbling decreased as the frightened cattle slowed their pace to a walk. Only about a third of the animals remained when the wranglers reformed the herd.

"Bob, Jim! Stay with the herd," Thad said, "the rest start looking for strays."

As the hours passed, wranglers came and went returning a few steers at a time. Fran returned to the location of the herd and set up camp. The sun grew small in the western sky, and the light began to fade when the last cowboy returned with a few more steers. It looked as if they had found most of the herd when off in the distance Thad saw about a dozen steers heading toward them. As the cattle came closer, a lone rider appeared behind them and Thad watched, wondering who the man could be since all his men had returned. Two wranglers rode out and helped drive the strays into the herd. Thad rode over to the stranger.

"Thanks for helping us find our cows."

"You're welcome."

"I didn't expect to see anyone out here on the prairie. What do I owe you, Mister ..."?

"Britt Thomas. Nothing. I'm glad to help."

"Thanks again, Britt. Had dinner?"

"No."

"Come into camp and join us."

Britt looked at Fran as she filled his plate then sat down next to Thad, away from the other men.

"Where you headed, Britt?"

"West."

"No place in particular?"

"Just west. A lot of country to see."

"That there is. I can see you know cattle. Are you looking for a job? I could use another wrangler."

"I see you're short of help. Don't think I've ever seen a crew like this before."

"They're pretty young but all good men. They just need time and experience. They'll have it when this drive is over."

"And a woman cook?"

"Frances owns a restaurant in Mexville. She's just doing me a favor."

"Okay, Mister Walker. I'll take the job. I want to see how this drive turns out."

"Call me Thad. Thanks. Now I have two experienced wranglers."

"You the other one?"

"I am."

"These your cattle?"

"The ranch belongs to the bank, but my partner and I may buy it. Put your bedroll wherever you want." Thad rose. "I'm going to relieve one of the guards so he can eat."

"How many are guarding the herd?"

"Two."

"I'll get the other one," Britt said as he got up and placed his empty plate on the chuck wagon.

***

Peace prevailed in Mexville before the drive started and continued as Thad drove the cattle toward their destination. Three strangers came to town and stayed a couple of days before leaving. None were trouble makers, but the mayor was pleased when they left. He didn't like being the law and longed for the day Thad returned, relieving him from the responsibility of maintaining peace.

***

Things were peaceful at the ranch as well. Buford decided to camp near the fenced pasture holding the breeding cattle, and the fifty not taken to market, providing meat for the town and ranch. He rode the perimeter twice each night to discourage predators from attacking the herd. At first, he found it difficult for one man to move the stock into the fenced area, taking them in small numbers. After the third day, however, the cattle seemed to know what to do when he appeared in the pasture just before sunset and started for the gate.

As the days passed Buford thought about buying the ranch and he liked the idea even though he didn't see how they could afford it. As a slave, he never imagined he could own land of his own. The dream of freedom was enough, but meeting Thad had seemed to make anything possible. Even though Thad's daring and boldness filled him with fear at times, he knew Thad was a God sent, making his dream of being a free man possible. Maybe running the ranch would eventually take them away from being the law, and end Thad's relentless quest for danger. Having almost lost their lives when attacked by Philmoor's men, did nothing to quench Thad's thirst for danger. In fact, he seemed to crave it even more by attacking Philmoor and his men barehanded and prevailing. Buford knew it would be wrong to leave the town and do nothing after the attack, but still, to go after eight men and Philmoor unarmed, seemed reckless at best. To Thad, it was just another adventure. The more Buford thought about it, the more he became convinced buying the ranch was the right thing to do.

***

The drive continued without incident and having an extra wrangler helped. One day they saw a small band of Indians on a far bluff, but they didn't follow the herd. Thad cut out three head and left them as a peace offering. They never saw the Indians again.

The drive continued, and Thad stopped early one evening as they approached Springfield, Missouri. That night after dinner Thad called all the hands together near the chuck wagon, except the two guarding the herd.

"Tomorrow we will be in Springfield. After I sell the herd and you have your pay you are on your own. You're never been here before, Springfield is a rough town, and you'll run into other wranglers. I know you want and deserve to have some fun. I'm proud of every one of you. I'm now looking at the men I told you about before we left. I want you to stay together and if there is trouble, help each other. If I hear any of you start trouble, I'll hold back half of your next pay. We came here to complete our job and relax, not start trouble. Joey, tell the guards what I've said. The rest of you are dismissed."

The men began to leave. "Britt." He turned and looked at Thad. "I can use you at the ranch if you want to stay."

"Okay. I'll stay for a while."

"If we buy the ranch you will be working with me half of the time, and with my partner the other half. His name is William Buford Chance, but I call him Butte."

"Is he anything like you?"

"Not quite, but I think you will like him. He's easy to get along with."

The next morning, they drove the herd to Springfield and waited behind another herd to have their steers counted and sold. After Thad paid the crew, he rode back to the camp and relieved Fran, watching the spare horses and chuck wagon. She rode to town and returned as the light faded in the cloudless evening sky.

"I thought you would spend the night," Thad said as she dismounted.

"Not my kind of town. I bought clean clothes took a bath and ate someone else's cooking. I'm ready to go home. Go back in if you want."

"Been here before. I'm ready to go back. I think the mayor will be glad to see me." As they talked, another rider rode in and dismounted. "Why didn't you stay in town, Britt? Thought you'd want to unwind before heading back."

"Good place to get shot or shoot someone. Big towns aren't civilized."

"Got some fresh coffee," Fran said.

"Thanks."

They sat around the fire drinking coffee and engaging in small talk before going to sleep, as a full moon rose in the dark clear sky.

All rose before first light, and Fran made breakfast before they started back to Mexville. By noon Joey caught up with them, and Fran prepared lunch. Three days later the ranch came into view, and they rode to the house.

When he heard the horses approaching, Buford came out onto the porch. Britt seemed a little surprised to see a black man.

"Sure glad to see you," Buford said, "I need a break from watching the herd and caring for the horses."

"Butte," Thad said, "this is Britt Thomas , William Buford Chance."

"Mr. Chance," Britt said, tipping his hat then looked at Thad. "You didn't tell me your partner was black."

"Does it matter?" Thad asked as he got off his horse.

"No," Britt answered as he and Joey dismounted. "I've never seen a black man in the west."

Buford walked over, extended his hand. "Call me Bill."

They shook hands: "Nice to meet you, Bill."

"Britt helped us round up strays when the herd was scattered by a storm. He's agreed to stay for a while and work the ranch."

"Then you think we should buy it?"

"I think so. Let's see what kind of a deal Sam offers us."

"I'm going to town," Fran said, getting down from the chuck wagon.

Joey started for the barn. "I'll get your horse, ma'am."

"Thanks for your help, Fran," Thad said. "You were an asset to the drive. We couldn't have made it without you."

"You're welcome. You paid me well, but don't ask again. This was my first and last cattle drive."

"I'm sure we can find a cook, but it's going to be difficult for him to live up to your standard."

"If you're looking for a free meal at the restaurant, forget it." She mounted her horse. "I'll see you boys in town." She turned her horse and rode off.

"I never met a woman like her before," Britt said.

"A little free advice my friend, don't ever pick a fight with her, you'll lose."

"No danger in that. I'd hate to be on her bad side but if you ask me, I'd say she has a heart as big as all outdoors."

"That she does, Britt, that she does."

"The boys should be back tomorrow Mr. Walker," Joey said, "why don't you and Mr. Chance go ta town and talk to Mr. Young. I'll be fine until the others get here."

"I'll stay with Joey," Britt said.

Thad looked at Buford: "Get your horse, we've got a ranch to buy."

When they got to town they stopped at the mayor's office and a big smile appeared on the mayor's face when he saw Thad.

"Now I can start breathing again."

"Town looks peaceful," Thad replied, "maybe you should stay sheriff and save the town some money?"

"You know I'm no lawman."

"Butte and I are going to the bank and talk to Sam about buying the ranch."

"Are you saying I need to look for a new sheriff?"

"We'll talk about it when we come back."

"Put this badge on before you go." Thad pinned on the badge as they left the office. When they walked into the bank, Sam came out of his office.

"I saw you go in the mayor's office; come on back, and we will talk." They went in and Sam closed the door. "Have a seat." Sam went behind the desk as Thad and Buford sat in chairs in front of the desk.

Thad removed a money pouch from under his shirt and handed it to Sam. "This is the bank's money from the cattle sale. I paid the hands and a new wrangler I hired on the drive."

"And yourself?"

"I wasn't a paid hand, but I kept out a little for Butte, working the ranch."

"You should pay yourself as well."

"Let's talk about buying the ranch," Thad said, "We would like to buy it if the price is right."

"With the acreage, buildings, and livestock I figure it is worth six thousand. I'll let you have it for four."

"If it's worth six why would you sell it to us for less?"

"I don't have that much in it, so it's a good deal for all of us. I'm not a cattleman I'm a banker, and I want you and Bill to stay. The town was in trouble until you came. Do we have a deal?"

"I only have two thousand." Buford's eyes opened wide. "We will still owe you two."

"You can pay me as the money comes in. I'm not going to charge you interest. I'm making enough from the sale. I'll put this money in your account to use for expenses until you sell more cattle or horses."

Thad looked at Buford, and Buford smiled. "You gotta deal."

"Great. I'll write up the contract and you both can sign it tomorrow."

They rose, and Thad shook Sam's hand. "Thanks, Sam."

"Yeah, thank you, Mr. Young," Buford said extending his hand.

As they crossed the street, Buford looked at Thad: "How did you win that much money gambling?"

"I'm good at it."

"You sure must be, but I guess you didn't trust me is why you never told me."

"It wasn't trust; I just didn't see the need."

"Okay, but that's a lot of money, how can I be buying the ranch with you when I ain't got no money?"

"We're partners. You can pay me back when the ranch starts making money."

"What about sheriffin'? How we...how are we going to run a ranch and sheriff, too?"

"The town only needs one lawman. I think we should take turns being sheriff and working the ranch."

"Do you think the mayor will go along with me being the law without you?"

"We're about to find out," Thad said as opened the door to the mayor's office.

The mayor looked up from his desk: "What did you decide?"

"We bought the ranch," Thad said.

"Are you turning in your badges? Where do you think I'm going to find another sheriff?"

"We will still be the law. The town only needs one lawman. We will take turns. Butte one month and me the next. We'll save the town money. If there's a need, we both will be here. As peaceful as it is now, I don't see a problem."

The mayor looked at Buford. "I don't have a problem with it, Bill. Everybody knows you, but I'm not sure how some will feel knowing you're the sheriff without Thad."

"I've never had no trouble."

"You have two choices, Trent," Thad said. "Our way or find a new sheriff." He turned to go.

"I didn't say no. I'm just not sure how some will feel. You know there are some that don't like Negroes ever though they had never seen a black man until you two came here."

"Let's try it," Thad said, "and see how it goes. We will sign the agreement tomorrow then I'll go to the ranch and Butte will be sheriff. Don't tell anyone what we're doing and see how they take it."

"Okay. We'll try it."

***

About noon the following day, Thad and Buford signed the agreement, and Thad rode to the ranch as Buford started through town as usual. No one said anything as they watched Thad leave. That evening Buford made his rounds, going into a few businesses and the saloon. No one said anything as he came and went, some tipping their hat as he entered. A few days later the mayor walked into the barbershop for a haircut. A customer was leaving as he entered.

Harry Grant nodded and shook out the apron as the mayor sat in the barber's chair: "Afternoon, Mayor." He placed the apron around the mayor's shoulders.

"Afternoon, Harry. Staying busy?"

"About normal."

"Hear any complaints from people in town about Bill being sheriff?"

Harry picked up a comb and scissors and began cutting. "Not really, but people are wondering why you kept the Negro as sheriff instead of Walker."

"I thought most liked Bill?"

"That's true, although some are afraid of him," he said as he continued his work, "and others are still not used to having a black man in town, let alone being the sheriff."

"I guess you heard Thad and Bill bought the Philmoor Ranch?"

"I heard."

"Thad said we only need one lawman now that Philmoor is gone, so he and Bill are going to swap off as sheriff, Chance for the first month than Walker."

Harry brushed loose hair from Trent's neck and the apron then picked up the shaving cup. "Why didn't you tell people?" He applied lather to the mayor's neck and began shaving.

"I wanted to see how they felt having a black sheriff and I think you should tell them about Thad. They will accept it better coming from you."

"How so?"

"You and Jerry at the saloon know everything that goes on in town, and people look to you to keep them informed. Everybody trusts both of you and tell you all their concerns. If they're upset with Bill being sheriff, they will tell you before they would me, but it doesn't seem to be a problem."

Harry wiped shaving cream from the mayor's neck and removed the apron. "People know Bill is an honest and fair man. Even those that are afraid of him know he will keep the peace. I guess some find his size and color a little intimidating."

"Well, spread the word," Trent said, getting up. "My concern is, in time they may want to stop being the law and just run the ranch. If that happens, it will be hard to find someone to replace them." He paid Harry and started for the door.

"Not sure Thad is cut out to be a rancher," Harry said as he shook out the apron.

"You could be right, but if ranching doesn't suit him, I don't think he will stay around long. Either way, I'm going to need a new sheriff."

"You worry too much, Bryant."

"Part of being mayor. See you at the restaurant." He closed the door as he left.

Chapter Nine
Learning the ropes

Thad spent his first week at the ranch getting things organized. He left Joey Smyth in charge even though Britt Thomas was older and had more experience. Since Britt was a drifter, he wasn't sure how long he would stay. Along with organizing, he started looking for ways to earn money and decided to ride to Fort Union to see if the army needed horses. The ranch had a herd of thirty horses, and if he could sell some of them to the army, he would have money to keep the ranch going. He went to the stable and found Britt cleaning out stalls.

"I'm going to Fort Union to see if they need horses. I would appreciate it if you would keep an eye on Joey for me while I'm gone. He still has a lot to learn."

"I'd be proud to, Thad. He's a nice youngster and in time will make a good foreman."

"Thanks. I'll tell Joey I'm going."

***

The gate was open when Thad approached the fort and he stopped in front of the guard by the gate. "I'm Thaddeus Walker from the Bar CW Ranch, near Mexville. I'd like to speak to the officer in charge."

"That would be Captain Stephens, sir. Follow me." The private led him to a building inside the fort and Thad got off his horse and followed him up some stairs. The private stopped and rapped on the door.

"Enter," came a voice through the door.

The private opened the door. "A Mr. Thaddeus Walker to see you, sir."

"Send him in."

Thad entered and stood in front of the desk as the captain stood. "I'm half owner of the Bar CW near Mexville, captain." He extended his hand.

They shook hands. "What can I do for you, Mr. Walker."

"I have a small herd of horses and thought perhaps you could use some fresh mounts."

"I could use a dozen, but I want them ready to ride. I don't want my men injured breaking horses."

"I can do that. Horses are forty dollars a head and eighty dollars broken."

"That's reasonable, provided my men won't have trouble riding them. Do you have any cattle? Indians raided our herd a week back, and I lost thirty head."

"We just came back from market, so I don't have many. I can sell you a couple of dozen."

"That will help. How much?"

"If you can wait until I break the horses and make one trip, twenty-five a head."

"How long?"

"Two to three weeks."

"You have a deal, Mr. Walker. I pay on delivery."

"Thanks, captain. See you in two weeks."

Thad rode back to the ranch and found Britt and Joey. "Either of you ever break a horse?"

"A couple," Britt said."

"Joey?"

"Well, I tried once but was on the ground more than in the saddle."

"It's time you learn. What about the other boys?"

"Not sure if they have but I'd say no," Joey answered.

"I want everyone at the corral tomorrow morning. We have twelve horses to break and deliver to the fort in two weeks, along with two dozen steers."

"Two weeks!" Joey said. "It's a two-day ride to the fort driving cattle and horses. That gives us only ten days to break 'em."

"What do you think, Britt?"

"Depends on how quick the others catch on."

"Guess we'll find out in the morning. I'm going to town and talk to Butte. I think he needs to have some of the fun."

"Fun. I don't recall it being no fun," Joey said, "gettin' throwd from a horse."

***

"Come out to the ranch in the morning," Thad said as he walked into the sheriff's office.

Buford stopped cleaning the shotgun in his lap and looked at Thad. "I'm the sheriff."

"Town can spare you for a few hours."

"You're supposed to be working the ranch. Can't you do it without me?"

"I can, but I think this is something you need to learn if you're going to be a rancher. Be at the corral first thing in the morning."

"Okay, I'll tell the mayor. How long will I be gone?"

"That depends on you." Buford looked straight at him, and Thad smiled. "See you in the morning."

I don't have a good feeling about this, Buford thought as he watched Thad leave.

***

When Buford arrived, Thad, Joey, and all the hands were at the corral. Britt and Jim were in the corral trying to saddle a nervous horse. Buford watched from the back of his horse as Britt held the horse's head, trying to comfort it, as Jim slipped a blanket then saddle on the back of the frightened animal.

"Morning, Butte," Thad said as the horse tried to rise on its hind legs when Jim began fastening the belly band. "You want to be first?"

"What you talking about?"

"We have a dozen horses to break for the Army at Fort Union."

"You know I've never broke a horse."

"Neither have any of these men, except for Britt and me. You're not going to learn sitting up there."

"You're trying to get me killed again, aren't you?"

"If you're going to be a rancher you need to know how to break horses."

"I don't have no idea how to break a horse."

"Pretty simple, get on his back and stay in the saddle."

"If you're so damned smart, why don't you show me?"

"Okay, but I thought any man that could ride a bareback horse with his hands tied behind his back, should be able to break a horse."

"It's not as if I did it on purpose and you know he threw me."

Thad went into the corral and closed the gate. Britt continued to hold the horse's head, and talk to it as Thad approached. Jim handed him the reins and backed away as Thad grabbed the saddle horn then swung onto the saddle. Britt let go of its head and ducked through the fence with Jim, as the nervous horse whinnied and rose on its hind legs then began bucking and running around the corral. Thad remained on its back, with one hand in the air as the horse continued to buck and twist. A couple of minutes passed, and the nervous horse began to tire. Thad began talking softly to the horse as the bucking subsided, replaced by kicking its hind legs, trying to lose its rider. Soon the horse began galloping around the corral and Thad let it run for a few rounds.

"Whoa boy." Thad pulled on the reins and the horse stopped, shivering, whinnying and shaking its head, raising its front feet off the ground then stood still but nervous as Thad dismounted. When he released the reins, the horse ran to the other side of the corral, shaking and snorting. Thad slipped through the fence and looked at Buford: "Your turn."

"That horse will kill me if I try to go in there."

Thad entered the corral and slowly approached the horse, talking to it with a reassuring voice. The horse backed away but let Thad take the reins then rub its nose.

"Come on, Butte," Thad said still trying to control the nervous steed.

Buford entered the corral and approached the horse, walking slow and talking to it. He took the reins from Thad, still holding its head. The horse shivered and pranced, trying to prevent Buford from mounting as he grabbed the saddle horn and swung onto the saddle. Thad released the horse and slipped through the fence as the horse whinnied, rose on its hind legs and tried to buck, kicking its rear feet. It began running around the corral, kicking and whinnying, shaking its head but was too tired to put up a fight after Thad's ride. Buford pulled on the reins, talking to the horse. The horse stopped then Buford jiggled the reins: "Gitty up." The horse started forward, still nervous. Buford walked it around the corral a few times then dismounted and left the corral.

"Now can I go back to town?"

"Not until you break a horse. I softened that one up for you." He looked at Joey. "Get another horse. Jim, you and Bob unsaddle this one and put him in the other corral. We'll let him rest until tomorrow."

While Joey roped another horse and brought it to the corral, Buford went to the house. Joey and Britt slipped the bridle on the horse and were saddling it when Buford returned.

"Well?" Thad said looking at Buford.

Buford pulled a carrot from his pocket and entered the corral. Joey left the corral as Buford took the reins, with Britt still holding the horse's head. "Let him go," Buford said, and Britt released him with the horse shaking its head, whinnying, and trying to pull away, but Buford pulled back, talking to it. He broke off a piece of carrot and held it out. At first, the horse pulled away then stopped and smelled the carrot then took it from Buford's open hand. "Come on boy."

Buford tried to lead the horse, but it pulled back. He held the carrot near the horse's nose, and it sniffed it, then followed as Buford walked backward away from it. He broke off another piece of carrot and gave it to the horse then gently rubbed its nose. The horse shied at first and shivered. Buford fed it the rest of the carrot while rubbing its nose. "Come on boy." He began walking with the horse following.

"Well I'll be damn," Thad said.

"I told you I know horses, just never broke one." He continued to walk the horse, stopping at times to rub its nose and stroke its neck. Minutes passed, and finally, Buford put the reins around the horse's neck while talking to it. "Easy boy, whoa boy," he swung onto the saddle, and the horse shivered but stood still. Buford smiled at Thad and as he did, the horse whinnied, kicked its hind feet, and began bucking, sending Buford to the ground.

Thad and Britt slipped through the fence trying to keep the frightened animal away from Buford as Buford scrambled to his feet. Thad grabbed the reins of the nervous horse, trying to control it and Britt grabbed its head, talking to it.

"Get on him," Thad said to Buford as the horse began to calm down. Buford, still stunned, looked at Thad. "Come on, you almost had him."

"You mean he almost had me." He approached the nervous animal with caution. He took the reins from Thad, put them around the nervous horse's neck, and swung onto the saddle as Thad and Britt slipped through the fence. The horse reared on its hind legs then kicked and began bucking and running around the corral. Buford hung on for a while then fell to the ground as the horse bucked and twisted. Bob, Jim, and Britt came into the corral, keeping the panicked animal away from Buford as he rose from the dirt.

"Come on out, Butte," Thad said, "we'll let him rest for a day and try again tomorrow. Put him in the other corral and bring out another horse and saddle." Jim led the reluctant animal from the corral.

"You gonna make me do it again?"

"No. You're had enough for one day, but you can come back tomorrow and finish the job."

"You mean let the horse finish the job of killing me."

"You'll tame him tomorrow. I liked your approach, and I think it would work if we had the time, but time is short. We need to break them and then ride them for a while before taking them to the fort. I want them to be used to having a man on their backs. I don't want them throwing a soldier. The captain may not do business with us again if his soldiers have trouble riding them."

they arrived at the fort, the twelve animals were content being around cattle and other horses with men on their backs'. The captain seemed pleased and agreed to do business with the ranch in the future.

"I'm going back to town," Buford said, "I think getting shot at is safer than breaking horses."

The next morning, Buford came back and broke the horse although it threw him a couple of times. He returned to town, and Thad and the wranglers continued breaking horses. It took a full week to break them all, and the next four days to get them used to being ridden. When they took them to the fort with the cattle, the wranglers rode some of them, swapping horses on the way. By the time they seemedrived at the fort, the twelve animals were content being around cattle and other horses with men on their backs'. The captain seemed pleased and agreed to do business with the ranch in the future.

Chapter Ten
Rescue

As the months slipped away, Thad and Buford began to enjoy working the ranch, and the area began to grow. Two farms were established near town, and another rancher moved his operation there also, establishing his ranch not far from the Bar CW. A traveling preacher came to town, and after holding worship services in some of the homes in town, the town asked him to stay and they built a small chapel and parsonage at the edge of town. Buford, along with most of the people in town began attending services. Thad went a couple of times but never became a member, spending his time at the sheriff's office on Sunday mornings.

Not all was peaceful, however, The small band of renegade Indians that sometimes attacked Fort Union, began raiding the farms and ranches. Thad and Buford went after the renegades a couple of times but never caught up with them.

Early one morning, Buford came into town and entered the sheriff's office as Thad was building a fire in the stove: "The Indians are back. They got fifty head last night."

"They've never stolen that many," Thad said, "we've got to stop them. We're going after them, and this time we are not turning back until we catch them."

"I hear ya, what's your plan?"

"Track them down and get our cattle back and either arrest them or kill them. We'll take a couple of the men with us. I'll get Britt to watch the town. He told me he worked as a deputy for a while. We'll tell the mayor before we go."

"Okay, let's ride."

When Thad and Buford got to the ranch they took Jim and Bob with them as they started following the trail left by the cattle and Indians. Britt headed to town wearing a badge. The four men followed the trail for several hours before it led them into a small canyon with most of the cattle in a makeshift pen, against the back canyon wall.

"I want you to take the cattle back to the ranch," Thad said to Jim and Bob. "Butte and I are going to see if we can track the Indians."

"You know there is at least a dozen of them," Jim said, "don't you want some help?"

"We may not find them, and I want the cattle back in our pasture before dark. If we find them and need help, one of us will come back for you. Be sure you keep your eyes open going back to the ranch. If they come looking for the cattle, they may come after you, if we don't find them first."

Jim and Bob opened the pen and began moving the cattle toward the gate as Thad and Buford continued following the trail.

"You know you ain't gonna send for them if we find them," Buford said, "you'll try to take them yourself."

"No I won't, you're with me."

"Yea that's the part that scares me."

A few hours later, as the sun continued its track west, Thad and Buford rode to the top of a small bluff and saw a small Indian village a couple of miles in front of them, in the valley below. Thad took his field glasses from his saddlebag and scanned the village.

"You think that's them?"

"I don't see any Braves, just a few squaws and kids, but there are five steers on the other side."

"Do you think they are ours?"

"Could be. It's the smallest village I've ever seen."

"How many?"

"At least half a dozen squaws and as many children. Could be more in the teepees, but there are no horses."

Buford looked around them. "They could be anywhere. We need to find cover."

"We're not far from the wagon trail. That may be where they are, looking for settlers going west."

"Okay. I know. We're heading to the wagon trail."

Thad put his glasses away. "If they're following a wagon train we may be able to surprise them."

"Or they spot us and kill us."

Starting down the bluff, they stayed far away from the village, heading for the wagon trail.

"It's getting late," Thad said, "let's pick up the pace. I want to catch them while we still have the light."

Both rode at a fast trot and within an hour saw the wagon trail ahead of them. Thad turned parallel to the trail going west. Dust appeared on the trail ahead of them and Thad urged his horse on with Buford beside him. The dust thickened and Indians on horses appeared in front of it and gunshots began filling the air. A small covered wagon, pulled by one horse, came into view with a band of a dozen Indians behind and beside it, shooting rifles and arrows at the panicked driver. When they got closer Thad drew and shot with one brave falling from his horse, then another as Buford joined the fight. One of the Indians rode toward the horse pulling the wagon, trying to grab the reins but the horse panicked, jerking left, and the wagon overturned, rolling on its top then side as the now freed horse scurried away. Two more Indians fell as Thad and Buford continued shooting.

The other warriors sped away as Thad and Buford reined in at the overturned wagon with Thad's last shot dropping another brave, fleeing the scene. While Thad continued watching for Indians, Buford bent down toward a black man trapped under the wagon, chest crushed, and blood coming from his mouth. He raised a shaky finger pointing to the broken and twisted wagon: "My...my..." The finger fell as the man breathed his last. Buford looked away from the dead man toward the interior of the wagon seeing nothing except broken furniture, clothing, bedding, and other household items, lying in a heap.

When Thad's attention turned to the wagon, he saw a black woman lying a few feet in front of it and ran to her. The woman lay dead with what appeared to be a broken neck.

"Is she okay? Buford asked.

Thad shook his head. "Neck is broken."

Before Buford could answer, a moan came from inside the wagon. Buford looked at Thad and started for the wagon, looking inside, as another moan filled the air. All they could see was a heap of personal household items. The moan came again with a little movement under a pile of bedding. Buford peeled the bedding away revealing the beautiful face of a young woman, buried under a mattress and a small dresser.

"You okay?" Buford asked.

Her eyes began to open then closed then opened wide as she screamed.

"We ain't gonna hurt ya," he said, but she screamed again, trying to move then screamed in pain.

"Don't move," Thad said, "Let us help you."

"Mama! Daddy!"

"They're outside," Thad said, "I'm going to come in; don't move."

"My arm hurts!"

Thad made his way into the wagon: "I'm not going to hurt you, just relax." He bent toward her then looked at Buford. "Her arm is trapped under the dresser. When I lift it, remove the mattress and see if you can get her out." Buford began working his way inside. Thad moved the dresser, and the girl again screamed in pain. Buford removed the mattress and threw it outside then tried to help her up;

she screamed again, crying. "Watch her arm," Thad said, "I think it's broken."

"I ain't gonna hurt ya, ma'am, I swear; I'm gonna pick ya up easy." He lifted her, and she screamed and cried, clinging to him with her right arm, her left arm hanging to her side. Buford made his way through the rubble and out of the wagon. As he did, the young woman saw her father crushed under the wagon, not moving.

"DADDY! DADDY! NO NO NO! DADDY!

"He gone, ma'am, I'm sorry," Buford said. "there was nothing I could do ... I'm sorry," The girl clung to him crying and shaking. Thad took the mattress around behind the destroyed wagon and motioned for Buford to bring the girl.

"Mama! Where's mama!" she said as Buford carried her away from the front of the wagon where her mother lay dead, not far from her father.

"I'm sorry, ma'am, she gone too."

"No," she screamed. "She can't be, I want to see her."

"Okay, but let me look at your arm first," Thad said. "Put her down on the mattress, Butte."

"No! I want to go to her, take me to her!" She yelled, as Buford lowered her to the mattress then screamed even louder when her left hand touched the bedding.

"Lie down; your arm is broke, ma'am," Thad said. "It will take the pressure off it if you lie down. We're a long way from a doctor. I need to restrain it or it may get worse. Please, ma'am." She lay crying as Thad took out his knife. "I need to split your sleeve." He took the knife and slowly split the sleeve and pulled it away from the arm. He could see the arm was bent between the wrist and elbow but the skin wasn't broken. "What's your name?"

"Norma Carter."

"I'm Thaddeus Walker, and this is William Buford Chance. I need to find a way to support your arm, but first I'm going to check your upper arm, Norma. I'll try not to hurt you." She nodded, still shaking and breathing heavily. Thad began at the elbow and worked his way up her arm, pressing gently as he worked his way to her shoulder. "Good, it's not broken above the elbow. Try to rest; I'll be right back."

Thad went to the front of the wagon and disappeared inside. He returned with a piece of board, a towel, and a pillowcase. "Hold this for me, Butte, so I can split it." Buford held the towel, and Thad split it down the middle. "I'm going to wrap this around your arm, Norma, and it may hurt some. Butte, raise her arm by the elbow and hand but go easy."

"I... I'll try not to hurt you, Miss," Buford said as he gently raised her arm. Norma moaned and continued to sob.

Thad wrapped the towel around her forearm, and she moaned again. He then ripped strips from the pillowcase and tied the towel in place. After splitting the board, he placed a piece below and one on top of her arm, tying them in place.

"You doing okay?" Thad asked.

"I think so."

"Do you think you can sit up?"

"I'll try."

Thad made a sling out of the rest of the pillowcase, placed the broken arm in it, and tied it around her neck: "Lift her up gently Butte, while I support her arm." Buford helped her sit up. "Are your legs okay? Do you think you can stand?" She nodded, and they both helped her stand.

"I want to see my mama." She started around the wagon. When she saw her mother in the dirt, she ran over and lay across the lifeless body, crying.

Buford stood close to her with tears in his eyes, wanting to help, but there was nothing he could do.

"I'm going to see if I can find the horse," Thad said. "Stay with her and watch for Indians."

An hour later Thad returned with the horse.

Norma still lay beside her mother. Buford, next to her.

Thad dismounted and tied both horses to the wagon. "Come with me, Miss Norma." He helped her up with her right arm and she followed him to the rear of the wagon. Thad looked into her eyes. "It will be dark soon, and I need to bury your parents, or the coyotes will get them." She began to cry, and he held her. "I'm sorry, but it must be done. I can come back for them later if you want. We'll have to spend the night. We're too far from the ranch and town. I'll have Butte build a fire while I'm gone. Do you think you can find us something to eat?"

"I... I think so."

Thad lowered the tailgate and rummaged through the wagon and found a shovel, then went around the wagon to the bodies of Norma's parents. Buford started foraging for firewood. Norma began looking for food in the wagon. A few minutes later, Buford returned with an armload of twigs and broken limbs. He dropped them on the ground and began building a fire.

"Did you find some food?" he asked as Norma made her way out of the wagon.

"Will you help me? I'm having trouble working with just one hand."

"Yes, Miss. Show me where it is and I'll get it."

"The food is in a box under the dresser."

"Come on out, Miss Norma."

Buford moved the dresser and collected can goods and other items from the box then went back to working on the fire.

Norma sat close to the fire, watching him work: "How does Mr. Walker treat you?"

"Mr. Walker? Thad? He treats me just fine." He emptied cans of beans into a pot over the fire.

"He seems like a good man for a white man."

Buford looked her in the eyes then returned to preparing dinner.

When Thad returned, the food was done, and Buford went into the wagon looking for dishes. Tears still filled Norma's eyes, so Thad sat beside the fire in silence. Knowing he had buried her parents was difficult for her to accept.

Buford came out of the wagon with plates, cups, and utensils. Thad poured a cup of coffee while Buford fixed a plate for Norma. He fixed one for Thad then for himself and sat next to the fire.

"Did you make these biscuits?" Thad asked.

"Course I did."

"They're almost as good as mine." Buford sighed and didn't answer, not wanting to start an argument in front of Norma.

When they finished eating, Norma looked at Thad with tears running down her face: "Take me to them." Thad rose along with Buford, and he and Norma followed Thad away from the trail to a secluded spot near a small grove of trees. The earth had been disturbed, and three stones were lying on top. Norma began to cry.

"You should say something," Buford said to Thad.

"You're the one that goes to church."

"I didn't know these people, Father, but I'm sure they were good people. I ask that you fill Miss Norma with Your peace and accept them into Your Kingdom. Amen."

"Amen," Thad replied, and they returned to the campfire.

Thad looked at Norma: "Do you want more coffee?"

"No thank you."

"Why weren't you with the wagon train?" Thad asked as he poured a cup of coffee and handed it to Buford.

"The Wagon Master wouldn't let us because of our color. He said to stay far enough behind so he couldn't see us."

"Your daddy was taking an awful chance coming out here," Buford said.

"People back east don't like us, and he thought it might be different out here, so he decided to go to California. Indians attacked Master Carter's plantation, and Daddy saved his life, so he wrote papers for us. When Daddy told him he wanted to go west, Master Carter gave us the wagon, provisions, and some money."

"Sound's like a good man," Thad said.

"He treats his people better than most, but we are the only ones he ever freed."

"How long have you been traveling?" Buford asked.

"Almost three weeks. We heard about a wagon train forming in Georgia so Daddy took us there but they wouldn't let us join, like I said. Daddy still thought we should go west." Tears began streaming down her cheeks and she lowered her head.

"We'll stop at the ranch on our way to town," Thad said, "and we'll have two of the men come back with a wagon and salvage what they can of your belongings."

"I'm all alone," Norma said as more tears wet her face. "What am I going to do?" Her emotions erupted and her body shook, her head bending low.

Buford moved close, putting his arms around her with tears running down his face: "You're gonna be just fine, Miss Norma." She continued to shake as her crying filled the air.

Thad made her a bed on the mattress, close to the fire, placing a blanket and pillow on it as Buford tried to comfort her. As time passed and the light began to fade, Norma's crying eased then stopped.

"Why don't you try to get some sleep?" Thad said. She rose, went to the mattress and laid down, worn out from her crying, and the tragedy that had befallen her.

"You want first watch?" Thad asked.

"Okay; don't think I can sleep."

Buford woke at first light, seeing Thad fixing breakfast and Norma still asleep on the mattress. He rose and poured a cup of coffee.

"We'll let her sleep until breakfast is ready," Thad said in a low voice. "But we need to get an early start. We have a long ride ahead of us." Buford nodded as he took a sip of coffee.

Minutes passed and Norma tried to roll over on the bed, bumping her broken arm, and moaned.

In an instant Buford was by her side: "Is you okay, Miss Norma?" Her eyes opened and she screamed. "Ain't nobody gonna hurt ya, Miss Norma. Don't be afraid." She looked at him for a moment then began crying as yesterday's tragic events appear in her mind. "Please don't cry, ma'am; we gonna take real good care of you. You gonna be just fine."

"I'm sorry," she said, looking at him through tear-filled eyes when the crying stopped.

"It's okay, Miss Norma. Ain't nothin' to be sorry for. You want some coffee?"

"Please." Buford poured the coffee and handed it to her. "Thank you."

"My pleasure, Miss."

"Breakfast is ready," Thad said. "You think you can eat something?"

"I'll try." She sat up.

It became quiet then Thad spoke as they ate: "We have a long ride ahead of us, so we need to get started. Have you ever ridden a horse?"

"Yes.

"Good. You can ride my horse and I'll ride the horse from your wagon. Butte, take care of the fire and I'll get the horses." He rose and went around the wagon.

He's very nice to you," Norma said.

"Thad's a good man."

"I can't believe he lets you have a gun."

"It's his gun. Used to be his brothers, but he got bit by a snake."

"Isn't he afraid you will shoot him?"

"Why would I do...oh no, I'm not his slave. We's friends."

"I never heard of a white man being friends to a black man."

"It's a long story. He saved me from being hung. Been helping me ever since."

Thad returned, leading two horses: "Time to go."

"I want to see them again," Norma said with tears in her eyes.

"Okay, but we can't stay long. It will be late when we get to the ranch."

Buford doused the fire and got his horse before they went to the graves. Norma knelt and cried for a while then Buford helped her onto Thad's horse. They rode for several hours before stopping for a cold lunch of beef jerky and water. The sun was in the western sky when they saw the Bar CW herd ahead of them. Jim, guarding the herd, rode toward them when he saw them approach, and appeared a little startled to see a young woman with them.

"Jim, this is Norma Carter," Thad said when Jim rode up to them. Her parent's wagon was attacked by Indians. Tomorrow I want you and Bob to take a wagon out to the wagon trail and follow it west until you come to the wrecked wagon. Salvage what you can and bring it to the ranch."

"Howdy, ma'am." Jim tipped his hat. Okay, boss. "We'll do it first thing in the morning."

"Thanks, Jim. We're going to take Miss Carter to the doctor after I get the buckboard. I'm tired of riding bareback. We should be back by nightfall."

Thad circled the herd as the three of them started for the ranch.

***

People stopped and watched as the buckboard came through town driven by Buford with a beautiful young black woman sitting beside him and Thad following behind on his horse. Britt Thomas came out of the sheriff's office.

"Doc in his office?" Thad asked.

"He's there," Britt said.

Fran Stone stepped out onto the boardwalk in front of the restaurant as the buckboard passed and stopped in front of a building with a sign on the porch. Buford helped Norma off the buckboard as the doctor came out onto the porch, holding the door for Norma.

"Take care of things, Mary; I'll be back." Fran starting toward the doctor's office.

"This is Miss Norma Carter, Doc," Buford said as they entered the office with Thad following them. "Miss Norma, Doctor Atkins."

"Nice to meet you, Miss Carter. Please have a seat. Are you in any pain?"

"A little. Nice to meet you, sir."

"Who applied the splint?" the doctor asked as he unwrapped the injured arm.

"I did," Thad said.

"Good job." Doctor Atkins looked into Norma's eyes. "I'm going to set it before I bandage it and it's going to hurt." Tears started down Norma's face and Buford held her shoulders, and, when the doctor straightened the arm, Norma screamed.

The door opened as she screamed and Fran walked in: "Are you okay, honey?" Norma sighed, looking at Fran and shook her head as the doctor applied the splint and wrapped the arm. Fran looked at Thad. "Where did you find her?"

"Indians ambushed her father's wagon on the wagon trail. The wagon flipped ... her parents didn't make it."

"No one else?"

"Just the three of them."

Norma began to cry.

"You're going to be fine, honey. I'll take you home with me."

"Miss Norma," Buford said, "this is Miss Frances Stone. Miss Stone, Miss Norma Carter."

"Nice to meet you," Fran said. "Do you have any other family?"

"No, Ma'am. We are slaves freed by Master Carter when daddy saved his life."

"How old are you, honey?"

"Nineteen."

"I always thought it'd be nice to have a daughter but never dreamed she would be as pretty as you. I'm big and loud but most people like me. I promise to take good care of you. Would you like to come and live with me?"

"Why would you want to help me?" Norma said with tears running down her face. "I'm different than you."

"Because she has a heart as big as the world," Thad said, "and helping people comes natural to Fran. She helped me on a cattle drive. Worked harder than anyone. The only difference she sees in you is you're a young woman in need of help and nothing else."

Fran looked at Norma: "I meant what I said, honey. When your arm is well you can help in the restaurant if you want. Once you are feeling better you can go if you want, but you have a home with me as long as you want to stay. Will you give me a chance?"

Norma, with tears streaming down her face, still looking into Fran's eye, bolted from the chair, hugging Fran and crying. Fran held her close, trying to comfort her.

"What do I owe you, doc?' Thad asked.

"Dollar will be fine."

Thad paid him and Fran looked at Thad as she continued to hold Norma: "I need to stay at the restaurant. Will you take Norma to my house and stay with her until I get there?"

"I'd be much obliged to do that, Ma'am," Buford said.

"Tomorrow two of the boys are going to the wagon and salvage what they can," Thad said looking at Fran. "We'll keep everything at the ranch until Norma is ready for them."

"Thanks, Thad. Honey, will you let Bill take you to my place and stay with you until I get there? Tomorrow you can go to the restaurant with me if you feel up to it, but I think you need to rest for now."

"Yes, ma'am." She released Fran and moved away.

"Butte, when you leave Fran's I want you to relieve Britt as sheriff. Tomorrow I'm going to the fort. I'm going to show the army where the Indian village is so maybe we will stop losing cattle."

"I'll do it. Sheriffin' gonna seem tame after fighting Indians."

***

Neither spoke on the way to Fran's as Buford drove the buggy through the open country. He helped Norma from the buggy and into the house: "I'm gonna unhitch the horse and let him graze," Buford said. "Make yourself ta home. I'll be right back." When he returned Norma was sitting on the couch in the living room. "Been a while since we ate. I can fix some victuals if you like?"

"I don't feel like eating."

"Understandable but ya...you need to keep up your strength."

"Thank you. I'll try." She burst into tears. "I'm all alone... I don't know what to do."

"No you ain...you're not. Miss Fran is a fine woman and she will take good care of you. You have Thad and me as friends, and when people in town get to know you you'll have more."

"But I'm a negro. You know most white folk don't like us. I feel so all alone."

"I know that feeling. I felt it each time I ran away, but then Thad saved me from hangin' and took me with him, no never mind my color. Gave me his brother's gun, taught me to shoot; herd cattle. I'm free because of him and some whites have taken a likin' to me. It ain't...it won't be easy for you Miss Norma, and it's gon...going to take a long time, but you're going to be just fine. I'm going to start a fire in the stove in the kitchen and see what I can find to fix."

"I don't want to be alone, Mr. Chance."

"Please call me Bill. Come in the kitchen and sit at the table while I work. I'll get some water and make some coffee."

"If you get the water I'll fix the coffee. I can't just sit here. I need to do something."

"Sounds good ta...to me. You can help all you want. I'll be right back with the water."

Buford returned with the water, poured some in the coffee pot, and started the fire: "I'm going to the root cellar and see what I can find."

When he left, Norma put coffee grounds in the coffee pot and placed it on the stove. The coffee pot was beginning to perk when Buford returned with a slab of bacon, two potatoes, and some eggs he gathered from the hen house.

Ain't gonna be...won't be much of a sup...dinner but it will have to do."

"It will be fine," Norma said.

"Does...do you want me to bake the potatoes or fry them?"

"I think fried will be better with eggs."

Buford finished cooking dinner and they ate in silence. Norma, still filled with grief, sat looking at her plate. Buford, unable to find words to comfort her, looked at his plate as well. Not being able to find words to console her wasn't the only problem Buford experienced. He found Norma's beauty intimidating. It seemed impossible for any girl, black or white, to be as beautiful as she, and he knew fear was not the only emotion he was experiencing. When he looked into her beautiful brown eyes his knees became weak. The girl at the bathhouse was beautiful and the fear he felt then wasn't because of her beauty but what he knew were her intentions. All he wanted was to get away from her but not so now. Even with his fear he felt drawn to Norma and wanted to be near her. This was a new feeling for him. As a slave, Buford never thought about girls; his desire for freedom consumed him. Even now, as a free man, his concerns were centered around making the ranch a success and dealing with Thad's insatiable appetite for danger. The thought of female companionship never entered his mind, especially here in the west, where blacks were few and most whites wanted little to do with negroes.

As Buford finished cleaning the dishes and putting them away, Fran came in, eliminating the tense silence in the house.

"Brought some food from the restaurant," She said as she entered the kitchen.

"Just ate," Buford said, "I'll go, got work to do."

"Thanks, Bill. Breakfast is on me in the morning."

"Much obliged. Miss Norma...see you tomorrow." She didn't answer as Buford left.

"Bill is one fine man," Fran said as the sound of horse hooves on the hard ground faded away.

"I thought he was a slave when they rescued me. I never met a free black man before, except for daddy." Tears appeared in her eyes.

"I don't know the story behind Bill and Thad, but this town came alive when they showed up. The West is different than the East but a lot of people are not fond of coloreds. I don't know why. It may be because you are different but hell, we all are different. That's the way God made us."

Some in town don't like Bill because he is black. Even so, all respect him. He has proven he is honest and trustworthy. Some are afraid of him because of his size but as I said, all respect him."

"Where did they come from?"

"As I said, I don't know their story but before they showed up, a rancher, Mr. Philmoor, was harassing the town. He ran off every sheriff we had until Thad and Bill came. Thad and Bill put him in his place for a while until his men caught them off guard and beat them almost to death. They took them out of town and dumped them, warning them, if they lived, not to come back to Mexville. Joey and I brought them here and, with Doc's help, nursed them back to health. Bill wanted to move on to California but not Thad. Unarmed they went to Philmoor's and somehow disarmed some of his men. Thad shot Philmoor when he tried to arrest him."

"I guess Mr. Chance is a runaway slave. He told me Mr. Walker saved him from hanging. Is that true?"

"Don't know, honey. Why don't you ask him?" Norma didn't answer and looked at the floor. "Come on, I'll show you your room and make the bed."

Buford returned to town and relieved Britt as sheriff. Britt would send one of the men to town tomorrow riding Buford's horse and take the buggy to the ranch.

***

As the sun rose the following morning, Thad headed toward Fort Union and Buford began his morning rounds, checking the town. Later, as the townspeople began to stir and the restaurant opened, Buford left the sheriff's office, heading across the street for breakfast. Norma, trying to find things to do to help prepare the tables for customers, saw him come in and went to the kitchen: "May I take Mr. Chance's order?"

Fran stopped what she was doing: "Okay, honey, but you let Mary carry the tray. I don't want you hurting your arm. Take Bill a cup of coffee." Fran went back to preparing food.

"Yes, ma'am." Norma got the coffee and approached Buford's table. "Would you like some coffee, Mr. Chance?"

Buford jumped to his feet and snapped his hat from his head. "Yes ma'am but please calls...call me Bill. Mister don't sound proper between friends. You shouldn't be working with a bust...broken arm."

"I need to do something; I can't just sit around. I want to help Miss Stone. She is doing so much for me and I'm trying not to think..." she looked away as tears formed in her eyes.

"I'm sorry, Miss Norma, I didn't mean... I just don't want you to hurt yourself."

She brushed away the tears and looked at him. Miss Stone... I guess I should call her Fran, won't let me do very much. Please sit, and drink your coffee."

"Yes, Ma'am." Buford sat.

"What would you like for breakfast M... Bill?"

"Steak, some eggs, and potatoes will do just fine, Miss."

"Please call me Norma. You said we are friends."

"Yes, ma'am. I mean, Norma, but I was just trying to show respect."

"Thank you. I'll give Fran your order, but Mary will serve you. Fran won't let me carry the tray. I'll come back later with more coffee, if you want?"

"I'd like that just fine."

Mary brought Buford's food as the restaurant began to fill, and Norma became busy refilling cups and helping Mary clear tables. When Norma refilled Buford's cup she didn't speak and hurried away, filling cups for other customers. Buford left the restaurant and walked the town again, trying to stop thinking about Norma.

***

Thad arrived at Fort Union around noon and a corporal escorted him to Captain Stephen's office: "I found your renegades, Captain."

"How many men will we need?"

"Maybe twenty."

The captain looked at the corporal: "I want two dozen men armed and ready to ride in ten minutes."

"Yes, Sir." The corporal did an about-face and left.

The captain looked at Thad: "How far from here?

"Maybe twenty, twenty-five miles."

"How did you find them?"

"They stole some of our cattle and we went after them. Found the cattle and tracked the braves to a small village but they weren't there so we headed for the wagon trail. Caught up with them attacking a covered wagon. We got four or five of them."

"And the wagon?"

"The wagon overturned and the driver and his wife were killed. We found their daughter inside with a broken arm and took her to town."

"You ready to ride?"

"Let's go get 'em, Captain."

***

While Thad and the soldiers were riding to the Indian village, Jim and Bob had salvaged what they could from the overturned wagon and were on their way back to the ranch.

***

At lunch, Buford went to the restaurant but, he didn't see Norma. The breakfast traffic was heavy, for a Monday, and likely she did more than she should have. Still recovering from the attack by the Indians and grieving for her parents had taken its toll. Fran sent Norma to rest on a cot in the back. Disappointed, Buford returned to the sheriff's office.

***

The Indians put up little resistance when the Cavalry encircled the village. The loss of some braves to Thad and Buford had decreased their will to fight. A few shot arrows and the rest dropped their weapons. The soldiers restrained the warriors and began dismantling the village for the long trek to the reservation.

Captain Stephens thanked Thad before he started back to the ranch.

***

As the days passed and Norma's strength returned, she began to accept the loss of her parents, although the pain of losing them would always be with her. Fran had fallen in love with her and treated her as if she were her biological daughter. Norma could feel the love between them but still was unable to see what lie ahead for her. Some day she would have to leave and try to build a life for herself, alone, but the thought of being alone scared her.

Chapter Eleven
Courting

At the end of two weeks, the doctor examined Norma's arm. It would be another four weeks before the cast would be removed, but he was pleased with her progress, the bones were knitting.

Still working as sheriff, Buford continued to take his meals at the restaurant. When he entered, Norma would take his order. Toward the end of the third week, Buford seemed a little nervous when Norma brought his coffee and prepared to take his breakfast order.

"I's... I would like to ask... I mean... I know you haven't been to church and I thought maybe you'd feel better about goin'...going if you didn't have to go alone." Norma looked at him a little confused. "What I'm trying to say is... I'd be mighty proud if you would go to church with me this Sunday."

Her eyes opened wide. "I... I don't know anyone in town except you and Fran."

"That's what I mean. People see you here at Fran's, but if you go to church they will get to know you better."

"We are the only coloreds here. I'm not sure I would be welcome."

"I go and no one seems to care that I'm different."

"But you're the sheriff."

"That's what I mean. It will be easier if you don't go alone." He paused. "That's not what I mean at all. I'd just be proud if you'd go with me."

A smile brightened Norma's face. "Thank you. I'll ask Fran. She likes to sleep in Sunday mornings since the restaurant doesn't open until noon."

"I'd be proud to come and get you."

"Thank you. Do you want your usual?"

"If you please."

When Norma entered the kitchen, Fran was in front of the stove preparing food.

"William. I mean Bill wants his usual and he asked me to go to church with him."

"It's about time. Do you want to go?"

"Yes, and he said he would come for me."

"He won't have to. I'll go with you if you don't mind?"

"You like to sleep in, Sunday morning."

"I still can, just not as late. I've met the Reverend but never heard him preach. About time I did...that is if you don't mind?"

She hugged Fran. "Thank you. I'll feel better if you are there."

"I know he's dying to know. Go tell him."

More customers were in the restaurant when Norma returned to Buford's table: "Fran said she would go with us if you don't mind."

"No. I'd like that. It's more than I could hope."

"And you won't have to come for me."

"That's nice, but I don't mind if I did come to get you. It would give me more time with you."

The look on Norma's face changed from happy to almost shock: "I better go... I have work to do."

Whoa, Buford thought, I don't think I should have said that. I hope she doesn't change her mind and not go.

Early Saturday morning the door of the sheriff's office opened and Thad walked in.

"What you doing here?" Buford asked.

"My turn to sheriff."

"I ain't been doing it that long."

"This is what we agreed to, remember?"

"I do, but it's too soon."

"I thought I'd give you a break."

"Don't need no break. I'm doin' just fine."

"You know you need more time at the ranch. You have a lot to learn."

"I know I know, but I don't want to do it right now."

Thad looked Buford in the eyes: "You feeling okay?"

"I'm fine. It's just... I... I'm takin' Miss Norma to church Sunday."

"I could do that for you."

"That ain't gonna happen, Thad."

"You're kinda sweet on her, aren't you?" Buford didn't answer. "I've had my eye on her as well."

"Huh!"

"Norma is a beautiful girl."

"She ain't your kind."

"What difference does it make?"

"What would people think if a white man took up with a colored woman?"

"It's none of their business."

Buford continued to look Thad in the eyes for a moment: "You just messin' with me, ain't you?"

"No. I'm serious, but I don't think I have a chance. I think she kinda likes you also."

"For sure?"

"I'm afraid so."

"Then you ain't gonna try to get in front of me?"

"Like to...but it won't do me any good."

"That's a load off my mind. I don't want her causin' a riff between us."

"There's one thing you need to watch."

"What?"

"Your talk. You need to talk like a gentleman, not a field hand or slave."

"I know, but when I get upset I forget."

"And when you're with Norma you get nervous and start talking like you did when we first met."

"It's true, Thad. What am I going to do?"

"When you are with her think about what you want to say before you say it."

"Okay. You're not gon...going to make me go back to the ranch, are you?"

"I'll give you a week."

"Make it two."

"Two it is. I hope you don't forget about the town, now that your head is filled with Norma."

"I do my job. It's just when I'm with her I can't concentrate."

"You've never been in love before, have you?"

"In love?"

"Worse case I've ever seen."

"What am I going to do, Thad?"

"Go easy. Remember she is still grieving for her parents. It will take a lot of time. She has Fran, and Fran is good for her, but you're the only one of her race, here. I don't know if she could handle it if it were not for you."

"Then you think she likes me because I'm black."

"No. It's also because you are big, handsome, and a gentleman...although you have some rough edges."

"It's those rough edges that bother me."

"Work on it."

"I will. Thanks, Thad, for understanding."

"I understand but I'm still jealous."

"Don't you start messin' with me again!"

"See you in two weeks." Thad left the office with a smirk on his face."

***

Buford bathed Saturday night. Brushed the clothes he wore to church and polished his boots. Church began at ten Sunday morning and Buford walked the town twice that morning, once before dawn and again after starting a fire in the stove and making coffee. Nothing helped however, and he paced the office floor waiting for Fran to arrive with Norma. A few people appeared on the boardwalks on either side of the street when the store and saloon opened. A horse trotted down the street, stopping in front of the saloon. The rider dismounted and went inside.

Sitting at the desk playing solitaire, Buford jumped to his feet when a buggy stopped in front of the jail. With hat in hand he hurried outside.

"Morning, Miss Carter, Miss Stone."

"Good morning," they both said.

"Hop in," Fran said.

"I's... I'll just walk beside you."

Fran jiggled the reins and the horse started down the street toward the church.

"Isn't this a fine day," Buford said, walking beside Norma sitting on the right side of the buggy. "The sun is bright, the air clear, and almost no clouds in the sky. Yes, sir, it is going to be one fine day."

When they entered the church everyone looked at them. The church was more than half full. The Mayor and barber were there, several women and a few husbands, and the Reverend Hudson standing behind the podium. Buford waited for Fran and Norma to sit before he sat beside Norma.

"Good morning," the reverend said. "Let us begin with one of my favorite hymns The Rock of Ages." After the hymn, the reverend read scripture from the book of Matthew and preached about brotherly love. When the last hymn was sung, people began filing out and shaking the reverend's hand. "This is indeed a pleasure Miss Stone to see you in church."

"Thank you, Reverend. I normally sleep in Sunday morning since I don't open the restaurant until noon, but I thought it was time to check on your preaching. Nice sermon."

"Thank you. I hope to see you more often."

"I plan on it."

"And this beautiful young lady must be Miss Carter that I have heard so much about."

Norma blushed: "Yes sir."

The reverend shook her hand: "You have created quite a stir in Mexville. Everyone has nothing but good things to say about you. You are a welcome addition to our little town. I hope to see you in church more often."

"Thank you, sir. I promise to come every Sunday."

"That will not only make me happy but God as well."

"Thank you, sir."

The reverend turned to Buford and shook his hand: "Thanks for bringing them, Bill. You are a true servant of the Lord."

"Thank you, sir."

"It's time for me to go to work," Fran said as she got into the buggy and Buford helped Norma into the right-hand seat. "See you later at the restaurant, Bill."

"Yes 'em, I'll be there."

When the restaurant opened for lunch, Buford was one of the first customers through the door and Norma hurried to his table as he sat. Eventually, the restaurant became full. Even so, Norma made many trips to Buford's table, carrying a fresh cup of coffee.

The days seemed long to Buford as he waited for Sunday and the chance to sit next to Norma in church again, feeling her warmth beside him and listening to her beautiful voice as she sang. When Sunday arrived the church service ended too soon for Buford, and he found himself looking forward to next Sunday when he would be with her again. Seeing Norma at the restaurant helped him make it through the week but didn't provide the comfort he felt sitting next to her during the much too short, hour service.

Once again the days of the week were too long and Sunday came and went too soon, which presented a new concern to Buford. At the end of the week Thad would become sheriff and he would be at the ranch away from Norma for the first time since they met. This time the days of the week were too short and Friday evening, as Buford entered the restaurant for dinner, he knew being able to see Norma every day would soon end. As she approached his table with a cup of coffee, he looked at her with sad eyes.

"Is there something wrong?" She sat the cup on the table. "You look sad."

"I am. Tomorrow Thad will take over as sheriff. It's my turn at the ranch."

"Then you won't be going to church Sunday?"

"Oh-oh yes, I'll be going to church but after that, I'll be at the ranch and won't see you again until next Sunday. I look forward to coming to the restaurant and seeing you."

Norma's face flushed and she smiled: "I'll miss seeing you too."

"Thank you. You don't know how much I wanted you to say that."

Her face flushed again: "I better go. You want your usual."

"Yes, ma'am, I do." She turned and hurried into the kitchen.

Saturday morning, after Buford returned from breakfast, Thad entered the office: "You can go whenever you want."

"I ain't... I'm in no hurry."

"You'll see Norma tomorrow."

"But not after church. Maybe I'll come to town for my meals."

"It's a long ride. Jeff is a good cook; he'll feed you well."

"She said she would miss me too."

"Don't worry, I'll keep her company."

"That's the part that worries me."

Thad smiled: "I know you're in love with her. I'm not going to try and get in your way."

"Do you think that's what it is, love?"

"If not, you have a bad case of indigestion. Go to the ranch. The time away from her will make Sunday more enjoyable."

"I'll go, but I know she is all I'll be thinking about."

"There are some horses that need to be broke. That will help get your mind off her. If not, they will stomp you in the ground."

"You know I don't like breaking horses."

"You don't have to like it, just do it."

Buford sighed, picked up his hat and left.

At noon, Thad walked into the restaurant and Norma came to his table: "What would you like to drink?"

"Coffee. Nice to see you again."

"Thank you and nice to see you as well. I'll be back with your coffee."

"Okay, and I'll have the special." She went to the kitchen and returned with the coffee. "Thank you."

"You're welcome, Mr. Walker."

"Please call me Thad. How are things going with Fran?"

"Very well. She really does treat me as if I am her daughter. I don't know what I'd do without her."

"And Buford also, I take it."

She smiled: "He is a nice man."

"That he is, and I can see why he will miss coming to the restaurant. I'm sure I'll feel the same when it is time for me to return to the ranch."

Norma's face flushed: "Thank you. Will you be going to church with us Sunday?"

"No, but you can say a prayer for me."

"I will. Mary will serve you." She turned and hurried away.

***

Sunday morning, Buford was waiting at the church when Fran and Norma arrived.

"Good morning," he said as he helped Norma from the buggy.

"Good morning," they both answered.

"I miss you coming to the restaurant," Fran said.

"I miss you too."

"I know who you miss."

Buford smiled and removed his hat as they went up the steps and into the church.

At noon, Buford and Thad ate lunch together before Buford rode back to the ranch.

***

Wednesday morning, Norma walked into Doctor Atkins office.

"Good morning, Miss Carter."

"Good morning, sir."

"Let's have a look at that arm." He removed the splint and wrapping. "Yes it looks fine," he said examining her forearm. "I want you to take it easy for a week or two. It will take time to regain your strength."

"Thank you, sir. What do I owe you?"

"Thad paid me yesterday."

"Oh. I'll pay him back when he comes into the restaurant."

"You can try, but if I know Thad, he won't take your money."

She smiled: "I'm going to help Miss Stone in the kitchen now that my arm is well."

"That should be fine. Just don't lift anything heavy for a while."

"Thank you, sir." She left the office, heading back to the restaurant.

***

While breaking horses that week, Buford was thrown many times before he was able to stop thinking about Norma and concentrate on the job at hand. Aches and pains accompanied him Sunday morning as he rode into town. The church service seemed too short to Buford, knowing it would be another week before he would be with Norma again.

When Buford and Thad entered the restaurant at noon, Fran walked up to their table: "Come with me, Bill." He rose and followed her into the kitchen and she handed him a picnic basket. "Norma is waiting in the buggy out back."

"Huh?"

"I thought it was time you two had some time alone. There are some large oak trees down by the spring; now get."

Buford went out the backdoor and handed Norma the basket, unwrapped the reins from the hitching post, and got in on the driver's side then jiggled the reins: "Mighty nice of Miss Fran to do this. The basket is heavy. Must be a lot of food in there."

"I helped," Norma said.

Neither spoke until they came to the spring and Buford stopped near a large oak tree: "This should do just fine." They spread a blanket under the tree, set the basket down, then Buford led the horse to another tree and unhitched it, letting it graze.

"Thank you for doing this," Buford said. Norma smiled and opened the basket, removing sandwiches and a jug of tea. She poured them each a cup and handed one to Buford. "I'm sorry. I like being here with you but don't know what to say."

"You could tell me about yourself."

"Ain...not much to tell."

"You said Thad saved you from hanging. Is that true?"

"It's true all right." She continued to look at him. He looked down then into her eyes. "I'm a runaway slave. I ran away two times before so when they caught me they decided to hang me, figuring I'd just run again."

"Did you run because they were mean to you?" She handed him a sandwich.

"Well, I was kinda rebellious growing up. I was born on the Gaylord Plantation in South Carolina. I was stubborn and so they would beat me. Finally Mr. Gaylord sold me to Mr. Owens in Louisiana and I ran away but they caught me. After a while I ran again and they caught me. The next time I ran is when they tried to hang me and Thad shot the rope when they made the horse run. Thad came after me and helped me get away and took me west with him."

"Aren't you afraid they will come after you again?"

"Not no more. Mr. Lynch came looking for me and found me. I had to kill him. I'm sorry for that, but he give me no choice."

"Why didn't Mr. Owns look for you?"

"Mr. Lynch made his living hunting down and bringing back runaway slaves. Well, that's about all there is to know about me. Would you mind telling me about you?"

"You know we were slaves freed by Mr. Carter. Mr. Carter bought mama and daddy at the slave market in Charleston South Carolina. He made daddy his manservant and mama did house cleaning and helped cook. When Mr. Carter went hunting he took daddy with him. The last time they went hunting, Indians attacked them and shot Mr. Carter with an arrow. Daddy killed two of the Indians and the others ran. Daddy removed the arrow and bandaged the wound and brought Mr. Carter back to the plantation. When Mr. Carter was well he freed us. You know the rest."

"That I do. Thank you for telling me. This is a good lunch."

"Thank you. Would you like more tea?"

"Please." He held out his cup and she filled it. "Would you like to walk along the stream?"

"That would be nice." He stood and helped her up. The sun was high overhead in a cloudless sky as they strolled along the meandering stream. "Isn't this a beautiful day?"

"Sure is, but being here with you makes it more beautiful."

She smiled: "Thank you. I think so too."

"I want to do it again. Maybe next Sunday we could go horseback riding?"

"I'd like that."

"How is your arm?"

"It's getting stronger all the time."

Their walk continued for almost an hour before returning to their picnic blanket, under the tree. After loading everything into the buggy, Buford harnessed the horse and they started back to town.

***

When Buford entered the sheriff's office, Thad was sitting with his feet on the desk drinking a cup of coffee: "Enjoy your picnic lunch?"

"You know, huh? Of course I did. Goin' horseback ridding next Sunday."

"The worse thing that can happen to a man is to fall in love. Don't let it interfere with running the ranch."

"You're right. I am in love with Norma, that's for sure. Why should that be such a bad thing?"

"It depends on the man and the woman." Thad let his feet fall from the desk and he rose. "I'm going to make my rounds. Want to join me?"

"Goin' back to the ranch. See you next Sunday."

***

After church the following Sunday, Buford and Norma ate lunch together at the restaurant before horseback riding in the open countryside. The pace slowed to a walk as they approached a pasture spotted with trees, not far from the ranch.

"Now that your arm is healed I hope you aren't working too hard?"

"I'm helping Fran cook and no, I'm not working too hard. You know Fran wouldn't let me overdo it, but sometimes she lets me do all the cooking. I love to cook and it gives her a rest. You know how hard she works. She has taught me a lot."

"That's nice. You want to walk some?" The horses stopped as they pulled on the reins and dismounted. With the reins in one hand, they walked side-by-side in front of the horses. "Sure is a beautiful day," Buford said as they walked.

"It is." She looked at him and smiled then stumbled over a small branch on the ground. Buford grabbed her hand to prevent her from falling. She smiled at him and didn't let go. He returned her smile and felt a tingle surge through him caused by her touch. Both looked away as they strolled hand-in-hand through the wooded area.

When they returned to town, Buford rode to the ranch, not stopping to see Thad. He could still feel Norma's hand in his and the tingle would not go away.

***

The next two weeks passed and Buford became sheriff again, which gave him more time with Norma. Sunday, after church, Thad would stay in town as sheriff until Buford returned from his time alone with Norma.

The month passed and then another and Buford and Norma continued their Sunday outings, becoming more comfortable together. When they walked along the stream or in the woods it was always hand-in-hand. On one occasion, when they finished eating

Buford looked at Norma: "Let's walk." She smiled and Buford got to his feet, pulling her up a little too aggressively and she found herself against him. Their eyes met and almost in slow motion, their lips touched as the world exploded around them. The kiss became more passionate and Norma pushed him away, breathing heavily.

"No!" We can't do this!"

"But...but I love you!"

"I love you too, but you know it isn't right."

"Oh Nor...honey I... I...will you marry me?"

Her eyes opened wide, "YES!" She jumped into his arms and kissed him again and he became more aggressive. "NO William! We must wait!"

"I... I don't think I can!"

"I don't want to wait either, but you know it isn't right."

"Let's go find the preacher and do it now."

"No. We are too emotional. We need to calm down.

"I don't want to calm down. I just want... I love you."

"You're too emotional. Would you feel the same, after?"

"I'll always feel the same."

"I believe you, but don't make me do it this way. You know it isn't proper."

He sighed looking down at the ground then into her eyes. "I know you're right. I want it to be right for you. I didn't know how being in love can make you feel. We better go before I lose control again."

Once the buggy was loaded and the horse harnessed, they started back to town. Both were still excited but the emotion was gone and they rode in silence. Buford pulled in behind the restaurant. After securing the reins to the hitching post Buford helped Norma out of the buggy and she ran inside.

"We're getting married!" she shouted when she saw Fran.

"Well, it's about time. He didn't..."

"Of course not. He kissed me then asked me!"

"Just like that, huh?"

"Not exactly, but we...nothing happened. We know we should wait. I'm so excited!"

"So am I and we're going to do this right. I'll take you to Barbara's and she can measure you for your wedding gown."

No, Fran. I don't want you to do anything except come to the wedding. We will have the Reverend marry us, and I want you and Thad to be there."

"You're my daughter, honey, and we're going to do this right. We'll have it at the restaurant and invite the whole town."

"I'm not sure anyone will come."

"Oh, honey, you've had the town in an uproar ever since you got here. They all love you. Not as much as me, but I can see it when they come in the restaurant. Business is better with you here. The men can't keep their eyes off you."

"Are you sure you want to do this?"

"I've been looking forward to this ever since you and Bill started seeing each other. Don't worry, honey, I'll take care of everything."

Chapter Twelve
The Wedding

As Fran and Norma were talking, Buford walked into the kitchen: "We are having a real wedding, William."

"Huh?"

"I'm going to have a wedding gown and Fran is having a wedding party after, in the restaurant."

"No. We's...we're just having the reverend marry us."

"He will perform the ceremony in the church," Fran said, "and the whole town is invited."

"N...no, Fran. I don't want you to do that. I just want it to be us and the reverend."

"You want to marry my daughter, don't you?"

"Yes 'em, I sure do."

"Then you will do it my way or no way. Is that clear enough for you?"

"I... I...yes 'em."

"Now get, I have a lot of planning to do."

Buford left the restaurant in a daze, almost walking into a horse and rider trotting through town, as he crossed the street. When he entered the sheriff's office Thad was playing solitaire at the desk. Without looking at him, Buford walked to a chair across the room and sat, looking at the floor.

"Are you ill?" Thad asked.

Slowly, Buford's head raised and he looked at Thad: "I... I...we... I'm gettin' married."

"No wonder you look sick. Is that what you want? How did it happen? Did you and Norma—"

"NO! She kissed me. I mean I kissed her or we kissed each other. I don't know how it happened but when it did my head exploded."

"You don't have to marry a girl just because you kissed her."

"It was more than a kiss. I mean... I kinda lost control and she pushed me away. We both were excited. She said we can't...it's not right and the words just jumped out of my mouth and she said yes! I'm scared Thad, nothing like this ever happened to me before."

"Relax. I'm sure you love her, but it doesn't have to happen right now. Talk to her when you calm down. You don't have to rush into it. I'm sure she is as scared as you."

Buford stared at him and his voice quivered: "Miss... Miss Fran is makin' wedding plans. She's invitin' the whole town."

"You've stepped in it this time, my friend. You're getting married and there's nothing you can do about it. Did you try talking to Fran?"

"There ain't no talking to that woman when she's made up her mind, you know that!"

"True statement. How soon?"

"I don't know. She is having a wedding dress made and has to tell everybody."

"I'll talk to her. I'll tell her there are things that must be done at the ranch before the wedding. Maybe it will buy you a few weeks."

"She ain't gonna believe that."

"Sure she will because it's true. You can't take your bride to the ranch with the house looking like it does. It needs to be cleaned. You need a new bed. We don't have one big enough for two people. And she will need a place to hang her clothes."

"This is scarier than fighting Indians and facing down Mr. Lynch."

"I told you the worse thing that can happen to a man is to fall in love. Now you're beginning to see why. Your life has changed forever."

"I know, and I want it to, but it's happening all too fast."

"There are other things you need to consider."

"Other things?"

"You need to stop being sheriff and become a full-time rancher."

"Then you will be the sheriff. It's your ranch more than mine. It's not fair to you."

"Maybe it's time we both stopped being sheriff. Britt is a good lawman. I'll have him take turns with me. In a couple of months, I'll see if he is open to becoming the sheriff. If he is, I'll talk to the mayor. People in town know him and respect him. If it works out, we both will become full-time ranchers."

"That could work."

"You and Norma can have the house and I'll sleep in the bunkhouse."

"That ain't right."

"You want Norma to sleep in the bunkhouse?"

"No. But you should be in the house, too."

"I'll spend a lot of time there, but I want it to be you and Norma's home. If things work out, later I'll build a small house. Let's see if Britt is willing to be sheriff and take it from there."

"You got it all figured out, haven't you?"

"You're the one that is getting married, not me. Now we have to make it work. I'll go to the ranch and talk to Britt. Tomorrow I'll be sheriff again and you can go to the ranch."

"But it's my turn."

"Your turn ended when you asked Norma to marry you. Try not to shoot yourself or fall and break your neck before tomorrow."

"Almost feel like runnin' again."

"You do and I'll come after you and you know I'll find you."

"I said almost. I ain't going nowhere."

"I'm sure glad it's you and not me."

"Why do you make it sound so bad?"

"Oh, Butte, you still have so much to learn."

"Just go. You're making me more nervous than I already am."

"See you tomorrow," Thad said as he turned to go, a smirk appeared on his face.

"Sometimes I don't know if he is serious or just messin' with my head."

When Thad got to the ranch he went looking for Britt and found him with the herd: "things are starting to change, Britt. Butte and Norma are getting married, so he won't be working as sheriff. Would you consider taking his place?" We will continue to swap off every month."

"Okay. I'm getting tired of ranch work and was thinking about moving on but I'll do it for a while. I kinda like being a lawman."

"Then maybe you would consider doing it permanent. I'm thinking of giving it up."

"Let's trade-off for a while and let me think about it."

"Fair enough. I'm going in tomorrow and let Butte come to the ranch and get things ready for his bride."

"I'll go if you want."

"Thanks. I want to be there until the wedding. I don't want Fran turning this into a coronation. She really loves Norma. I want to slow her down some to give Butte time to get things in order in the house. It won't be easy making it acceptable to a woman."

"You're right. It doesn't look like a woman has ever been in it. I'll help him."

"I would appreciate it. He will need all the help he can get and I'm not sure he knows what to do."

When Thad walked into the office Monday morning Buford was sitting, slumped over the desk with a cup of coffee.

"You look like hell. Haven't you slept?"

"Not much."

"Well...you better pull yourself together. You have a lot of things to do and if you look like that on your wedding day, Norma will turn and walk away."

"I'm gonna be okay. I just keep thinking about it and how it is happening so fast. I'm afraid I can't make her happy. I'm not sure I know how."

"You'll figure it out once your married. I'm sure Norma is feeling about the same."

"But that house is a mess. I don't know where to start."

"Britt said he will help you and the first thing is to clean it. And when you are done, clean it again. It doesn't matter how good it looks to you, women look at things differently than men. What is acceptable to you and me will look like a pigsty to Norma."

"Will you stop messing with me! I'm having a hard enough time the way it is."

"I'm not messing with you this time, Butte. Women like things clean and believe me...what is clean to you won't be to Norma. I've watched her in the restaurant and she is very neat and clean."

"Okay... I hear ya."

"And you need to find a bed and some furniture for the bedroom."

"I don't know anything about furniture."

"Okay, I'll see what I can do."

When Buford rode to the ranch, Thad went over to the restaurant. Mary met him as he walked in.

"You having breakfast?"

"No. I ate at the ranch. Is Fran available?"

"I'll get her."

Fran came out of the kitchen and walked up to him: "How are you, Thad? What can I do for you?"

"We need to talk about the wedding."

"It's all set for Sunday."

"Too soon, Fran. There are things that need to be done."

"What needs to be done?"

"First there's the house. I'm not sure Butte can have it ready by Sunday, there's a lot to do."

"It'll be good enough. I'm not sure either one of them will even know what the inside looks like for the first few weeks."

"You may be right, but the bed is too small. I'll have to send someone to Texas and I don't think they will be back for a couple of weeks. Postpone it a week or two."

"Hell... I'll give them my bed. I'll sleep in Norma's room until the wedding and have Olson order me a new one."

"I saw your bed when you were taking care of us and it is beautiful. You don't want to give it away."

"It will be my wedding present."

"Well, who is going to give her away?"

"The Mayor. He's looking forward to it."

"You need more time to notify people."

"The whole town knows and looking forward to it. Well...there's a few that don't like negroes but most will be there." She looked him straight in the eye. "You got something against this wedding, Walker?"

"No. I just think Butte needs more time."

She laughed, "hell he'd need more time if it was a year from now."

"No doubt."

She laughed again. "I think it was his hormones talking when he asked her, but it's the right thing for both of them. This town has never had a wedding, and I'm going to make sure it's a dandy."

"Okay. I'll forget about the bed and see if Taylor can make something for the bedroom to hang clothes in. There's nothing but a small bed and chest of drawers in there, and Norma will need a place for her things. Not sure he can do it in a week, though."

"Jeb is a good carpenter and makes nice furniture. I'm sure he can get it done in time. Send a couple of the boys to my house tomorrow to get the bed."

"Guess I better talk to Jeb and head for the ranch. See you for lunch."

Thad rode to the ranch and found Joey checking the herd: "Send a couple of the boys to Fran's house tomorrow and get her bed and bedding. She's giving it to Butte and Norma as a wedding gift."

"I can't believe Bill is gettin' married," Joey said.

"Surprised me too. I hope he knows what he is doing."

"Mighty pretty woman he's a marryin'."

"That she is. Butte in the house?"

"Yes, sir, he is. Him and Britt been cleaning since breakfast."

"The wedding is Sunday at two. See you then."

"Looks like you have a good start," Thad said when he walked into the house. Britt was busy dusting and Buford on his hands and knees scrubbing the floors with a brush. "You should have it ready by Sunday."

"Sunday! This Sunday!" Buford said, looking up from his work. "I'm not sure we can be ready by then."

"You have the rest of the week. Move the bed out and work on getting the room ready. Fran is giving you her bed as a wedding present, and two of the hands are going to get it tomorrow."

"You said you would talk to her."

"I did, but she's a headstrong woman. Once her mind is made up there is no changing it." Buford stared at him. "Don't worry...you'll have the house ready by then."

"I ain't worried about the house. I don't know if I'll be ready. I... I'm not sure I want to do this."

"You love her, don't you?"

"That I do. She is all I think about and all I want is to be with her. But..."

"A smirk appeared on Thad's face. "I think every man has cold feet before his wedding. You'll be fine."

"You're gonna be with me, ain't ya?"

"I'm your best man, of course, I'll be up there with you, but I can't stop your voice from quivering or your knee from knotting."

"Damn you, Thaddeus Walker! You ain't helpin' none!"

"See you at the wedding." Thad turned to go, smiling.

"He's saved my life many times but sometimes I don't know why I put up with him."

"He's just teasing you, Bill," Britt said. "You'll be fine at the wedding."

"I hope you're right. C 'mon, we better work on the bedroom."

***

Sunday morning came too soon for Buford and after church, he walked into the sheriff's office with a nervous stomach: "I don't think I heard a word of the sermon. I never felt this nervous when I was running away."

"You will be fine once the ceremony is over."

"Maybe. If I can live through it."

"You're a brave man, Butte. You've fought Indians, rustlers, stampeding cattle, and faced down men at gunpoint. Relax, this should be easy for you."

"Those things seem tame compared to what I'm about to do. I don't know if I can make her happy."

"I'm sure she feels the same. You both will have some adjusting to do."

"Do you think she is as nervous as me?"

"No. This is something women look forward to, getting married. She is probably more excited than nervous."

Buford looked straight at Thad: "I've never made love to a woman before."

A smirk appeared on Thad's face. "Don't worry, that will come natural. I think she will be more nervous than you and no doubt a little scared, so don't be too aggressive."

Buford sighed: "I wish it was over."

"Which part? The ceremony or making love? Do you have the ring?"

"The ring?"

"You're supposed to put a ring on her finger during the ceremony."

"I don't remember slaves having no rings."

"Let's go to the store; I think Olson will have some."

***

As Buford and Thad stood at the front of the church with the reverend, waiting for Norma and the mayor, Buford was almost shaking. Then, when the bride and mayor appeared in the doorway, Buford became calm. The sight of Norma, standing at the entrance to the church in her wedding gown and a white veil over her face, filled him with a peace he had never experienced.

In complete silence, the two started down the aisle with everyone in attendance standing and looking at Norma as she passed.

"Who gives this woman to this man?" The reverend asked.

"I will," the mayor said and stepped aside as Buford moved next to Norma.

Neither Norma or Buford's voice wavered as they said their marriage vows, and Buford spoke with resolve and pride. To Buford's surprise, Norma placed a ring on his finger as well and a tingle filled him from her touch. The words Reverend Hudson spoke after the ceremony didn't register with Buford, nor the prayer that followed, but a smile brightened his face when Hudson said: "Ladies and gentlemen it is my pleasure to present, Mr. and Mrs. William B. Chance." All stood and applause filled the air. "Mr. Chance, you may kiss the bride." Cheers rang out as their lips touched.

Norma and Buford were the first to enter the restaurant, followed by those attending the ceremony, along with a few others. A free meal at the restaurant was too good to pass up.

The party went on for about an hour with people passed through the serving line, before the bride and groom fed each other a piece of cake. As they were finishing, Fran looked at Thad, sitting next to her: "Isn't there something you could say?"

"What's to say? They're married. He's a lucky man."

"He's your best friend. I've heard it's proper for the best man to speak at a wedding dinner."

"I've never been proper in my life."

"You're gonna be this time. Quiet!" Fran shouter as she stood, "Thad has something to say."

Thad reluctantly stood: "When I first met Butte he was going north, but with a little prodding I persuaded him to go west with me. I've seen him fight Indians, calm stampeding cattle, and face down a man bent on killing him. I've also seen him save a man's life, twice, that didn't like him because of his color. Butte didn't care whether the man liked him or not, his life was worth saving. Needless to say, they became good friends. Butte is not only the bravest man I've ever known but kind as well. I consider myself a lucky man to have him as my friend. But not as lucky as Butte. Somehow he has convinced the most beautiful woman I have ever met to become his wife. Norma's beauty is not only external but internal as well. She has a heart as big as her second mother, Fran." He picked up a shot glass from the table and held it up. "To the bride and groom. May their life together be long and happy." All stood and raised a glass to the happy couple.

"Let's go," Buford whispered in Norma's ear. Both rose and headed for the door and everyone followed. A cheer went up when Buford helped Norma into the waiting buggy and drove away.

"Mighty fine party Miss Fran put on for us," Buford said, glancing at Norma then back to the road. "I didn't know there were that many people that liked us."

"It was very nice and everyone has treated me well since I got here."

"I can't believe we are married," Buford replied, with his eyes looking straight ahead.

It became quiet as the horse trotted over the road until Buford stopped in front of the ranch house. "We're here." He helped Norma down and they walked onto the porch. Buford opened the door and stepped aside but Norma didn't move. "Ain... Aren't you going in?"

"A man is supposed to carry his bride over the threshold."

"Oh." He scooped her up and she put her arms around his neck, smiling. "I think this is a mighty fine idea." He crossed the threshold and kicked the door closed behind to them, heading for the bedroom.

***

Even though on duty, Thad stayed at the restaurant and helped remove the dishes and rearrange tables: "What do you think they are doing about now?" he said, carrying dishes into the kitchen.

Fran, busy scraping food from plates didn't look at him, but a smile appeared on her face: "How many guesses do I get? I think what I should do next, is find a wife for you."

"Stick to running the restaurant. I'm not the kind that settles down."

"You're running a ranch, aren't you? What do you call that?"

"An experiment. I want to see if we can be successful. So far it's working. I'm going to walk the town and check on things. See you later."

"Thanks for your help."

***

As the sun cleared the horizon the following morning, Buford rose before Norma and went out back to the outhouse. When he returned, Norma was in the kitchen preparing breakfast and he came up behind her, putting his arms around her waist.

"We don't have to be in no hurry to eat," he said.

She smiled as she continued cooking: "Aren't you hungry?"

"Yeah. For you."

Turning toward him, she kissed him then pushed him away. "Later. Go set the table."

"I'll do it but it's not what I want to do."

When the food was ready she filled two plates and they both sat. With heads bowed she began: "Father we thank You for this food and ask you to bless this house and our marriage. In Jesus' name, amen."

"Amen. This is real good," he said as they began to eat.

"Thank you. Fran is a good teacher.

"Well, you won't have to cook at the restaurant now that we're married. You can just be a rancher's wife."

"No, William. I want to keep helping her. She works too hard and she has done so much for me. She really has become my mother. I'm going to continue working. You will be gone most of the day working the ranch. I'll be home in time to fix dinner."

"No need. We can eat what Jeff fixes for the hands. He's a good cook and I don't want you working when you get home. We have other things to do." A smile appeared on his face and Norma blushed, looking at her plate as they continued to eat. When they finished eating Norma rose and began gathering the dishes. Buford stood and removed the plate from her hand. "Later." He scooped her up in his arms, heading for the bedroom. A smile appeared on

Norma's face and she put her arms around his neck, kissing him on the cheek.

Chapter Thirteen
New Beginning

A month after the wedding, Jeff decided to quit and go west, so the ranch would need a new cook. When Fran heard, she decided it was time to let Norma go.

"You need a cook at the ranch. Why don't you be the cook? You can cook for eleven people. It shouldn't be a problem for you and you should be at the ranch, not here."

"But I want to help you. You work too hard the way it is, and I like being with you."

"And I love having you here, honey, but your place is with your husband. We can still spend time together."

"No. You need help cooking. I won't go."

"You know the new family that came here a little over a month ago, the Jorgon's. Their daughter, Arlene, came to me looking for a job. You were here so I said no, but if you go to the ranch I could hire her. She's only sixteen but seems smart and full of energy. I think I can teach her to cook and wait tables. I think the family could use the money."

"You're just saying that because you think I should be at the ranch. I'm afraid if I go you will try to do the cooking by yourself. And I don't let you pay me, so it will cost you money to hire someone."

"I can afford the cost, and I promise I will hire Arlene."

"If you hire Arlene now, I will stay on for a week or two and see how she is doing. I will only leave if I'm sure she is able to take my place helping you."

"Hey! Just who is the mother here, you or me?"

Norma hugged her: "You are a great mother and I love you very much. But I worry about you."

"God smiled on me the day He brought you to me. I love you too. Okay, we will do it your way."

"Thanks, mom."

"Now see what you did! You got me crying." Fran released her, wiping her eyes. "I'm going to go talk to Arlene."

Norma continued to work at the restaurant for two more weeks before leaving. She could have left at the end of the first week since Arlene caught on much faster than she and Fran thought. It almost made Norma a little jealous to see how well Arlene took to Frances. But it was no surprise since everyone liked Fran and she adored young people. So, finally Norma stopped coming to the restaurant. This made Buford happy not only because they would be together more, the men were complaining about his cooking.

***

Thad and Britt continued to take turns working the ranch and being sheriff. Six months after the wedding Norma became pregnant.

"Have you thought about being sheriff full-time?" Thad asked Britt when Norma began to show.

"I have and I like the idea."

"Now that Norma is going to have a baby, I want to take over most of the management of the ranch so Butte will have more time with his family."

"Makes sense. Do you think the mayor will have a problem with me as the only sheriff?"

"He likes you and I've mentioned it to him before, but I'll talk to him again. He knows Butte and me are available if needed. As tame as this town is I'm not sure they need a sheriff."

"Does Bill know?"

"Not yet. I'll tell him tonight. I'm going to talk to Trent."

When Thad walked into the mayor's office he was sitting behind his desk looking at some papers. Thad sat in a chair and put his feet on the desk.

"Make yourself to home," Trent said.

"Thanks." Thad let his feet fall from the desk. "I have something to discuss with you."

"Usually when you want to talk it's something I don't want to hear."

"I want you to hire Britt as sheriff. I'm going to be running the ranch."

"You and Britt have been swapping off, what's changed?"

"What's changed is Norma is pregnant."

"I know that. She's Bill's, wife, not yours."

"We are getting ready for another cattle drive and Butte can't go because of Norma. When I get back he will want to spend most of his time with the baby and Norma. I won't have time to be sheriff."

Britt was a drifter when you found him, what if he doesn't stay? If he leaves will you come back?"

"I think he will stay; he likes being a lawman."

"You didn't answer my question."

"I think my days of being a sheriff are over. Now that Butte has a family to take care of, I need to be a full-time rancher."

"So...if Britt decides to leave, the town is without a sheriff."

"I think you're wrong about him. I think he will stay but you know nothing is permanent. If he, in time, decides to leave you will have to find another sheriff."

The mayor sighed and sat back in his chair. "As usual you leave me no choice."

"Thanks, Trent. When I get back to the office I'll swear him in and give him my badge."

***

When Thad got to the ranch he found Buford cleaning out stalls in the stable: "I didn't think you could get this far away from Norma."

"You know I do my job."

"I know, and now that I'll be here all the time you can spend as much time with Norma as you want."

"Chores still need to be done."

"True. I'm going to use Jim as cook on the drive so he can take over as cook now until the drive starts. We could use another hand."

"What about the Carson twins?"

"Ned and Ted? They're only fourteen."

"Almost fifteen. I know they want to be cowboys. They talked to Joey about a job about the time Norma became pregnant, but I told him no."

"They've never worked cattle."

"Ain't gonna learn no younger. You need all the hands on the drive. If we hire Ned and Ted I can use them here while you are gone. They know how to ride and rope. I can teach them to work cattle. I can also use some help mucking out stalls and caring for the horses. We have too many breeding cows for me to handle by myself."

"You're right. Talk to Joey. We can use them now."

"I'll do that as soon as I finish here."

"I'll finish. Norma is due to have the baby while we are on the drive. When it happens you won't have much time for taking care of the ranch. The sooner we get those boys started the better."

Buford smiled and handed Thad the shovel: "Don't have to tell me twice."

"Hmm. I think I said the wrong thing. I'll find Joey."

"Ain't gonna happen. I'm gone," Buford turned and walked away.

***

Buford woke with Norma lying beside him the following morning, still sleeping. He gently rubbed his hand over her belly. She smiled and opened her eyes: "Sorry. I didn't mean to wake you." She moved close to him and he put his arms around her. "I wish we knew what it's going to be."

"Will you be disappointed if it is a girl?"

"Oh, no, honey. I just want a healthy baby and I know if it is a girl it will be as beautiful as its mama."

"I know men want a son to carry on their name."

He grinned: "You just might have more than one baby, you know."

"I'm a little afraid, William. I don't know what to expect. Since we lived in the Carter house I never saw someone having a baby."

He pulled her close. "I don't want you worrying about a thing. Mrs. Johnston will be here and she has been midwifin' most of her life and the doctor will be here also. You gonna be just fine."

"Let me go. I need to start breakfast. The men will be waiting."

"No need. Jim is going to be cook on the drive so he's starting as cook today. You can sleep in if you want."

"Why didn't you tell me?"

"Thad and me just talked about it yesterday."

"I can still cook."

"You know what Fran said. You shouldn't be on your feet too much. You need to start taking it easy."

"Does that mean you are going to serve me breakfast in bed?"

"Sure enough, if that's what you want."

"No, but let's have breakfast together, just you and me. Not with the hands."

"You gotta deal and I'll fix it."

"Let's do it together."

***

After breakfast, Joey rode to the Carson place, a small farm about a mile from town. Besides Ned and Ted, the Carson's had three other children. Two boys, one twelve and one ten, and a daughter seven. Mr. Carson raised vegetables for the restaurant and some of the townspeople. He also raised a few hogs, providing pork and bacon for the restaurant.

When Joey rode up to the Carson house, Mr. Carson came out. "Mornin' Mr. Carson."

"Morning, Joey."

"Ned and Ted asked me about a job a while back. Mind if I talk to them?"

"I know they did. They don't like farming and I can't keep them busy. They're in the barn."

"Thank you, sir." When Joey stopped in front of the barn the twins came out. "You boys still interested in working for the Bar CW?"

"Yes sir," they both answered.

"Be at the ranch in the morning."

As Joey rode off Ned and Ted looked at each other: "We're gonna be cowboys!" Ned said.

As the sun began to rise the following morning Ned and Ted rode up to the stable at the Bar CW, where Buford, Thad, and Joey were standing.

"You know Mr. Walker and Mr. Chance," Joey said.

"Yes, sir, we do," Ted said, "and we can't wait to go on the drive."

"Good way to lose your lives," Thad said. "You're too young and inexperienced. You will be working for Butte here on the ranch. "You boys know how to shoot?"

"Yes, sir," they both answered.

"What kind of guns?"

"Shotgun and rifle."

"Handguns?"

"No, sir," Ned said. "Pa is the only one that shoots a handgun."

"We will loan you guns...after we teach you how to use them," Thad said. "You can buy your own when you have the money." He looked at Buford. "You take them."

"Unsaddle your mounts and put them out to pasture. Find an empty bunk in the bunkhouse for your bedrolls," Buford said, "then I want the stable cleaned and the horses curried."

"We already know how to do that," Ted replied.

"Good. Then I won't have to show you." The twins looked at each other. "Well...get moving. Got a lot of work to do. When you're done, I'll be in the house."

The twins unsaddled their horses and led them to the pasture.

"I think you're going to have your hands full with those two," Thad said.

"They'll come around."

It took all morning to clean the stable and curry the horses, so the sun was high overhead when the twins came to the house. Buford saw them and went out onto the porch: "Get some lunch and saddle your horses then come back here." When they returned Buford's horse was at the hitching post. Buford left the house and swung into the saddle. "Let's go."

"When are we going to get to do what real cowboys do?" Ned asked.

"Cleaning stalls and currying horses is a part of being a cowboy. We're going to the herd. You have a lot to learn."

Buford reined in a few yards from the herd. "You and your horse have never had cattle around you, so I want you to walk your horses into the herd. Go slow and talk to your horse when he becomes nervous. Show him you're not afraid. If he sees you're afraid he may spook and try to run. If he does the cattle may stampede."

"Well... I... I am a little afraid," Ted said.

"Me too," Ned replied.

"Course you are, but don't let your horse know it. I want one of you on each side of me with a few cows in between us. Go slow. If you can't do this I'm sending you home. This is real cowboy stuff. C'mon, we're wastin' daylight."

At a very slow walk, they started for the herd. Buford stayed near the edge of the herd for a while then moved in toward the center. He continued through the herd, watching Ned and Ted as they talked to their horses to keep them calm. After a couple of hours, Buford left the herd and sent the twins through the cattle alone.

"You're off to a good start," Thad said as he rode up to Buford. "I'll take it from here. Go check on Norma."

"I thought you wanted me to work with them since they will be with me when you're gone?"

"You've not only got them used to being in with the cattle but working with you as well. They trust you. Now you need to check on Norma. I'm sure she is a little nervous about giving birth to her first baby."

"That she is and so am I. I heard some women on the plantation screaming when the baby was comin' so I know it ain't no fun."

"I hope you didn't tell her that."

"No! she's scared enough as it is, but since I know I'm scared for her, too."

"Go on back to the house. I'll see you at dinner."

Thad continued to work with the twins the rest of the day, showing them how to separate a few cows from the herd and return them. In three weeks the drive would begin and Thad wanted Ned and Ted to be able to handle the herd without Buford.

For the next two weeks Thad continued to work with the two young boys, improving their skill at working with cattle and building their confidence. One day toward the end of the second week, Thad taught them how to use a forge and shoe a horse. They caught on fast since they had watched their father replace a shoe at home.

"Get your horses," Thad said to the twins at the start of the third week. "We're going for a ride." About an hour later Thad reined in near a small grove of trees. They dismounted and Thad removed two gun belts with hosters and revolvers from his saddlebags. The boys' eyes opened wide. "Put these on," Thad said, "but don't touch the guns." The boys strapped the guns on with big smiles on their faces. "When is a gun empty?"

"When it don't got no bullets," Ned said.

"Wrong answer," Thad said. "What do you say, Ted?"

"Well ... I think Ned is right. If it don't have bullets in it, it's empty."

"The answer is never."

"Never!" they both said.

"If you treat a gun as if it is always loaded you will never accidentally shoot yourself or someone else. And never point a gun at someone unless you intend to shoot them. Okay, the first thing you need to know is how to load it."

Thad loaded his revolver then watched each boy load their guns. He then demonstrated how to aim and shoot objects sitting on a fallen tree. The shooting training continued throughout the week, with Thad showing the boys different shooting techniques. By the end of the week, Ned and Ted were shooting offhand and sometimes hitting their targets.

***

Just before sunup the morning of the drive, Buford and the twins rode out to the campsite near the herd. Some of the men were sitting next to the fire, drinking coffee and talking, while others were with the cattle. Thad was talking to Jim, the cook, when they reined in near the chuckwagon. The eastern sky began to change from inky black to a hazy dark gray as they dismounted.

"Looks like you're ready," Buford said.

"That we are," he said as Jim busied himself loading things on the chuckwagon.

"Hope it's a peaceful drive."

You know how drives are, this will be no different."

"I had the Reverend say a prayer for you, Sunday."

"Thanks. I'm sure we will need it. How is Norma this morning?"

"Still sleepin'. Startin' to have a few light pains. I'm going to have Mrs. Johnston come and stay until the baby comes."

"Good idea." A dim red glow began to appear just above the eastern horizon. Thad swung into the saddle. "Move 'em out."

"Move 'em out," rang throughout the camp as wranglers mounted their steeds and headed for the herd.

"See you in a few weeks," Thad said as Jim doused the fire and finished loading the chuckwagon.

"You'll be in my prayers," Buford said.

"Pray for Norma and the baby." Thad swung his horse around and headed for the herd.

"Wish we were going with them," Ned said as the chuckwagon sped away, heading for the front of the herd.

"Maybe next year," Buford said. "C'mon. we've got work to do."

Two days after the drive started a buggy stopped in front of the ranch house. Buford helped Mrs. Johnston down from the buggy. "Thank you, ma'am, for coming," he said. "She's been havin' some pains."

"Now don't you worry about a thing. She will be fine."

"I won't stop worrying until this is over." Buford removed her bag from the buggy and they started up the steps. "I'll be happy when it is."

"Not as happy as Norma."

Buford opened the door and Norma, sitting on the couch, started to get up. "You stay right there, honey. You look like you are ready to pop."

"I feel like it too." Norma's eyes filled with tears.

"Now now now," Amanda Johnston sat beside her and gave her a hug. "Eveything is going to be just fine."

"I'm not sure I want to ever do this again."

"Well... I've heard that before. I think you will change your mind once the baby is here."

Buford took Amanda's bag into the spare bedroom, feeling ashamed, knowing he'd been the cause of Norma's pain and fear.

A week passed with her pains coming and going before they stopped altogether. Then, two days later she awoke in agony as the pains returned more severe and closer together. Buford jumped out of bed and ran into the spare bedroom in his longjohns: "Come quick! I think it's a happenin.'" Amanda looked a little shocked. "Oh...oh... I'm sorry."

"Go get the doctor."

"Yes 'em." He left the room as Amanda got out of bed with a smirk on her face.

Buford hurriedly dressed and ran to the bunkhouse: "Go get the doctor," he said to Ned, still in bed. Ned jumped out of bed and dressed as Buford returned to the house.

Norma's pains continued then stopped: "I guess it's not time," Norma said.

"It's time, honey; they are going to come back and much worse but you'll be fine. I'm here. It won't be long and you will be a mother." Norma began to cry and Amanda sat on the bed and pulled her close. About an hour later the pain returned, slow at first, then increasing as the doctor arrived along with Fran. The doctor entered the bedroom and closed the door.

"You doing okay, Bill?" Fran asked.

"I don't want her to suffer," he said as moans came from the bedroom.

"There is always some pain when a woman gives birth," Fran answered as the moans became louder.

"Breathe deep," Amanda said as Norma's pain increased and she took deep breaths and the moans became louder. "Push, honey." The moans turned into screams. "Harder, Norma, push harder." She pushed harder and screamed louder as the baby's head emerged from the birth canal.

"We are almost there," the doctor said, "keep pushing." She pushed again and screamed. "I've got him."

"Him! Norma said, "it's a boy!"

"A beautiful boy," the doctor answered and held him so Norma could see, then placed the baby on her stomach and tied the cord and removed the placenta.

When Norma stopped screaming Buford jumped to his feet: "I'm going in there!"

"Not yet, Bill. They'll come and get you when it's time."

"Too quiet. I want to know she's all right." Then he heard a faint cry of a baby and a moment later the door opened.

"Come and see your son," Amanda said.

"Son!" Buford hurried through the doorway into the room and saw Norma smiling, holding a little baby. He bent down and kissed her. "I'm sorry you suffered so much."

"It was nothing. Isn't he beautiful?"

"Almost as beautiful as his mama."

"Hold him."

"I'm afraid I might hurt him."

"He's a strong and healthy boy," the doctor said. "You won't hurt him."

"But he looks so small."

"He is a pretty big baby for the size of his mother. He will probably be as big as his father when he grows up. Be sure to support his back and head."

Buford gently picked up the baby and a tingle ran through him. He smiled.

"I want to name him after you," Norma said.

Buford smiled as he looked down at his son. "I'd be mighty proud to have him carry my name, but I've thought about it ever since I knew we were going to have a baby." He looked at her. "I thought if it were a girl we'd name it after you but...if it weren't for Thad I wouldn't be here. He's saved my life many times and he even gave me my name, so, I thought we should name him Thaddeus."

"I like that," Norma said, "but I still want him to have your name as well. Let's name him Thaddeus William Chance."

Buford smiled: "Sounds like a mighty fine name to me."

"Norma needs to rest," the doctor said.

Buford kissed the baby and gently placed him in Norma's arms and kissed her. Everyone left the room except for Amanda.

"They are both doing well," the doctor said, "I'll come back in a week and check on them."

"Thank you sir. What do I owe ya?"

"This one is on me, Bill, but not the next."

"The next?"

"I can see it in her eyes. She is going to be a wonderful mother and one baby is not going to satisfy her, but don't get too romantic for a while."

"Dinner is on me tonight, doc, for you and your wife. I'll see you at the restaurant later."

"Thanks, Frances. I'll take you up on that."

"You should let me pay," Buford said to Fran when the doctor left.

"Not on your life. I'm a grandmother now and I'm celebrating."

Mrs. Johnston stayed through the first week and left when the doctor came and pronounced them both strong and healthy. Buford thanked her and paid her for her time.

***

As the weeks passed Norma and young Thaddeus grew stronger. The drive ended four weeks after the arrival of young Thaddeus. When Thad returned he found Buford working in the stable.

"We made a lot of money on this drive, partner. It won't be long and we will have Sam and the bank paid off."

"That's good. Come on, I want you to see my son." They left the stable and went into the house. Norma was in the rocking chair rocking the baby when they came in. She placed her finger on her lips and rose, taking the sleeping baby into the bedroom. "Guess you will have to wait until he wakes."

"Looks like a fine boy. I can see he's going to be as handsome as his mother is beautiful. Glad he doesn't take after you."

"That ain't nice Thad." A smirk appeared on Thad's face.

Norma returned and gave him a hug. "That's the welcome home I've been waiting for."

"He usually sleeps for two hours. You can hold him when he is awake."

"I'm looking forward to it."

"Did William tell you what we named him?"

"No. I'd guess William Buford Chance Junior."

"It's Thaddeus William Chance," Buford said. Now don't you feel bad about what you said."

"Thaddeus? Why would you do that to your son? I hope he doesn't hate you when he grows up."

"He won't," Norma said, "once he gets to know his uncle."

"Uncle. That's a name I never thought I'd be called. I'm going to town and deposit the money. Maybe when I get back young Thaddeus will be awake. Poor kid." He put his hat on and left.

***

As time passed the ranch continued to prosper and the town grew. More farmers moved to the area along with new businesses in town. A sawmill opened, a lawyer put up his sign, and a newspaper began publishing a weekly paper. Britt continued to be sheriff and one year passed then two and Britt fell in love with Arlene Jorgon, now a pretty and well developed young woman. Shortly after her eighteenth birthday, they were married. Britt continued to be the only lawman in town and Arlene continued to work for Fran in the restaurant.

Two months after Young Thaddeus' second birthday his namesake walked into the house with a paper in his hand: "It's past time for me to move on. I'm going to California."

"You can't," Buford said, "you're half owner of the ranch."

Thad handed him the paper. "I signed it over to you."

"No! It's more your ranch than mine. I still owe you for what you put down on it."

"The ranch is paid for. No one owes anyone. You and Joey are doing a good job of running it. I've been restless for some time. It's time to move on."

"I don't want you to go," Norma said, hugging him. "You're family."

"If anyone could change my mind, Norma," he pulled her closer, "it would be you, but I've made up my mind."

"I owe you everything, Thad. We've been partners ever since you saved me from hanging. You can't go."

"Please stay," Norma said pulling away from him.

"My bedroll and saddlebags are packed. When I go through that door it will be for the last time."

"I've always relied on you," Buford said, "You taught me everything. I'll be lost without you."

"Nothing more to teach, Butte. You'll be just fine. Take good care of Norma and my nephew."

"Promise to write," Norma said, with tears running down her face.

"I promise."

She kissed and hugged him. He returned her hug and kiss then turned and left. They followed him out and watched as he mounted his horse and rode off. Both had tears running down their cheeks as he and his horse grew small before disappearing across the open range.

Chapter Fourteen
War

Things continued to go well for the ranch after Thad left and he was good about answering all of Norma's letters, as he promised. Even though Norma taught Buford to read and write, he never wrote to Thad. In time Buford and Norma adjusted to not having Thad around and concentrated on running the ranch and raising their son. Norma continued to write to Thad but not as often. Shortly after Thaddeus' third birthday Norma became pregnant and gave birth to a girl, which they named Frances after Frances Stone since she considered Norma her daughter.

The ranch continued to prosper and the area to grow as did the country but tensions were building. As new territories opened, a disagreement arose as to whether new states should be slave or free states. Northern states, which were against slavery, wanted new states to be free to check the growth of slavery, hoping in time slavery would disappear. The South, which relied on slave labor to exist, thought new states should be slave or have the right to decide whether to be free or slave. With the election of a new President, Abraham Lincoln, who opposed the expansion of slavery, South Carolina ceded from the Union and encouraged other southern states to join them. A few months after the election, war began on April 12, 1861, when South Carolina fired on Fort Sumter. In July, the Union and Confederates Forces fought the first of two battles of Bull Run, in Virginia. Although outnumbered and at first on the defensive, the Rebels were able to break through the Union's right flank, creating a panicked retreat of northern troops, ending in a humiliating defeat for the Union.

Once Norma taught Buford to read, he faithfully read the Mexville Gazette and, even though the national news was somewhat dated, became concerned with where the country was headed. When war broke out he became moody and a little withdrawn.

"Are you working too hard, William? You've been very quiet lately. Are you feeling okay?"

"It's the war, Hon."

"I know. It's awful but it's not out here."

"Not yet, but it will be, and I think I need to go fight."

"No! It's not your war. Your place is here with your family."

"It is my war, Norma, it's our war, all people of color. If the South wins we will all be slaves."

"Let the East fight the war. That's where the problem is, not out here."

"You know Texas is a slave state."

"It's not fair!" She turned her back to him.

"Life's not fair, Hon. We have to make it fair. That's why I have to go fight. I'm going to go talk to the men. I'll leave in the morning."

"No!" She turned and held him. "Give me time to adjust."

"How long?"

"A month."

"Two weeks. I'll leave in two weeks. I'm going to talk to the hands." He went to the stable and found Joey currying a horse. "Get the men in here. I need to talk to them—all of them."

"Okay, boss. I'll be right back."

In thirty minutes all of the hands were standing outside the stable:

"You know there's a war. It's a war about my people. I need to go fight."

"We'll go with you," they all said.

"Thanks. I need you here to look after things and my family. Rebs may come here before it's over. If they do, they will take my family to Texas as slaves. I need you to take Norma and the kids away, hide 'em, whatever you have to do. Just don't let the Rebs get them."

"Don't worry about a thing, boss," Jim said, "I'll take good care of them."

"We all will," they all said at the same time.

"I'll see to it," Joey said. "When you leaving?"

"In two weeks."

"I wish we could go with you," Joey said, "but I know our place is here."

"Thanks. "I'm mighty proud to have you all as a part of this ranch."

***

Buford spent more time with Norma and the kids during the next two weeks. Even so, Norma was quiet most of the time, breaking down and crying when she was alone. The night before Buford was to leave, Norma held him close throughout the night. They made love and tears ran down her face afterwards, knowing she may never see him again.

Before the sun the following morning, everyone was up and ate in silence. Buford helped Norma clear the table before hugging Thaddeus and picking him up. "We've talked about this," Buford said as he put him down. "You know daddy will be gone for a while so you will be the man of the house. I need you to take good care of your little sister and mama."

"I will daddy, I promise."

Buford picked up Frances and hugged and kissed her then handed her to Norma, hugging and kissing her as well. Norma put the baby in the crib and followed Buford to the door.

"Don't go! Give me another week, two days—a day!"

"You know if I do, Hon, you will want more time." He opened the door and saw a lone rider sitting on a horse a few feet from the porch. Buford looked at Norma: "What's he doing here?"

"Nice to see you too, Butte," Thad said as he dismounted.

Norma hurried down the steps and hugged and kissed him: "Thank you."

"I'd fight the fires of hell for you if you asked me." He looked at young Thaddeus. "You remember me, son?"

"Uncle Thad."

"Smart boy. You must take after your mother."

Buford sighed as Joey brought his horse to him. He hugged and kissed the kids again then Norma. "I'll be back, honey." Tears were streaming down her face as he released her.

She hugged Thad again: "I'll bring him back, I promise."

Both mounted their horses and rode off at a gallop. Neither spoke for a while then slowed the horses to a walk.

"I shoulda known she'd write you." Thad didn't answer. "Thanks for coming."

"You didn't think I'd let you have all the fun, did you?"

"War ain't no game, Thad."

"Depends on who's rules you follow."

"Never did understand you. Seemed like all you wanted to do is get us killed. I'm surprised you ain't got yourself killed yet."

"I keep trying but most are too slow and bad shots."

"Do me a favor. Don't try no more."

"I won't have to. The Rebs will do it for me."

A few hours later Fort Union came into view. They could see a detachment of soldiers outside the gate along with two officers and a sergeant. The sergeant was swearing in a dozen recruits. A corporal marched the recruits away as Thad and Buford reined in near the sergeant and officers.

"We come to join," Thad said.

What's your name, Mister?" The General asked.

I'm Thaddeus Walker and this is William Buford Chance."

"Do you have any fighting experience?"

"Fought some Indians once and some rustlers."

"Swear them in sergeant major." The sergeant swore then in. "You men are now the property of the U.S. Army. Private Chance, we are sending you east. We don't have a colored regiment in the west."

"We're a team," Thad said, "we want to stay together."

"I give the orders, private."

"If we can't be together we are not staying."

"You belong to the army now, mister. You're not going anywhere."

Thad turned and started to mount his horse. Buford hesitated then mounted his horse. "Ready arms," the general said to the detachment of soldiers and they raised their rifles. Aim..."

The colonel stepped in front of the general: "Don't shoot general. I know these men. Let me have them."

"You're willing to have a negro in your regiment?"

"Yes, sir."

"At ease." The soldiers lowered their guns. "I'll hold you personally responsible, colonel, if there is a problem."

"Yes sir, I understand, sir."

"Very well."

"Walker, Chance!" Both stopped when they heard a familiar voice and looked at the colonel. "You both will be in my regiment. Get off your horses. They dismounted. "Sergeant Major get these men some uniforms and equipment."

"I know that voice," Buford said as they followed the sergeant.

"Yeah, it's Captain Watson but he's no longer a captain."

"The captain of the fort in Indian country?"

"That's the one."

"Glad he stopped them from shooting. We ain't been together a day and already you're trying to get us killed."

"You know I'm a gambler."

"But do you have to gamble with our lives?"

"I didn't think he would let them shoot us."

"You recognized him?"

"As soon as we rode up. I remembered him as being a compassionate man."

"What if you were wrong?"

"I guess we'd be dead. You want to serve together, don't you?"

"Yeah, but not in the grave."

"Cut the chatter!" The sergeant yelled, "and get in step!"

After receiving uniforms and equipment the new recruits set up their tents then the sergeant began drilling the new troops.

"I didn't come here to learn to march," Buford said to Thad marching beside him, "I come to fight."

"Did I tell you to talk, private!?"

"No, sergeant major."

"Company, halt!" The sergeant came up close to Buford's face. "You will address me as sir! You got it!?"

"Yes, sir."

"Am I going to have trouble with you, Private Chance?"

"No, sir! I come to kill Rebs, not march."

"That time will come, mister. Until then you will follow orders! Is that clear!?"

"Yes, sir!"

"Forward, march!" A smirk appeared on Thad's face as the march resumed. Buford glanced at him then straight ahead. "Get in step, Chance!" Left, left, left right left!" The smirk broadened on Thad's face as Buford's eye rolled up.

After the evening meal, Buford and Thad were sitting in front of their tent, watching the sun disappear below the horizon: "Don't see the point in all this marching," Buford said.

"Discipline. They're trying to teach us to follow orders without thinking. We are supposed to react without questioning what they say."

"Sounds like you're gonna have a harder time with that than me."

"Good chance."

***

A bugle sounded before sunup the following morning: "Fall in with your rifles!" Buford and Thad dressed and got their rifles, taking their place in the formation. "Shoulder, arms!" Some had the gun on the left shoulder and some on the right. "Right shoulder you dim wits! Right face! Forward, march!"

The sun was above the horizon when the new troops got to the firing range and took their positions on the firing line, with the sun to their backs.

"Prone position!"

Buford looked at Thad: "On your belly."

"Stow it, Walker!" Buford looked at Thad and grinned. "Ready arms! Aim!" Before the command was given a shot rang out. "Wait for the command, Walker! You wasted a round. You missed!"

"No, I didn't."

"What did you say, mister!?"

"I don't miss, sir."

"I don't see a hole, private!"

"Sir." He looked at Buford. "Look through your field glasses, sir."

The sergeant glared at Buford then looked through the glasses. He refocused and looked again. "Damn lucky shot, Walker. Next time wait for the command." Thad reloaded. "Ready arms! Aim! Fire!" Walker's gun fired before the others. "Take your time, Walker! You missed this time!"

"Sir." The sergeant looked at Buford and Buford pointed at the glasses. The sergeant looked through the glasses, refocusing several times.

"At ease. Drop your weapons!" He walked out to Thad's target and examined it, looking at both sides before returning. "Another lucky shot, private. Next time take more time."

The target practice continued with the recruits changing from the prone position to kneeling and then standing. Thad's target was patched several times since he continued to put every shot thought the bullseye.

"At ease! Rest!" The sergeant walked off, almost in a daze.

"Begging your pardon, sir." The sergeant turned to see Buford standing behind him. "You're wasting bullets having Thad shoot. He don't miss, sir."

"No one is that good, private."

"Thad is. He taught me to shoot and as you can see I'm pretty good but not as good as Thad. No one is."

"I've seen it with my own eyes," the sergeant said, "but I still don't believe it."

"Thad has got this thing about him. When he taught me to shoot he said he can see the bullet hit the target before he shoots."

"That's impossible."

"Yes, sir, I know, sir. But that is what he believes and as long as he believes it he don't miss. I can throw four cans in the air and he can draw and shoot offhand, hitting everyone before they hit the ground."

"Maybe I should use him as a sniper."

"I don't think so, sir. He likes danger. Seeks it out. I don't think he would be happy anywhere except fightin' with the other troops."

"Thanks, private. Get back to your position. We're going back to the fort."

***

Training continued for the new troops through 1861 and Thad was promoted to corporal because of his ability to shoot and his boldness in training. The sergeant-major also used him as a shooting instructor, helping the recruits improve their marksmanship skills. Through November of '61, no major battles were fought in the New

Mexico Territory. Then in December, Brigadier General Henry H. Sibley in Texas, claimed New Mexico belonged to the South. In February 1862 Sibley headed north from Fort Thom, following the Rio Grande.

In February Colonel Watson called his officers and sergeant major to his quarters: "We have word the Texans are heading toward Fort Craig. We have been resigned. Prepare the troops to march to Fort Craig."

"Pack your gear and prepare to march," the sergeant major said to the formation of troops in front of him. "We leave in the morning. Dismissed!"

"Where do you think we are going?" Buford asked Thad.

"Can't say. Maybe the sergeant major will tell us tomorrow."

"Do you think we'll get to fight the Rebs, soon?"

"Good chance. Rumor is General Silbey in Texas said New Mexico belongs to the South."

"Do you think we are going to Texas?"

"I doubt it, but if the Rebs think New Mexico belongs to them they will probably come to claim it."

The march started before sunup the following morning and days later they arrived at Fort Craig.

"Why are they making wooden guns?" Buford asked. "Are they crazy? You can't shoot wooden guns."

"The Rebs won't be able to tell them from real guns and think there are more of us than there is," Thad said.

"Whoa! That's pretty clever."

"We don't know how many Rebs are coming. We have less than 4,000 men. If they see we are a small force we may not have a chance."

"That Colonel Canby must be a mighty smart man."

"I hope so. If the Confederates outnumber us and know how few men we have, we could be sitting ducks."

"You mean we could all die?"

"Good chance."

"I'm beginning to think maybe we shouldn't have joined."

"The first shot hasn't been fired. You don't win a war by giving up."

"I ain't giving up. I'm gonna kill as many Rebs as I can."

Upon approaching Fort Craig and seeing so many guns, General Sibly decided the Fort was too strong to take by direct assault and tried to entice Colonel Canby to leave the fort and attack him. Canby, however, refused to attack Sibly.

"I guess the Quaker guns are working," Thad said.

"Quaker gun?"

"The Quakers are a religious group that doesn't believe in fighting, so they call guns that can't fire, Quaker guns."

"Sounds like more people should be Quakers."

"That would be great except there will always be those that will fight, so you can either fight back or become their slaves."

"Guess I ain't gonna be no Quaker. Been a slave and know I ain't gonna be one ever again."

"That's why we must win this war."

"That's why I joined. Nobody is going to make my family slaves."

***

After three days and Canby still refusing to leave his fortifications, Silbey's rations began to run low. Silbey convened a council of war and decided to cross the Rio Grande and capture the ford at Valverde. This would sever Fort Craig's communication with Santa Fe. The Confederates moved their forces and camped east of the Valverde Ford.

When Canby realized what Sibley was trying to do he dispatched a force, under the command of Lieutenant Colonel Roberts, consisting of cavalry, infantry, and artillery, to the ford. This force included Colonel Watson's detachment from Fort Union.

"I'm feeling kinda shaky," Buford said as they headed for the ford.

"Well, get over it. It may cause you to miss when you shoot. This is no different than fighting Indians or rustlers."

"Some...more of the Rebs than Indians, and rustlers don't have cannon."

The artillery guns slowed Roberts advance so he sent the cavalry ahead to secure the ford. The infantry also advanced to the ford. Surprised to see Union forces there, Confederate Major Pyron called for reinforcements from Lieutenant Colonel Scurry's 4th Texas Mounted Rifles. Major Pyron positioned his forces in a dry river bed and Scurry deployed his men to Pyron's right, as Union cannons moved into place.

Lacking artillery, the Confederates were unable to return fire on the Union's forces. Even though outnumbering the Confederates, Colonel Robert's did not attempt to assault the Rebels.

When Colonel Canby learned of the standoff, he left Fort Craig with most of his force. Arriving at the scene, he left two regiments of infantry on the west bank and took the rest of his forces across the river.

After pounding the Confederates with artillery, the Union forces began to gain the upper hand. Aware of the situation, General Silbey sent in reinforcements under the command of Colonel Green.

As the fighting raged on, early in the afternoon, Green authorized an attack by some of his forces but was met by heavy fire from some of the Union soldiers. With their assault foiled, the remnants of the Confederates withdrew. Assessing the situation, Canby decided against a frontal attack and sent some untested troops across the river along with Captain McRae's artillery, to a forward position. With the Union assault forming, Green ordered an attack by Major Raguet's troops against the Union right, to buy time. The assault was repulsed and the Union troops began to advance. With Raguet's men turning back, Green ordered Scurry to attack the Union center, where Colonel Watson's men were deployed. Advancing in three waves, Scurry's forces, in fierce fighting, overran McRae's artillery, capturing the guns and shattering the Union line. During the scurry of the battle, Thad and Buford were separated. As Canby's position collapsed he ordered a retreat.

"Fall back!" Came the command. Some of the troops had already turned back before the order was given and a handful of Union soldiers, including Buford, found themselves encircled by men in gray.

"Drop your weapons!"

Buford looked toward the voice, staring into the barrel of a rifle. He dropped his gun.

"What are you doing off the plantation?" The corporal said.

"I'm a free man."

"Ain't no such thing as a free black man."

"You're wrong," Buford answered.

The corporal clenched his jaw and smashed Buford in the mouth with his right fist. Blood ran down Buford's chin as the taste of blood filled his mouth

"Don't you smart mouth me, boy!"

"The name is William Buford Chance."

The corporal's face filled with rage and he swung again, blooding Buford's nose. "You're awful mouthy for a slave."

"I told you I'm a free man."

The corporal's face again filled with rage and he ripped off Buford's coat and shirt, turning him around. "Don't look like no back of a free man to me, boy! I'm going to have a lot of fun with you when we get to camp, now move!" He shoved him forward as the others started walking.

"Leave him alone." One of the other Union soldiers said.

"You want some of what he's gettin', bluebelly?" The man looked at him then looked away. "Move your butts," the corporal said, pushing Buford again.

***

Colonel Canby and his troops returned to the fort but Watson camped a few miles away from the fort to assess the damage to his regiment.

Thad walked through the camp looking for Buford but couldn't find him. Seeing a soldier that was with them in the battle, Thad approached him: "I can't find Butte."

"Ain't gonna. Him and some others got captured by the Rebs."

"Are you sure?"

"They got 'em all right. I saw them coming and started back just before the call was given to fall back. Private Chance and the others were surrounded by Rebs. Nothing I could do but get killed, so I ran with the others."

"You sure they didn't kill them?"

"I don't think so. I looked back long enough to see them drop their rifles."

"How many were captured?"

"Not sure. Half a dozen I'd say. Sure wouldn't want to be a black man in the Rebs hands. Ain't no tellin' what they will do to Private Chance. Sure is a shame. He's a fine soldier."

"Thanks."

Thad walked toward the horse picket line, took a horse from the rope line, and threw a blanket and saddle on its back. He fastened the belly band and walked the animal to his tent and got his rifle before walking the horse to the edge of the camp. A sentry stood a few feet away when he put the reins around the horse's neck.

"Where you going with that horse, corporal?"

Thad looked toward the voice and saw Colonel Watson standing not far away: "To get Butte, sir."

"If you leave the camp you will be considered a deserter."

"I'll be back, sir."

"If you do come back I'll have you shot."

Thad swung into the saddle: "Okay." He tapped the animal with his heels and the horse moved forward. The sentry raised his rifle toward Thad.

"Lower the rifle, soldier."

"He's deserting, sir."

"As you were, private!"

"Yes, sir." He lowered the gun.

When Thad was a short distance from camp he picked up the pace, galloping toward the battlefield. From the battlefield Thad followed the trail left by the Confederates, returning to their camp.

***

"String him up on that tree at the edge of camp," the Confederate Corporal said to a private. "I'm gonna enjoy hearing him scream."

The private tied Buford's wrists together and threw the rope over the limb of the tree, securing it in place.

The corporal got his whip and made it snap as he walked toward Buford and stopped a few feet from him. "I'm going to make you scream your guts out, boy." He swung the whip and put a gash across Buford's back. Buford's head jerked and his body twisted but he didn't scream as he took a deep breath. "Scream, damn you!" The soldier snapped the whip across his back the second time as Buford twisted and jerked with no sound coming forth. The whip cracked a third time with Buford fighting the urge to scream as pain surged across his back. "Scream you black son-of-a-bitch!" the corporal yelled as another gash appeared on Buford's back and this time his knees buckled as his head jerked, causing his lip to start bleeding again and the taste of blood filled his mouth when he sucked in air, suppressing the scream. Buford straightened his legs, waiting for the next lash to come.

"Put the whip down, soldier," a lieutenant said walking up beside the corporal. "I want him strong enough to walk to Texas. I'm not wasting a horse on a slave."

"Yes, sir. Just one more."

He started to swing the whip, but the officer grabbed it, almost ripping it from the man's hand. "You want me to use this on you, corporal, or have you shot for disobeying an order!"

"No, sir! Sorry, sir!"

"You want me to cut him down, sir?" the private that tied Buford to the tree, asked.

"Leave him till morning. I won't have to worry about him trying to escape."

Buford breathed a sigh of relief when the whipping stopped. However, the pain in his back wouldn't go away, and the rope around his wrists restricted the flow of blood to his hands if he didn't stand as straight as he could, almost with his heels off the ground.

In time the blood from the whiplashes stopped running down his back and began to dry. After a while, he turned around so he was facing the camp. A few inches in front of him lay a piece of tree limb a few inches in diameter. With agonizing pain he stretched his right foot forward, trying to move the limb closer to his feet. It took several attempts, but finally the stick moved toward him and he positioned it under the heels of his boots, relieving the pressure on his wrists. As the light faded Buford tried to sleep but even with the stick under his heels, rest was almost impossible.

***

The sun was almost down when Thad saw the Rebel Camp about a mile in front of him. I'll wait until midnight, he thought, as he dismounted in some trees about half a mile from the camp. As darkness closed in around him Thad checked his gun, making sure all chambers were loaded. Several fires were burning in the camp and a few men were walking around but he didn't see Buford tied to the tree or know where the prisoners were in the camp. Neither did he have a plan as to how to rescue Buford, if he did find him. That would come later when he was closer to the camp. For now, he waited for the hours to pass until all in camp were asleep, except for the guards. As the night grew darker he saw a star lit moonless sky above him. In time the activity in camp ceased and some of the fires began to dim, so he moved closer.

The camp was large, making it difficult to find the area where the prisoners were housed then his eye caught the shadow of a man under a tree with his arms above his head. A guard, no more than fifty yards away, was napping, leaning on his rifle. In stealth silence, Thad made his way through the trees and around the brush toward Buford. Unaware of Thad's presence, Buford tried to sleep but when he drifted off his body would go weak and the tug of the rope around his wrists, jolted him awake. Just as he was starting to doze he felt his arms and body start to fall as the rope was cut above his head then felt an arm around his chest, preventing him from falling. As Buford straightened his legs he saw Thad grab his left forearm and cut the rope, freeing his hands.

Thad glanced at the guard then grabbed Buford's hand and started through the trees, crouched low, moving away from the camp. Minutes later they approached the horse and Thad swung into the saddle, pulling Buford up behind him. With the gentle tap of Thad's heels, the horse started forward at a walk. The slow pace continued until they were on the trail made by the Confederate Army returning to camp, a couple of miles away. Thad urged the horse on at a gallop and Buford began to moan.

"Are you okay?"

"The bouncing is killing my back."

"Sorry, we need to put some distance between us and your Reb friends. If that guard wakes and sees you're gone the whole camp will be after us."

Thad continued at a gallop until they reached the deserted battlefield then slowed the pace.

"You're stupid," Buford said. "If they'd caught you they'd done worse to you than they did to me. You called me stupid when I told Captain Watson about Mr. Lynch but this beats that."

"Do you think I could go back and face Norma if you're not with me?"

"That's my point. If you'd stayed in camp at least one of us mighta made it back."

"You're free, aren't you? We're both here."

"Yeah, until they catch up with us."

"Good point. You going to be okay when the horse starts running?"

"Just go!"

Thad spurred the horse and it started running with Buford hanging on to Thad, gritting his teeth as the pain in his back increased. The fast pace continued until they were a couple of miles beyond the battlefield then Thad slowed the horse to a walk.

"I think we're safe. The camp shouldn't be more than three-four miles away."

"Good. I'm gonna sleep for a week when we get there."

"Why did you let yourself get captured?"

"Do you think I wanted to? One second I'm surrounded by blue uniforms and the next gray."

"You didn't hear the call to retreat?"

"If I did I'd be the first one gone."

"You should've stayed with me."

"You think I had time to look for you? I was too busy killin' Rebs and stayin' alive."

***

The guard close to where Buford had been hanging from the tree continued to doze then woke and looked at the camp before dozing again, not noticing Buford was gone. About three hours after Thad cut Buford loose the guard woke and looked toward the tree where Buford should be. He started to doze again then realized something had changed. He looked again at the empty space beneath the tree. In a panic, he ran to the tree and saw the rope still in the tree and pieces of rope on the ground beneath the tree.

"He's gone"! The prisoner is gone!" He yelled.

Men began coming out of tents, dressing. The lieutenant and corporal were the first to arrive. "What happened?" the lieutenant asked.

"I looked and he was just gone, sir."

"I want a dozen men on horses," the corporal said. Within minutes men were on horses and returned to the tree. "Three men north, south, east, and west. Spread out. I want him back!"

"You fell asleep," the lieutenant said, looking at the guard.

"I just closed my eyes for one second, sir."

"One second! Whoever cut him loose must be faster than lightning to do it and disappear."

"I swear, sir, I just barely closed my eyes."

"How often did you check this spot, private?"

"Well I... I... I'm not sure, sir."

"When was the last time you checked before you saw he was missing? How long? Ten minutes. An hour. Two hours?"

"I don't remember, sir."

"Put him in the stockade." Two soldiers grabbed him and marched him away.

An hour later the riders returned. "We searched in all directions, sir and found hoof prints from one horse going up to the trail then we lost them, sir."

"One man did this?"

"We think so, sir."

"Get some rest. It's going to be a long day tomorrow."

***

The Rebel search team returned to camp as Thad and Buford were approaching the Union Camp.

"Halt and be recognized," the guard said when he saw the horse approaching.

"Corporal Walker and Private Chance."

"Advance."

They enter the camp. "I'm taking Private Chance to the doc," Thad said. Then walked the horse into the camp toward the hospital tent. "Got another patient for you, sir." He slid down from the saddle then helped Buford down.

"Come into the light," the doctor said to Buford. The doctor looked at his face and touched his nose. "It's broken but straight. Lip is swollen and torn. Open your mouth. Any loose teeth?"

"No, sir."

The doctor looked at his back. "You'll live but it will take some time to heal."

"I want to get back to fightin', sir. I got a lot of Rebs to kill."

"Sit on this cot and I'll clean and dress your wounds."

"See you later, Butte," Thad said and walked the horse back to the picket line then unsaddled it.

Thad headed for the colonel's tent and walked past the private, standing outside.

"You can't go in there," the private said.

Thad kept walking, opened the flap, and went inside. Colonel Watson jumped when Thad dropped his revolver on the cot, waking him: "Use my gun when you have me shot, Sir"

"Put the gun away!"

Thad holstered the weapon.

"Did you find him?"

"He's with the doc. They beat him pretty bad, but he will fight again."

"The other men?"

"I didn't see them, sir. Butte was alone. They beat him and left him tied to a tree. If they hadn't he probably would still be there."

"You're a real pain in the butt, Walker. You're arrogant, independent, and you don't follow orders. But you're no doubt the best shot in the army and a good instructor. Even though you disobeyed my orders not to leave, what you just did, saving another soldier's life was brave and heroic. I don't know whether to give you a medal or have you shot."

"I didn't join for medals, sir."

"Get the hell out of my tent, Walker!" Thad turned to go. "Walker!" He looked at the colonel. "Leave those strips!" He slowly tore them from his uniform and placed them on the table before leaving.

***

In the weeks that followed, most of Buford's wounds had healed. Colonel Watson returned to Fort Craig a few days after the Battle of Valverde. Confederate Brigadier General Sibley, believing his forces were not sufficient to take Fort Craig, continued north toward Albuquerque and Santa Fe, hoping to resupply his army.

After occupying both Albuquerque and Santa Fe, General Silbey sent Major Pyron with a force of about 300 Texans to the Glorieta Pass, a strategic location on the Santa Fe Trail. Major Pyron camped at Johnson's Ranch, located at one end of the Pass. Union Major Chivington with a contingent of 400 troops was sent to the Pass and on March 26, engaged the Confederates. Chivington's men captured some advanced Rebel troops but Rebel artillery pressed him back. Chivington regrouped and split his forces, positioning them on both sides of the Pass, catching the Rebels in a crossfire. Pyron retreated to a narrow section of the pass, forming a defensive line before Chivington's men caught up with him.

The Union forces flanked the Rebels again and overpowered them with gunfire. Pyron fled again and the Union troops captured the Confederate rearguard, with a cavalry charge. With the battle over, Chivington retired to the Kozlowski Ranch.

The following day reinforcements arrived for both armies. Lieutenant Colonel Scurry with 800 men for the Confederates and Colonel Slough, filling in for Colonel Watson, down with a fever, arrived with 900 of Watson's men. Both forces decided to attack the following day. Scurry advanced down the canyon and found the Union troops approaching, so he established a battle line. Slough attacked before noon and the Confederates held their ground. After the first attack, Private Thaddeus Walker approached the Colonel.

"Sir, the rebel supply wagons are at the Johnson Ranch. If we destroy them it will stop the Rebs northern movement. If you give me twenty men, sir, I'll burn them."

"Good idea, private. Choose your men but don't let the Confederates see you leave."

"Thank you, sir. They won't know we're gone."

"If we are not here when you return, go to Kozlowski's Ranch."

Thad assembled his volunteers and they walked their horses behind and through the trees, going about a mile from the battle area before mounting and riding toward the Johnson Ranch.

"I hope you know what you are doing, Thad," Buford said as they rode. "Could be a number of troops there."

"I thought you said you wanted to kill Rebs?"

"I do, but I don't plan on them killin' me back."

"Where is your spirit of adventure?"

"Oh, I got that all right. It's your thirst for danger that worries me."

"You want to go back?"

"Hell no. You ever know me to run from a fight?"

"Now that's the Butte I know and love."

"Yeah, I hope you still know me when this is over."

When they got to the ranch, off in the distance, they saw the wagons in a circle as if it were a wagon train going west. Some soldiers were outside as guards and some within the circled wagons. Thad reined in about a mile from the wagons, on a tree-covered hill.

"Here is the plan," Thad said, "I want half of you to attack from the far side. When you leave here stay back in the trees. When you get to the other side of the wagons I want you all to come out of the trees together, shooting. Surprise them. Try to take out some of the guards outside first. I think those you don't kill will go inside the circled wagons. Keep shooting and stay on that side, outside the wagons. Ride in a circle. Once they are inside and shooting at you, we will come in from this side. Watch for us. I don't want us shooting each other. We will ride in fast, shooting in the air at first, until we jump the tongues of the wagons, then shoot anyone pointing a gun at you. No more wild shooting from those of you on the far side once you see us coming. Pick your target before shooting. Once we are inside, move in close and only shoot if necessary. Any questions?"

"Which of us are going to the other side?" one soldier asked.

"I need ten volunteers."

"I'll go they all said at the same time."

"Thanks. It's nice to be serving with brave men. You ten to my left. Take your time and make sure you are not seen." The ten started off, going deeper into the trees before starting toward the far side of the wagons.

"Check your guns, men," Thad said, pulling his from its holster. Each man checked his gun and then returned it to its holster.

"There's twelve of us," Thad said. "When we start for the wagons I want to see four men together, riding toward the break between the wagons. "You four," Thad pointed to four men on his left, "I want you riding for the wagon tongue on our left. Butte and I and you two next to Butte, will take the one straight ahead. You to my right take the wagon tongue to our right. I don't want to see any heroes. Stay together and leave room for each to jump the tongue. Do it in a line. Keep your gun in the air and start shooting when we are close to the wagons. Once you jump over, only shoot if a gun is pointed at you. I think they will give up when they see they are pinned between us. Any questions?"

"Why can't we shoot at the men in the circle?" One private asked.

"Because ten of your buddies will be on the other side of the wagons. A wild shot from a fast-moving horse could kill one of our men. We have too many Rebs trying to do that. Let's not help them." He looked at each man as he continued. "We came here to destroy supplies and wagons, not to kill. Kill if necessary but the wagons are the reason we are here."

***

It took almost an hour for the ten men to get into the trees on the far side. They moved to the edge of the woods and drew their guns. "Ride!" One of them said and they burst out of the trees in a line, shouting and shooting. In shock, the guards on the outside of the ring of wagons jerked their heads toward the oncoming riders. One then another guard fell to the ground as the remaining began shooting and heading for the cover of the circled wagons. Another guard fell from his horse as it cleared the tongue of a wagon. The guards in the circle began returning fire as the guards from the outside jumped from their mounts and began returning fire from behind the wagons. The Union soldiers returned fire, riding in a circle several yards from the ring of wagons.

Thad, Buford, and the other ten soldiers burst from the trees on the opposite side of the wagons in groups of four. Halfway to the wagons, they started firing in the air, heading for the circle with the shocked confederates jerking their heads toward the oncoming riders, as they jump into the ring of wagons. The Rebs stood, dropping their guns as Thad and his men reined in, in front of them. The ten men outside the wagons rode up close to the circled wagons, guns drawn.

"Disarm them," Thad said. Buford and the ten inside the ring dismounted and began removing weapons from the stunned Confederates. Buford looked at each man, looking to see if he recognized any that may have been involved with his beating.

"Take them outside and destroy the wagons," Thad said.

Buford and the ten with him marched the twelve Rebs over to the trees, tying their hands and feet while the other ten soldiers dismounted and began setting fire to the supply wagons.

The flames grew high and bright as some wagons exploded when the flames reached barrels of gun powder. Cheers rang out with each explosion. The fires continued for hours and brightened the surrounding area as night closed in around them.

When Thad was sure all supplies and wagons were rendered unusable, he walked over to the prisoners: "I don't take prisoners. If you promise to go back to Santa Fe I will let you go."

"We promise," the sergeant in charge said.

"Untie them."

"We can't just let them go!" One of the Union Soldiers said.

"We can't, but I can. Untie them." Several men began untying the Rebel Soldiers. The prisoners started to stand. "Take off your boots."

"Do you think it is going to be easy to walk to Santa Fe without boots?" the sergeant said.

"It will be even more difficult to fight without boots. Take them off."

"It's dark," the sergeant said, "there are wild animals around here. Are you going to send us away unarmed?"

"No. You can keep your fists. If I see you men on the battlefield, I will kill each one of you myself."

"And he's just the man to do it," Buford said.

The twelve men started through the woods as the flames of the wagons continued to burn.

***

A bright moon lit the sky as Thad, Buford, and the twenty soldiers made their way back to Glorieta Pass and the battle area, finding it void of soldiers. From there Thad went to the Kozlowski Ranch and entered camp.

"I'm Private Walker, I need to talk to the colonel," Thad said to the private stationed outside the tent.

The private faced the tent: "A Private Walker to see you, sir."

"Send him in."

Thad entered the tent and saluted the Colonel. He returned the salute. "Were you successful?"

"Yes, sir. It went well."

"Did you lose any men?"

"No, sir. We killed five Rebs and captured twelve."

"What was your strategy?"

"I watched you on the battlefield and divided the men into two groups and attacked from two sides. It was a complete surprise."

"Where are the prisoners?"

"I let them go."

"You let them go?"

"Yes, sir."

"Why?"

"I thought they would be a liability coming back, so I made them swear not to enter the battle and to return to Santa Fe. We disarmed them and took their boots."

"Probably a smart move." The colonel looked at Thad's sleeves. "Looks like you were a corporal at one time."

"Yes, sir."

"What happened?"

"Colonel Watson and I had a disagreement."

"You may have saved many lives and even shortened the war here in the west. I'll talk to Watson."

"Not necessary, sir. The colonel was right. I deserved to lose my stripes."

"Very well, private. You're dismissed."

"Thank you, sir. Who won the battle?"

"It was a draw." He saluted the colonel and left the tent.

The next morning a private came to Thad and Buford's tent. "The colonel wants to see you, Private Walker."

"Okay."

"What do you think he wants?" Buford asked.

"I don't know? I talked to him last night when we got back." Thad entered the tent and saluted."

"Have a seat, Walker," the colonel said returning his salute. "You weren't quite honest with me yesterday, were you?"

"I don't understand, sir."

"Drop the sir for now, Walker. I talked to several of the men that went with you. They said your strategy was not only well thought out but brilliantly executed."

"I told you yesterday, colonel, I followed your lead on the battlefield."

The men gave me a detailed description of what happened. It sounds like it was executed by an academy officer. Have you thought about making the army your career?"

"I'm not a soldier, colonel. I'm just trying to help a friend stay alive and help win this war."

"I can recommend you for a citation."

"No medals, Colonel Slough."

"You're a strange man, Thaddeus, but if that's the way you want it."

"It is."

"Will you at least let me shake your hand."

Thad extended his hand: "My pleasure Colonel."

"What did he want?" Buford asked when Thad returned.

"I don't know, I think he was lonely."

***

With their supplies gone, the confederates returned to Santa Fe, the first stop on the long march to San Antonio, Texas. The loss of the battle of Glorieta Pass stopped the Confederate's effort to capture the New Mexico Territory, which included the area that would one day become the State of Arizona.

The battle of the southwest may have ended but not the war. That would continue for another three years. The war began with South Carolina's artillery attack on Fort Sumter on April 12, 1861, before sunrise. And the official end came when General Robert E. Lee surrendered to Union General Ulysses S. Grant on April 9, 1865, after the Battle of Appomattox Court House. However, that was not the last battle. The Battle of Palmetto Ranch, also called the Battle of Palmetto Hill, came after Appomattox, on May 12 and 13, 1865 along the Rio Grande River, east of Brownsville, Texas.

Thad and Buford didn't fight in this battle even though it was fought in the west. The Battle of Palmetto Ranch should not have taken place since in early 1865 both the Confederate and Union troops in south Texas agreed to cease fighting, under a gentlemen's agreement. Although the decision, reached by subordinate officers, was repudiated by their superiors, both sides honor the agreement.

There has been much speculation as to the cause of the Battle of Palmetto Ranch but the results were the same as the first battle of the war, the First Battle of Bull Run, with the Union losing.

***

After the war's end, Thad and Buford left Fort Union for the last time, early one morning, heading back to the ranch.

"I know I was a little upset when Norma wrote you and asking you to go with me, but she was right. If you hadn't come with me I wouldn't be going home. The Rebs would've killed me."

"Yeah...and you got me thinking by what you said after I cut you loose in the Rebel Camp."

"What did I say?"

"You said I was stupid for rescuing you. You said if the Rebs had got me neither one of us would go back."

"So?"

"You said if I hadn't gone after you then as least one of us might make it back."

"Well...it's true."

"I know, and I started thinking... Norma...the most beautiful woman I've ever met...a widow."

"Damn you, Thaddeus Walker! Just when I'm trying to thank you for saving my life you tick me off!" A smirk appeared on Thad's face and things were quiet for a while. "You didn't mean that did you?"

"That Norma is the most beautiful woman I've ever met? Sure I did."

"That's not what I'm talking about and you know it."

"I made a promise to Norma before we left and I was determined to keep it."

"But you would've anyway, right?"

"Of course, but what man could say no to Norma."

"Don't you start again!" The smirk appeared on Thad's face again as they rode in silence.

Young Thaddeus was playing in front of the house with his little sister when, off in the distance, he saw two riders coming toward him. Although little more than two dots at first, they began to grow larger. He continued to watch then bolted up the steps and into the house: "Mama! There's two men on horses coming and one of them looks like daddy!"

Norma dropped the pan she was drying and gasped, trembling, before hurrying to the door, wiping her hands on her apron. Running across the porch and down the steps, Norma stopped a few feet from the porch, gasping and trembling with tears running down her face. One of the men spurred his horse on as she screamed and ran toward him. The horse sped toward her skidding to a stop as Buford jumped off and Norma sprang forward into his arms, screaming, trembling, and crying. Buford grabbed her and spun her around as he erupted in tears. He pulled away enough to kiss her then held her, both still crying. Thad rode up beside them as young Thaddeus ran toward his parents with little Frances coming up behind him.

"Daddy," young Thaddeus said as he tried to hug him. Norma let Buford go and he hugged the boy and bent down looking into his eyes.

"Oh my! Thaddeus, you have grown and are so handsome. You are a fine young man." He looked at Frances. "You have grown too and as beautiful as your mama." He stretched out his arms but she stayed away.

"It's daddy, honey," Norma said, going over and picking her up and walking over to Buford. "Don't you remember?" but she turned her head away.

"I remember you." Buford kissed her on the cheek and she turned her head away then looked at him and reached for him. He took her in his arms and she hugged him. "That's what I've been looking for." He held her close.

Norma walked over to Thad, hugged and kissed him. "Thank you."

"You're welcome," he said returning her hug and kiss.

Norma turned toward Buford and he put Frances down, taking Norma in his arms again. They kissed and stood looking into each others eyes: "Watch your sister, Thaddeus. Mama and daddy are going inside and talk." They started for the house, holding hands.

Thaddeus started to follow them. "Stay with me, son," Thad said.

"But I want to hear what they are saying."

"It's a private talk, Thaddeus. Stay with your little sister like your daddy said."

"What could they be talking about that is private?"

"Maybe getting you a baby brother."

"Really!"

"Good chance."

"How can you be my uncle when you're white?"

"Does seem strange, doesn't it? Your daddy and I are so much alike and have been together so long we kinda adopted each other."

"Do I have an Aunt?"

"No. I couldn't find a woman as nice or as beautiful as your mama. You remember me, honey?" Thad said to little Frances. She backed away.

"It's Uncle Thad, Francy." Thad bent down and held out his hands and she moved toward her brother. "He won't hurt you." She hid behind Thaddeus. "You don't have to be afraid of him cause he's white." She stayed behind Thaddeus.

Thad led his horse over to the water trough and let him drink.

"Mama said you're the bravest man alive."

"No. That's your daddy."

"For sure?"

"For sure. I saw him go into a herd of stampeding cattle once and save a man that got knocked off his horse. Stampeding cows are more dangerous than fighting a war. He went in, scooped the man upon his horse, and got him back on his horse. Bravest thing I ever saw."

"I would've been afraid."

"The difference between a hero and a coward, son, is the direction they choose to go. One toward danger and the other away from it. Your daddy was afraid but put it behind him and saved the man because it was the right thing to do." He put the reins around the horse's neck and swung into the saddle.

"Are you leaving?"

"Stay out here and take care of your sister until your ma and pa come out."

"But mama said you would stay."

"Got places to go, son. Tell your ma to write." He walked his horse for a ways, broke into a gallop then disappeared from view.